*To my children, Brandon and Julia,
who keep me in the light.*

Also by Bernard Schaffer

Superbia

Guns of Seneca 6

Grendel Unit

The Girl from Tenerife

Whitechapel: The Final Stand of Sherlock Holmes

THE
THIEF
OF
ALL
LIGHT

A SANTERO AND REIN THRILLER

BERNARD SCHAFFER

PINNACLE BOOKS
Kensington Publishing Corp.
www.kensingtonbooks.com

PINNACLE BOOKS are published by

Kensington Publishing Corp.
119 West 40th Street
New York, NY 10018

All Kensington titles, imprints, and distributed lines are available at special quantity discounts for bulk purchases for sales promotions, premiums, fund-raising, educational, or institutional use. Special book excerpts or customized printings can also be created to fit specific needs. For details, write or phone the office of the Kensington sales manager: Kensington Publishing Corp., 119 West 40th Street, New York, NY 10018, attn: Sales Department; phone 1-800-221-2647.

ISBN-13: 978-0-7860-4293-7
ISBN-10: 0-7860-4293-1

First Kensington hardcover edition: August 2018
First Pinnacle premium mass market printing: June 2019

10 9 8 7 6 5 4 3 2 1

Printed in the United States of America

Electronic edition:

ISBN-13: 978-0-7860-4293-4 (e-book)
ISBN-10: 0-7860-4293-X (e-book)

I
ATROCITY EXHIBITION

1

That night, he was Ed. the last time, he had been dean, and before that, Earle. He maintained a list in his mind, and he was marking names off of that list. Working his way toward the top.

Being Ed was a big deal.

He looked down at his guest's feet, studying the painted color of her toenails. A smooth, luxuriant bronze, applied perfectly. He would remember that shade when he was no longer Ed. He squeezed her bare calf, feeling its shape and musculature. Long, lean, firm, and tight, the way only a young woman's can be. Her head bobbed at the touch of his hand. The chemical locomotive slowed its pace through her system. Soon, the conductor would blow his whistle, and the engine would brake, and then the doors of her mind would slide open in a cloud of benzodiazepine-opiate steam, delivering her into his waiting arms.

"In terms of numbers, America is pretty low on the list," he said. "People always forget to include the other countries. Believe it or not, Colombia has the top three spots. In terms of provable numbers, we only have one in the top ten, and he just barely squeaked in.

Gary Ridgway," the man calling himself Ed said. "You've heard of him? Green River?"

When she did not answer, he leaned back against the cool basement wall, setting his hands down on the damp cement. The water heater was leaking again. He was going to have to fix it himself, obviously. His guest would stay there for a few days, at the least, and he imagined he'd need hot water at some point. There was always something.

"Top three, are you ready? Luis Garavito, Pedro López, Daniel Camargo Barbosa," he said, counting the names off with his fingers. "Crazy numbers. Big, impossible numbers. Luis got a hundred and thirty-eight, and he had a fantastic nickname, too. *La Bestia.* The Beast. Pedro got one hundred ten. They called him the Monster of the Andes. In all fairness, López might have done a lot more than just those hundred and ten. When they caught him, he said he'd done as many as three hundred. Can you believe that? Three hundred. Most of them kids. And just to give you an idea what a different world it is down there, he got released from prison. See, that's why you can't really rely on the numbers anybody puts up in Colombia. If you can do three hundred kids and still get out of jail, well, that's not really trying, now, is it?"

The woman muttered something inaudible.

He turned toward her. "What was that?"

The red rubber ball strapped between her teeth prevented her from speaking clearly, and she grunted against the weight of the chains binding her wrists and ankles.

Typical, he thought. They never contribute anything.

He hadn't expected her to, really. "So, anyway. Barbosa was another one. High numbers on paper, but in reality? He had twelve years to work, from '74 to '86, and the most they'll credit him for is one fifty. Even then, that's only twelve a year. Twelve! If you can't strangle more than twelve little girls a year, with nobody stopping you, I don't see why you even bother. You ask me, that's just lazy," he said, shaking his head.

"Most people here have only heard of Ted Bundy and John Wayne Gacy. Their numbers are pretty low, comparatively, but they're definitely the most famous. Gacy, because he dressed up like a clown, and most people agree that's pretty terrifying. Bundy was famous because he was so good looking and well spoken. People just couldn't believe he was doing what he was doing. I guess there's a lesson to be learned in that somewhere. Say what you want about his lack of production, but in terms of style and originality? You have to give credit where it is due. Now, sure, Green River did bigger numbers than either Bundy or Gacy, but he also came along after they did, and it's always easier to build on what's come before. You know what they say the mark of greatness is?"

When she didn't answer, he told her. "When everything before you is obsolete, and everything after bears your mark."

He sifted through her purse and found her driver's license, glanced at it, flicked it away, and removed her cell phone. The screen was locked, but he was able to scroll down through the multiple missed calls and text messages she'd been receiving all evening. They were mainly from her mother asking where she was and why she wasn't responding. He grabbed her hand and stretched out her index finger as she squirmed. He forced her finger against the bottom of her phone, holding it there until it unlocked.

She slumped forward when he released her, whimpering mutely. He ignored her, focused instead on finding her phone's airplane mode, to prevent anyone tracking its location. It was an unnecessary measure, he knew. There were homes in his area that did not even have indoor plumbing. The nearest cell tower was twenty miles away.

"Well, I guess we should get started," he said as he placed the phone on his workbench. "There's a lot to do." He picked up his mask and fit it down over his face, adjusting its large eyes and droopy mouth so that he could see and still be heard. The microphones placed around the basement were of the highest quality he could afford, but the acoustics were tricky because of the cement walls. He reminded himself to speak clearly and keep his voice raised. He would want to hear every word when he watched the video later.

A vast array of tools lay assembled on the workbench, and he waved his hands over them like a magician about to perform a mystical deed. He hovered over the handle of a long machete, then picked up a small ball-peen hammer. Its wooden handle was warm in his palm. He looked down at the woman, squirming on the floor like some kind of crab, and he decided the hammer would be best to start with.

She trembled as he came forward in his mask, trying to scream but gagging on the rubber ball strapped between her teeth. He looked down at the dark stream traveling from between her legs across the basement floor toward him, and stepped out of the way, hearing its soft trickle inside the industrial drain he'd installed four years prior.

"You know, I'm starting to worry that I gave you the wrong impression. I apologize if that's the case." He reached forward and unbuckled her ball gag, smiling when her eyes rose up to meet his.

She spat the ball out and worked her jaw, trying to stretch out the ache in the sides of her face. She blinked, unsure of what she was seeing. In the foggy chemical haze, she thought his face might be melting. "You're not going to kill me?" she panted. Hope blossomed inside her eyes, spreading like a rash across her entire face. "This was just some kind of joke, right? Did someone put you up to this?"

"Well, actually, I mean that I gave you the wrong impression that I just care about numbers. It's not about that. It's about *impact*. Do you remember what I told you my name was?"

"You're Ed," she said quickly, desperate to invoke his name. To let him know she'd been paying attention. This was all just a sick game, she told herself. There was a way to play it. She just needed to figure out how. "You're Ed, and I'm Denise. My name is Denise Lawson, Ed." She repeated her name, needing him to know it, needing him to see her as a real person, not a plaything. Force him to see you, she told herself. Buy time to think. Keep him talking. "Can you say it?"

His head tilted sideways as he listened to her.

"My name is Denise. My parents are going to know I didn't come home, Ed. Do you know why I sat down with you at the bar tonight? Because you have kind eyes. I know you're not going to hurt me, okay? I believe you won't do that." She rattled the chains holding her to the wall and said, "Can you please undo these? I promise, it's okay. Things just got out of hand, right? I should have been more clear that this wasn't what I was into. I know you're a good person, Ed. I know you won't hurt me. Right?"

He studied her, never wanting to forget any of it. The cameras and microphones would record everything, but only he could see the colors in her face change. The pure waters of hope in her eyes clouded over and darkened for him alone. She was still unsure. Her voice quickened, a long stream of words spilling out of her all at once.

"Listen to me, Ed," Denise continued. "People know where I am. I told everyone where I was going, and they are probably coming here right now, because I said I would call. If you just let me go, I will never say a word. I promise. I swear on my life. Ed? Please."

His voice was gentle when he said, "Do you know why I picked Ed? Ed Gein only had two, or at least two that we know of, but it was what he did with them that we remember. It's not about quantity. It's about quality. Impact. True greatness. Do you know Ed Gein?"

"No!" she said, trying not to lose it. "Take these chains off of me. Right now and let me go home! Okay, Ed? Right now. I need you to listen to me. This isn't funny anymore. I need to go home."

He stroked her cheek with the tips of his fingers. "Ed Gein was an artist. That's why we remember him. He inspired us with his beauty. Now you're going to help me make something beautiful too."

2

"You ever seen a ghost?"

Carrie Santero turned away from the passenger-side window to look at the older man sitting next to her. His hair was dyed brown a few shades too dark, making his eyebrows and the scruff of hair on his chin look mismatched. He was in good shape for a man his age, tall and lean, it was obvious he cared about his appearance. She watched as he tapped the underside of his cigarette pack and popped one out, pursing it between his lips.

"You mind?" he asked from the corner of his mouth.

She rolled down the window a few inches and lied, saying she did not. The gun was uncomfortable on her hip. It dug into her ribs. It was her large-frame duty weapon, meant to be carried on a thick patrol belt in a sturdy polymer holster with Level III Retention levers and buttons, not the flimsy nylon holster she'd borrowed earlier that day. Still, it was her first time working plainclothes and she did not mind. She moved the gun's handle aside and leaned back in the seat.

Harv Bender snapped his lighter open, and the flame licked the tip of the cigarette until it flared, brightening his face inside the dark car and catching the curve of the plain gold band of his wedding ring. "I was on the street back then, not even a detective yet. You were probably still in middle school."

"More like grade school," Carrie said, flashing a smile.

"All right," he said, nodding as he inhaled. "So it's midnight shift and the town is real quiet. Kind of a night like this. Warm, dark, fog rolling through like something out of a bad movie. I used to think about sailors back then."

She raised an eyebrow at him. "I had no idea you went that way, Harv."

"Not like that, smart-ass," he said. "I used to think about ancient sailors, out on the black water in the dead of night, thick fog everywhere, no idea what was out there. Must have been enough to drive some of them crazy. Every little light and sound must have seemed terrifying. Hell, that's where all them stories about ghost ships and mermaids and sea monsters came from."

"Actually, a lot of things they took for monsters, like giant squids, turned out to be real. They found a few. I watched a show on it."

"Mmm," he said, taking another long drag. "Well, look at you. Not just pretty but smart, too. That's a shame. Smart women don't do well in this job. They come off bitchy and make people nervous." His hand reached for her knee, giving it a slight squeeze, and he laughed, trying to play it off as a joke in case she objected. She didn't pull away so he left it there, keeping still, not wanting to spook her. "Anyway, I was out in the middle of the sticks one night, driving real slow because I didn't want to hit any deer, and I took a ride through this cemetery at the far edge of town. I'm cruising through the trails, just trying to watch where I'm going, and I see something in the shadows. I can't spotlight it, because in fog like that, all it does is reflect the light right back at you. So I stop my car, and I just sit."

His hand moved up her thigh the slightest fraction of an inch. "The fog starts to part, and I see this tiny thing standing in front of one of the graves, looking down at it. She had long, blond hair, but not dark like yours is. Golden. Shining so brightly I could still see it in all that fog. Scared the living shit out of me, I'll tell you."

"What did you do?" she asked.

"What do you think? I got the hell out of there."

"You didn't."

"You're damn right I did." He laughed.

"What if it was a lost kid? Some kind of runaway? What if it was one of the Krissing girls who somehow got away?"

He finished his cigarette. "I checked on all that afterward, believe me. No kids were missing, and the Krissing girls weren't from around that area. Anyway, none of them ever escaped. Old Man Krissing kept all the ones he took. The girls anyway. He had other plans in mind for the boys. Believe me. I was there. Right in the thick of it."

"So you just left without seeing if it was a lost kid?"

"You're a one-track-minded person, aren't you. It's cute. Honest. Let's talk about something else, though. How do you like being on the Task Force so far?"

"I'm real glad to be doing it," she said, looking down at his hand. She told herself to play it cool. Harv Bender was the Deputy Chief of the County Detectives. He needed to personally sign off on her overtime details with the Anti-Crime Task Force, and telling him to get his fucking hand off her knee before she broke it was not going to help her stay assigned to those details at all. "It's good to get away from the barking dog complaints and stop sign violations to do some real police work for a change."

"Well, you keep up the good job and we might be able to make it permanent," he said, now stroking her leg with his thumb. "You ever get bumped to County D's, you get a take-home car, all the overtime you can stand, no more wearing any polyester monkey suit. Get you out here with us big boys, making real cases. Is that what you want?"

He smelled like cigarettes, and now her clothes were going to stink like them too. His hand rested on the inside of her thigh, with his splayed fingers creeping inward. "The only reason I became a cop is because I want to make detective," she said.

"Let me see what I can do," he said, smiling at her. "I'm always happy to help a friend."

She shifted in her seat and closed her legs, pulling away from him enough that he let his hand rest on the gearshift instead of following her. "Speaking of Krissing, you said you were there? I know my chief and his old partner worked that job. Did you help them?"

"Did I what?" He sniffed. "Your chief's a good guy and everything, but I didn't just help them work it. I was doing all the behind-the-scenes heavy lifting while him and that asshole Rein were taking all the credit."

She frowned, thinking of the man she'd worked for since graduating the police academy, the one she'd begged to let her join the Task Force and made her swear to *Stay clear of Harvey Bender. He thinks he's a tomcat.* "I guess all that matters is that the girls got found when they did and Old Man Krissing won't ever hurt anyone again"

Harv drew another cigarette and chuckled. "You got that right. Rein might be a psychopath, but one thing he got right was how he did Krissing. I can't believe he got away with it, either. Really took *some balls*, and bigger ones than what they took from Old Man Krissing, if you know what I mean," he said, laughing so hard at his own joke that he had to stifle a cough with his fist. He cleared his throat and said, "But if you think about it, everything shook out the way it was supposed to in the end. I mean, look at me. I'm second-in-command of the County Detectives, while Bill is stuck in a department with idiots who think finding a dime bag is the bust of the century." He looked at her and said, "No offense, I mean."

"None taken," she said.

"I guess all that credit and glory they got after finding Krissing didn't amount to much. But at least Bill has a job. Rein's lucky they didn't keep him in prison for the rest of his life. Bill said I just assisted them?" he muttered. "Tell you what, if you want to see who was really pulling their weight on the Krissing job and who was just in it for show, all you need to do is see how the players involved turned out. The goddamn truth is sitting in this car next to you."

They were the last ones back to the meeting spot, a gravel driveway set behind the rotting frame of an old barn. It was midnight, and the woods around them croaked with life. The autumn moon hung low in the sky, close enough to reveal its craggy face, the air sur-

prisingly cold for so early in the season. Harv cut their
headlights as they pulled up to the group, a half-dozen
older detectives in flannel shirts and tactical pants that
had too many pockets up and down the sides of their
legs. As Carrie got out, she heard one of the men say,
"Aw shit, I bet she's pregnant."

Harv heard them too, and when he thought Carrie
wasn't looking, he pretended to zip up his fly. The group
laughed, except the officer running the operation. Sergeant Dave Kenderdine quieted the others and said,
"Thanks for finally showing up, you two. Get anything?"

"Nothing we can't take a pill to fix," Harv said, wink-
ing. "There's just trees and deer out here tonight."

"Same for everybody else." Kenderdine made a few
quick notes on his legal pad and then looked back up at
Carrie. "Well, sorry your first time wasn't more event-
ful. Unfortunately, this is the majority of what we do.
You sit around for hours and hours, and when something does happen, it's over in a few seconds. It's a lot
of monotonous work, but the payoff is worth it, I
promise. I'm sure Harv told you that already, though."

"He told me a lot of stuff," Carrie said.

Sgt. Kenderdine looked at Harv. "You make her sit
through that stupid ghost story?"

The rest of the guys groaned, and one of them covered his mouth and said, "I bet that's not all she sat on."

A burst of laughter followed. It stopped when Kenderdine's head snapped around, flashing disapproval.
The men looked at Carrie, waiting for her reaction.
Was she a cop, who knew how things went? Or was
she a member of the protected class, just waiting for a
chance to sue them? "Sarge, I have a question about
gear," she said.

"Go ahead."

"Harv told me I'm gonna need kneepads if I plan on sticking around here. Do you supply them, or should I?"

The cops in front of her gaped, too stunned to respond. It was Harv who laughed first, and loudest, and the others followed after. He clapped her on the back and said, "I love this kid. I told you guys we had nothing to worry about."

She was the first female police officer in the history of Coyote Township, Vieira County, out in the western part of Pennsylvania that people from big cities like Philadelphia and Pittsburgh called Pennsyltucky. Bill Waylon swore he'd hired her on the spot because he saw something in her, some kind of spark, but she knew it was to avoid any problems with the EEOC. Women just didn't apply for police jobs that far out in the country. The smart ones went to college and moved the hell out. The pretty ones too lazy to move away married local business owners. The rest got jobs at Walmart.

Older cops treated her like some kind of glorified secretary. Younger cops spoke about her in hushed tones that ceased when she approached. She'd heard all the rumors. There were at least fifteen police officers she'd allegedly slept with during the short span of her career. Actually, fifteen was a soft number. It probably went higher, she thought.

Bill Waylon was a good boss, very old-fashioned, and he didn't tolerate anyone hassling her. Still, she kept her mouth shut any time she wanted to punch someone in the soft spot between their nose and upper lip. He made a big-enough deal about it that she never had to. That was not her favorite thing about him, though. Waylon backed up his people when they did their job, and he wasn't afraid to tell locals to go fuck themselves when they complained about cops who were in the right. She knew this was a celebratory quality in a chief. Just like patrolmen who didn't wear their uniforms off-duty to get free food from all the local restaurants, chiefs who stood up for their cops were rare.

There were fifteen similar small police departments in Vieira County, most of them places where Barney Fife had long been the community standard for cops. The townships and boroughs they patrolled were recently developed communities that only a decade prior had run off well water and received only AM radio. It was coal country, years after all the coal mines had shut down, leaving behind nothing but cheap housing and unemployed hillbillies. New people had flooded the area, buying up land for cheap, turning fields into housing developments and shopping centers. Chain stores like Starbucks and Regal Cinema began sprouting up, taking the place of abandoned gas stations and cement lots. People complained about the local towns losing their character.

The residents took pride that their towns could not be compared to big-city cesspools. They lived in a place where they could call the cops to complain their neighbors weren't mowing their grass or bitch about trash trucks coming through too early in the morning. They could get ordinances passed and speed bumps installed on public roads, and enforce a thousand other arbitrary needs, so long as they complained loud enough and long enough.

These were communities where the Pennsylvania State Police went on call overnight and took two hours to respond, if at all. No one minded, because it kept the taxes down. The thing most often said—like a mantra when it came time to ask for an increase in police salaries, or equipment, or manpower, and as an excuse when their houses were burglarized and they hadn't bothered to lock the door—was, "Nothing ever happens out here anyway."

Carrie parked her car in front of the station and unlocked the front door. She flicked on the light in the front office and cleared aside a stack of unsorted papers and dirty Styrofoam cups to make space on the desk. A typewriter took up most of it, a bulky thing made of solid metal. Bill Waylon had complained to the township council that it was starting to cost more per year to order typewriter ribbon from specialty distributors than it would to outfit the entire building with brand-new computers in every room.

When the council agreed to buy them computers, the older officers filed a grievance, saying it was a change in working conditions. They threatened to file an age discrimination lawsuit, claiming computers were something for young people and forcing them to learn how to use one was just a sneaky way of driving them off the force.

Waylon took the money and spent it on typewriter ribbon, whiteout, and a used mobile data terminal laptop for one of their two police cars. Most of the times, the laptop stayed locked up in the station.

The station had just one jail cell, outfitted with a concrete bed and aluminum toilet. The cell was occupied by sleeping cops more often than it was by criminals, and Carrie had gotten so used to the guys pissing in them that when she walked past, she called out,

"Your wife been cooking asparagus? Jesus, that stinks" or "You might want to get your prostate checked, that sounds a little weak to me."

She wrote out her overtime chit, making sure to circle the words *Task Force* so the pencil-pusher geeks knew she wasn't costing the local taxpayers any money. She punched in Waylon's phone number and let it ring.

"Chief Waylon speaking," he said, sounding official for a man who'd just woken up.

"It's Carrie, boss," she said. "I'm all done."

"Oh, good," he grumbled. "How did it go?"

"Kind of slow. We didn't see anything. They told me that's normal."

"How was Harv? He get grabby with you?"

"You think I'd let that happen? I just rode with him, to get it out of the way. He told me a bunch of stories, that's all."

"Let me guess. He's the unsung hero of this whole county."

She could not help but laugh. "Something like that."

"I bet."

"Well, apparently, he had a lot more to do with the Krissing investigation than people realize," Carrie said.

"Someday, if you ever get sick of sleeping at night, I'll tell you a little bit about what that old son of a so-and-so was doing to those little girls. For Harv to say he had anything to do with it, that's just a sin. I ought to punch him in the mouth next time I see him."

"Maybe I misunderstood," Carrie said. "I don't want to cause any trouble on this unit, or for you."

"Knowing Harv, you understood him perfectly. Six little girls are still walking the earth because of what Rein did. I know it because I'm the only person who was with him, so I'll be hog-tied if I let people forget that. I'm sure as heck not going to let some dimwit like Harv Bender run around taking credit for it."

She whistled into the phone. "*Son of a so-and-so? Dimwit?* Geez, Bill, that's mighty strong language coming from you. You feeling okay? I didn't get you all riled up, now did I?"

Waylon grunted, "I'm fine. Listen, go get some sleep. It's dark and foggy out, so be careful driving home. I'll see you tomorrow."

She flicked off the lights and locked up the station, glad to be going home. The chief's rule was that she could work the local Anti-Crime Task Force as long as it never interfered with her patrol duties. She didn't care if she had to pull an all-nighter doing surveillance, she was going to make sure she showed up on time and in uniform, just to not let him down. Anyhow, there was a cot in the back office, even if it did permanently reek of stale alcohol from all the times the older guys had showed up for work hungover and had to sleep it off.

She felt her cell phone vibrate in her pocket as she walked to her car. She pulled it out to look at the screen. It was past midnight. "Hello?"

"Where you at, bitch?" a female voice barked into the phone. "I got my mom to watch Nubs for a few hours an' you ain't here!"

Loud jukebox music in the background played pop country, and billiard balls cracked against one another like gunshots. Tailfeathers, she thought, knowing it must be ladies-drink-for-a-dollar night if Molly was there. "Sweetie, I can't. I'm exhausted. We just got done, and I have to be in tomorrow at seven."

"Just go in late."

"My job's not like that," Carrie said. "I can't just *go in late.*"

"Blah, blah, blah. You're no fun, you know that? Zero fun. I got a kid, and I ain't got no man, and I ain't got no money, but look at me. I still have fun. Know why? Because that's how I do, bitch."

Carrie wedged the phone against her ear with her shoulder as she started her car and said, "I'm hoping you walked there. Do you need a ride home?"

"No, sir, I ain't drunk, officer, sir," Molly said.

"I can tell you're drinking," Carrie said. "You only talk gangsta when you're drunk."

"Excuse me for not using proper English, my good lady. Perhaps this suits your delicate ears more sensibly?" Molly let out a long, slow burp that made them both laugh. "Can't you *please* just come have fun with your friend and stop being so lame?"

"Listen, it's not like you're not busy too. Whenever I'm free, you have Nubs."

"Oh, I'm sorry, is my child interfering with your social life, officer?"

"No, it's not like that. I just meant—"

"God, you're so stuck up now. When those cops you hang out with get tired of trying to feel you up, don't come crying to me."

Carrie held her tongue, trying to figure out what to say, but then it stopped mattering, because the line went dead. She knew better than to try to call back. They were like sisters, and nothing would ever change that, but things were different now, somehow.

After high school, most of their friends went off to college, and they both stayed in town. Molly's life became a nonstop party, filled with men, booze, a little smoke from time to time. When she got knocked up, it was no surprise. When the baby's father didn't stick around, that was no surprise, either. People who knew her never expected her to have the baby.

But Molly blossomed as a mom. She took it seriously and cleaned up her act. Nubs was born six years ago, and even when Molly was too broke to put gas in her car, that little girl still had clean clothes, brushed hair, and a packed lunch. If Molly wanted to go blow off steam, who could blame her, Carrie thought. In the morning, she'd get a text apologizing for the argument, filled with hearts and smiley emoticons. They'd make plans to get together and never speak of the matter again.

Actually, that wasn't true, Carrie told herself. The text wouldn't come in the morning. Probably midafternoon, after the pounding in Molly's head stopped.

No one who knew Carrie growing up would have suspected she'd become a cop. Hell, most of them would have bet real money on her having a kid even earlier than Molly did. It was always a shock when she ran into someone she knew while on duty. Crazy Carrie, they used to call her. Smoking in the bathroom, painting her fingernails black, using safety pins for earrings. Wearing T-shirts of long-defunct punk bands like Minor Threat and Black Flag, but actually listening to the music, too.

The last thing any young person wants to be labeled as is inauthentic, and soon she acquired an expanding interest in the culture referenced by the goth scene. Rock star suicides. Obscure foreign horror films. Infamous acts of extreme cruelty and violence throughout history. Government-sponsored medical experiments on prisoners. Serial killers.

She'd devoured books by Robert Ressler, a legendary FBI profiler who dealt with most of the famous ones firsthand, and then began obsessing over the Manson Family murders. In one particular moment of insanity, she'd written a letter to Manson, sending it to him at Corcoran State Prison, telling him she was learning all she could about his life. She enclosed a picture in the envelope that showed her making devil horns with her fingers and wearing a cut-off T-shirt with "Helter Skelter" printed across the front.

Two weeks later, she'd gotten a letter back. Her fingers trembled as she opened the flap and pulled out the folded paper tucked inside. There, in blue ink, was a response from one of America's most notorious psychopaths:

> *Hey pretty little thing. If you want to learn about me, come on out here. I could use the company.*

It was signed across the bottom in Manson's swirling script, with strange designs scribbled on the paper like Nordic runes.

She'd stuffed the letter under her mattress and never told anyone about it. For months she'd been terrified that the police would come arrest her for having contacted a psychotic killer. It was one thing to fantasize about evil, to reach into the darkness and play with it a little. It was something different when it knew your name and called you Pretty Little Thing.

At fifteen years old, both she and Molly got jobs at the local record shop, True Vinyl. She was the last of the mixtape generation, one of the earnest teenagers who spent hours crafting the perfect collection of songs, then cutting out pictures from magazines to create a customized cover. There was an art to the entire process, and when she gave a mixtape to someone as a gift, it was her way of saying, this is me, all of me, at this exact moment in time.

By that summer, she was the proud owner of seven piercings. Four of them you could see, in her ears, nose, and lip. The other three were just for the lucky ones.

She'd smoked weed and done pills but never stuck anything up her nose or in her arm. A few of the locals were into crystal meth, and she'd seen it around enough times to know that sooner or later, she was going to tweak.

On a Friday, early in the afternoon, an old man had walked into the store. Liver spots covered his arms and neck, and a shock of bleached-blond hair stuck straight up from the top of his head. He wore purple sunglasses that covered most of his face, and he kept his head low as he moved throughout the store, ignoring the records and checking the walls instead. It was unusual enough to see someone older than forty inside the store, but when Carrie had looked up from behind the register, she saw something that made her eyes widen. The faces of the boy band NSYNC emblazoned across the old guy's bright blue T-shirt and the words "CELEBRITY TOUR" printed below it.

He saw Carrie looking at the shirt and said, "Do you carry posters?"

She looked up from the shirt, confused by his question, then said, "I think in the back corner we have a few."

"Of who?"

"Nothing you've heard of, probably."

He looked annoyed and said, "How about Britney Spears? Aaron Carter. Justin Timberlake, obviously. I'll even take Lil' Romeo if you don't have anything else."

Carrie had smirked at the old man rattling off the pop acts as if he actually knew who they were, trying to decide if he was a weirdo or just some overly enthusiastic grandparent shopping for the kids in his life. "Sorry. That's not really what we carry here. You might want to try the mall or something."

"I already have everything they carry." He'd lowered his sunglasses to inspect her more carefully. "How old are you?"

"Old enough. Why?"

He'd twirled his finger in a circle, tracing the outline of the heavy makeup around her eyes, and said, "You should go a little easier on the goth look. I bet you were a lot prettier when you were younger. You should take that piercing out of your lip, too. Boys are probably afraid it will catch on their peckers when you suck them off."

The old man had left the store, the heavy brass bells rattling the glass door as it closed behind him. Carrie turned her head and shouted, "Hey! Can you guys come up here for a second?"

Molly had come through the beaded curtain first, followed by two other teenagers, a puff of marijuana smoke billowing out toward the fluorescent lighting. Carrie had pointed at the old man crossing the street and said, "Do any of you know that creep? He just came in here and said some crazy shit to me."

Molly had squinted as she'd lowered her head to look. "That's just Old Man Krissing. He stops in every few weeks to see if we have any new posters. What's he wearing, a Bieber shirt? Last time I saw him he had a Wiggles T-shirt on."

"The kids' group?" Carrie had asked.

"Yeah. He's so cute. He must have grandkids who love music."

"He's not cute, Molly. He's an asshole."

"Okay. What did he say to you?"

None of them looked concerned, or even interested. "It was nothing," Carrie had said. "Just forget it."

"Well, I think he's cute."

The group filtered back through the curtain separating the store from the large room in the rear, their voices replaced by the gurgling of a water bong and subsequent fits of coughing. "Carrie, come get in on this before it's gone!" Molly had shouted.

She'd watched the old man get into a small, green VW Bug and drive away. She'd looked over her shoulder and said, "I'm good, thanks."

Two little girls had been reported missing. One of them from twenty miles away, in the southern end of the county, and another from New Jersey. Just two of the thousands who were reported missing that year, but these two were different.

In the years to come, the newspapers would label them the first Krissing girls.

Bill Waylon's office had a framed photograph with portraits of ten smiling, perfect little angels. Some of them wore braces, some wore large, thick glasses. Some were awkward, and some were so beautiful they looked destined to be supermodels. Each of them smiled at the camera, full of life and youth, unaware that their flames were about to be snuffed out by the darkest of people in the darkest of ways. Words were inscribed under the portraits: *We Will Never Forget You. Your Light Will Shine Forever.*

Beneath that was a framed, yellowed newspaper article that showed Waylon in a suit, looking much younger and fitter, without the bulging pot belly that threatened to bust through his white uniform shirt, standing next to another detective. The headline read DETECTIVES QUESTIONED ABOUT KRISSING ARREST MUTILATION.

She'd read that newspaper article when it was first printed, the same way she'd read every article when the investigation first came to light. Somehow, it was different than reading about the Manson Family murders, or any of the serial killers Robert Ressler talked about profiling. She'd come face-to-face with Krissing, and he wasn't grandiose or seductive or powerful at all. He was just some dirty pervert wearing a ridiculous T-shirt with ridiculous sunglasses and hair. Just a son of a bitch who ruined the lives of multiple families that lived within ten miles of her house.

That same day, Carrie had surprised everyone she knew by removing all the jewelry from her face. She'd thrown the letter from Charles Manson in the trash the same morning she'd taken her first community college class in criminal justice.

Her phone buzzed again, and she looked down to see a new text from Molly: *Joke's on u bitch I found a boyfriend!*

"Great," Carrie said, tossing her phone onto the passenger seat.

It buzzed again. *He's got these awesome friends, they want to take me to a party. OMG they said it's the best party ever!*

Carrie slowed to a stop at the next light and picked up her phone, typing, *What the hell are you talking about?*

A new text appeared before she could send it. *BTW never ever never get a margarita at Tailfeathers. They suck. They taste like medicine or something.*

Carrie jabbed the call button with her thumb and pressed the phone to her ear, starting to drive again. It rang as she drove, mentally instructing Molly to pick up. She heard thumping music in the background and Nubs's sweet giggle, saying, "Mommy can't come to the phone right now. Leave a message!"

"Pick up the phone, you asshole," Carrie said, then hung up.

An incoming picture appeared on her screen. Molly was slumped forward, grinning stupidly at the camera. Her eyes were half-lidded, heavy with too much mascara that ran dripping from their corners. Her frosted blond hair was a tangled mess, and one of the men surrounding her was pulling it back, like he was holding a dog by a leash.

The picture was crowded with men surrounding Molly, staring at Carrie through the phone's screen. The one pulling her hair wore a red hooded sweatshirt with a Greek fraternity symbol emblazoned across the chest. He was leering down at Molly, hungry for her.

Carrie yanked the wheel right, making the tires squeal, and jammed the gas pedal to the floor, heading for the distant lights of Old Town.

*   *   *

Tailfeathers' parking lot lights were already turned off by the time she arrived, a message to people trying to get there before last call that it was too late. The bartenders weren't making enough money and they were closing early. The neon beer advertisements flickered in the front windows, washing the entrance in fluorescent yellows and greens. Carrie's headlights panned a tinted-out SUV as it backed out of a parking space near the front door, the driver looking at Carrie's car with annoyance as she turned on her high beams to see who was inside. There were figures in the back, hidden behind the car's darkened windows. She caught a glimpse of a red sweatshirt in the front passenger seat and threw her car into park, jumping out to block their way. "Stop the car!" she commanded, pointing at the driver.

She heard Red Sweatshirt say, "What the fuck?" through the open car window as she wrenched her gun from the holster on her hip and raised it, leveling it at the driver's suddenly wide eyes. "Police department. Stop. The. Mother. Fucking. Car. You heard me that time?" she said.

The driver slammed the transmission forward and held up his hands, saying, "What's going on?"

"Who else is in the car?" Carrie said.

"What?" he cried. "What are you talking about?"

Carrie circled around to the driver's side, trying to peer through the darkened rear windows. "Where is she?"

"Where's who?" the driver spat.

"The girl from inside! The girl you told about the party!" She turned the gun on Red Sweatshirt and shouted, "Don't sit there looking at me like I didn't see you all standing around her five minutes ago!"

"Officer, there's a misunderstanding," the driver said. "That was just—"

Carrie grabbed the rear door and pulled it open. The SUV's interior light came on, revealing the two other men who were in the picture holding a case of Budweiser on the seat between them. Both of them waved their hands in the air, crying out, "We didn't do anything!"

She tried looking in the seats behind them, unable to see down on the floor, where Molly would be lying curled up, passed out, or maybe even covered by a blanket so no one could see her being driven away by these bastards to their *party*. "Open the rear."

"What?"

Carrie reached through the window and grabbed the driver by the shirt, twisting it and snarling, "Open the goddamn rear gate."

He looked down at her grip on his shirt and said, "Get your hands off me, lady! You have no idea what you're doing!"

"I know that I'll be blowing your motherfucking brains out all over your boyfriend here if you don't open the trunk!"

"Stop pointing a gun at us! There's nothing in there!" Red Sweatshirt screamed, his voice breaking with terror.

"Open the rear gate!" Carrie shouted back.

"There's nothing back there!" the driver cried out. "Just let me go. Please, please let me go!"

With that, the bar's front door opened and Molly

burst through it, laughing aloud, needing to press her hand against the outside wall to steady herself. She turned her head and her eyes widened at the sight of Carrie pressing a gun to someone's forehead. "What are you waving that thing around for, you maniac?"

Carrie looked at the driver. Tears were streaming down his face. Snot dripped across the top of Red Sweatshirt's quivering upper lip.

"You made it sound like you were about to be gang raped by these assholes!" Carrie shouted.

"You mean the picture?" Molly said. "Jesus, that was a joke, Carrie! I was just trying to give you shit for not coming to hang out with me!" She looked at the men in the car, both of them overcome with fright, and rolled her eyes, "Look what you did. Go sit in your car."

When Carrie didn't move, Molly snapped, "Now, so I can fix this!"

Carrie slammed her gun back in its holster and turned around, grabbing her car door and pulling it open and shut as hard as she could. The slam echoed all around them. She grabbed the steering wheel with both hands, feeling anger bubbling up inside of her.

When your chief finds out about this, there is going to be major shit, she told herself. Pointing a gun at un-armed civilians, off-duty, out of your jurisdiction. For no reason. Major, major shit.

She watched Molly lean against the driver's door, talking to the men inside. Saw them looking from Molly, to her, and back again. Molly reached in and touched the driver's face, wiping it for him and then cupping the side of his cheek with her hand. She waved as they sped off.

Molly shuffled toward Carrie sheepishly, her hands stuffed in the back pockets of her tiny shorts. "You okay?" she said, leaning against Carrie's door.

"I'm going to get fired."

"No, you're not. You'll be fine. God, chill out."

"How would you know?" Carrie shot back at her. "You got fired from your last job three weeks ago!"

"I didn't get fired. Technically, I got laid off."

"Well, in my job you don't get laid off, Molly. I get fired, and no one will ever hire me again. Christ, I could even get arrested over this."

"You're not going to get fired, okay?" Molly snapped. "I made a deal."

Carrie looked at her suspiciously. "What kind of deal?"

"I told them if they kept their mouths shut and just went home, I wouldn't tell you they were all snorting crystal in the bathroom."

"Were they?" Carrie said.

"Uh, yeah."

"Were you?"

Molly folded her arms and glared at her. "Seriously?"

"That picture you sent me was a dick move, Molly. A really dick move."

"It was a joke, Carrie. Honest to God, I thought you'd know I was just messing with you." Molly covered her mouth with the back of her hand to try to stifle a laugh. "I cannot believe you came in here, guns blazing like that! Holy shit, that was the most badass thing I ever seen in my life." Molly punched her lightly in the arm. "You made those dudes piss their pants."

Carrie looked away, fighting the urge to smile. "I'm still mad at you."

"Yeah, but you love me," Molly said. "Otherwise you wouldn't have come here ready to shoot up the place trying to rescue me."

"Just get in the car. I'm taking you home."

Molly pointed across the parking lot. "I have my car here."

"Get in. I can smell alcohol on you. You're not driving."

"Can't you just follow me home to make sure I get there okay?" Molly whined.

"Yeah, so I can witness you swerve into a telephone pole? That's a great idea. You can get your car tomorrow. Get in."

Molly went around to the passenger side and got in. "I'm only listening to you because you have a gun and now I know how much you like threatening people with it."

Carrie went to put the car in drive, stopped, and looked at Molly. "Seat belt."

"Seriously? We're only going a few blocks!"

"Seat. Belt."

"Oh my God, you're such a cop bitch!" Molly grabbed the seat belt and yanked it across her body. "There, are you happy now?"

"Not even close," Carrie said, starting to drive.

"What did you think of the guy in the red sweatshirt?" Molly said as they pulled out of the parking lot.

"The one with snot coming out of his nose?"

"That was just from the meth. He's not like that all the time, probably."

"If you say so. Why do you ask?"

"He gave me his number."

Carrie glared at her. "You're kidding me, right?"

"Mama has needs, hon. Mama has needs."

"Mama needs to stay away from strange men she meets in bars is what Mama needs."

"See? Right there. That's why you're single," Molly said. "You're too picky."

3

Morning weekday shifts were normally quiet. They'd have an occasional wreck, where someone took a sharp turn too fast and wiped out a length of chicken wire fence. Mainly, mornings consisted of phone calls to the station complaining about cars parked where they shouldn't be. Normally, the owner of the car sobered up enough by ten a.m. to come retrieve it. No police response necessary, as Carrie wrote on most of her reports.

She spread out her newspaper across the ancient, unsteady table in the locker room, picking at the jagged pieces of contact paper that had long covered it, preferring the unfinished wood beneath.

She sipped her coffee as she flipped through the paper, looking for the local news section. It was three pages long, tucked behind the national news. This was irredeemably stupid, in her opinion. Nobody was reading the local newspaper for yesterday's global events. The Internet had real-time updates from all corners of the earth, free of charge, but every backwoods news rag wanted to pretend it was still the 1950s and act like they were the ones informing the public.

What local papers *could* do was report on things the Internet didn't care about. They should have had reporters at every police station and township meeting, digging up all the drama that people scurried to cover up like cat droppings in a litter box. Maybe then citizens wouldn't be so quick to say, "Well, it's not like cops do anything around here anyway" or insist the police treat every barking dog complaint like the crime of the century.

She scanned the news and saw a few articles about local high school sports teams, a seniors group raising money for the troops, and what the weather was going to do. She closed the paper in disgust and got up, realizing that the familiar weight around her hips was missing. She laughed at herself as she walked over to her locker and spun the dial to open it. She'd never even put on her gun belt that morning.

Bill Waylon arrived precisely at eight A.M. His white shirt gleamed, and the sleeves were creased sharp enough to cut anyone walking past him too closely. His black leather shoes were polished to reflective surfaces, and the brim of his chief's hat shined with bright yellow braids. His silver hair was brushed back, the same color as his fine, thick mustache. In a way, he looked like some kind of sheriff from the Old West. The kind who walked into saloons alone and let the wanted men have one last whiskey before deciding to go quietly or die where they stood.

"You know what the best thing about being chief is, Carrie?" he'd once asked. "There's not some pain in the behind being chief over you."

He was good to her, if overbearingly stuffy. From the start he'd been protective, making it known far and wide that the first cop who so much as said "Hello" to her in a harassing way was going to find their ass in a sling. The way Bill protected was awkward and over-done but well intentioned, the way an aunt introduced you to all your cousin's friends on the football team, as if saying, "I know she's pretty, but none of you can have her."

He glared at anyone who cursed in the station around her and tried to set a good example himself. She caught him struggling to come up with replacements for what he meant to say, forcing awkward phrases like, "That mother slick-talker" and "Goddarn son of a b . . . bis-cuit-eater," and it always left her laughing.

"You need to stop, Chief. I hear worse all the time. Shit, I *say* worse all the time," she'd told him.

He'd get red in the face and say, "You're just a little bit older than my girls, Carrie. I wouldn't want anybody talking dirty in front of them if they were here."

Waylon had been with the Coyote Township Police Department just a few years longer than she had, but he'd brought a wealth of experience and connections from his previous job as a Vieira County Detective. His office walls were decorated with awards from every federal agency and multiple photographs with various politicians, including then vice president Joe Biden. "I don't vote for their kind, of course," Waylon explained whenever someone saw the picture, "but he's from Delaware and his wife's from just outside Philadelphia, so they took interest in the Krissing case. When the vice president asks you to be somewhere, you be somewhere, I don't care what party you are. They almost threw me out of the council meeting over that one, though, that's for sure."

She'd heard him say it a half-dozen times before

taking him aside and saying, "I'm a Democrat. Why do you keep saying 'their kind,' like it's something bad?"

"You'll grow out of that," he'd said, waving his hand dismissively. "A few more years on the job and you'll be as Republican as they come."

"I'll grow out of a woman's right to make decisions about her own body?" She'd looked him up and down and said, "I don't think I like the way this conversation is going, Chief."

His mustache had twitched as he looked at her, caught between smiling and having a slight panic attack. It was as if all the man's fears about having a female in the station house had come true and he was the one all the women's liberation groups and EEOC attack dogs were going to come gunning for. He stuttered a little and said, "I-I didn't mean anything by it, Carrie. Of course you have that right."

She'd squinted at him and leaned forward, "Hey, boss?"

"What?"

Her hand snapped out, cracking him in the belt buckle, making him flinch and protect his groin with both hands. "I'm fucking with you," she'd said. "Lighten up."

She'd left him standing in the hallway, trying to catch his breath, hands still covering his crotch. After that, they hadn't have any more discussions about politics.

Waylon unlocked his office door and called into the back room, "You awake back there, kiddo?"

She threaded a belt keeper through her belt on either side of the holster and snapped it shut, locking the holster in place. "What, you think I can't handle a little late-night surveillance?"

"God knows, if I had to spend an evening in a car with Harvey Bender, I couldn't."

She came up the hallway fixing the next two belt keepers into place. "It wasn't so bad," she said. "The way I see it, I can learn from anyone at this point. If someone can teach me anything about being a detective, I'll take it, no matter how much of a flaming douchebag they are."

"A detective, huh? One night out with the Task Force and you already want to leave Coyote and ship off to the County."

"That's what you did, isn't it?"

"Only because I never had anyone smart enough to tell me not to," he said. "You see the older guys around here, how excited they get over stopping a tractor trailer and writing him a few thousand dollars' worth of tickets? That's a big bust to them. The simple stuff makes them happy. Fat, dumb, and happy. If I could go back in time, I'd tell my younger self, Don't go looking for all that craziness. Just stay put and keep your head down. Do your twenty-five and don't take anything personal. Be fat, dumb, and happy."

Carrie pointed at the chief's gut. "Well, I'd say you're making a good head start on it, sir."

He patted his stomach. "I was both blessed and cursed with a wife who loves to bake."

Carrie's mind was already working ahead, framing the next question. It had to be asked carefully. "So, boss, I was wondering something. You know how we don't have any money in the budget for training?"

"Intimately."

"Well, what if I find an interview and interrogation school but I pay for it on my own? I'll even use vacation time to go if you need me to. The way I see it, there's no better skill to have as a detective than being able to get a confession, and I want to learn how to do it the right way."

Bill leaned back in his chair, considering her. "You're that serious about it?"

"I honestly am."

Bill stroked his mustache, a clear sign that he was thinking about it. "Actually, I agree with you, there's no better skill," he said. "Any idiot can sit in a back alley staring at a building for hours on end, but it takes a real special breed to be an interviewer. Now, I've been to all the schools. I've studied the Reid method and the behavioral forensic analysis techniques, and the qualitative interview curriculum, and you know what?"

"What?" she said.

"It's all bull. They teach you that if you ask a certain question a certain way, if the suspect shifts in his seat to the left instead of the right, or looks up when he should look down, you'll have him dead to rights. Can you imagine some idiot going into court and testifying that he knows a suspect committed a murder because his eyes shifted a certain way? It's embarrassing."

"So how do I learn to do it, then?"

Bill thought for a second and said, "You need to watch a true interviewer perform his magic. I say magic, because that's what it is. When you watch a good man in the box, he's like a dark sorcerer, spinning a web of illusion around the suspect until the poor soul don't know whether to mess himself or go blind. It's like he's leading the fool down a long hallway into a dark room, and by the time the door shuts, it's too late."

"Okay," she said. "So tell me who to go watch, and I'll go."

Bill scratched his chin and said, "Hang on. I think I have something that can help you." He got up from his desk and walked over to the small closet behind her chair, slid the rack of old police uniforms aside, and reached down for a box on the floor. He removed the lid and came up with a large manila envelope. "I saved this. Not for any special reason. I filed it away years ago in case we went to trial, but the guy pled guilty before we ever stepped foot in court. When I cleared out my desk, I guess I kept it as a kind of memento." He waved the envelope at her. "Technically, I may have committed a small act of theft, removing this from the County instead of putting it in their evidence locker. You understand what I'm saying?"

Carrie drew her fingers across her lips to zip them shut, then said, "I never saw a damn thing, Chief."

He snapped his fingers at her and said, "You're talking like a detective already. Come on, I think there's a VCR somewhere we can hook up to that hunk of junk TV in the back."

The camera was fixed on the side of a long interview table in a police interrogation room she did not recognize. The image moved in and out of focus as the operator twisted the lens to get a better view of the man sitting there. He was in his late twenties, good looking, well built. He wore his hair long in the back and kept it short and spiked in front. Carrie leaned forward to hear someone close a door off-screen and say, "We rolling, Bill?"

The man who sat at the table was pencil thin, his

thick brown hair swept up like Elvis. He hadn't developed the jowls and craggy lines along his cheeks yet, but Carrie recognized Harv Bender's smirk the moment he set a thick manila folder on the table and folded his hands. "I'm Detective Bender, and this is Detective Bill Waylon," Harv said, nodding toward the person standing out of view of the camera.

"How you doing?" the man said. "I asked them what this was all about, but they just said I had to come talk to you guys."

"That's right," Harv said. He tapped the folder with his index finger. "I'm the lead investigator on a case we've been putting together for two months. You know what's in here, Freddie?"

"No, sir."

"The absolute end of your existence, you scumbag."

The chief pressed stop on the thick remote control and pointed at the screen. "This kid, Freddie, he was a karate instructor at some little Tae Kwon Do place. No record. No history with any of the local PDs, not even a traffic ticket. His methodology was he'd befriend the families of prepubescent girls, looking for single moms, ones who really needed help babysitting and what not. He'd offer to watch the kids so Mom could go out and blow off some steam. Sure, why not, right? Good-looking guy, loves kids. A few of the moms even had him sleep over, cooked him breakfast. One even had an intimate relationship with him. Then, three twelve-year-old girls reported that he raped them during that same summer."

"Wait, if he was banging the moms, why did he go after the kids?" she asked.

"A lot of these guys will do whatever it takes to get closer to their intended target."

As he moved to press play, Carrie stopped him. "Are you talking about Harv? The a-hole I listened to brag all last night is the kind of cop I'm supposed to emulate?"

Waylon just smiled. "Let's see."

On the screen, Freddie looked down at the folder in confusion and said, "Is this a joke?" He burst into laughter and said, "This is a joke, right? Man, you guys almost had me there for a minute."

Harv's face flushed red and he slammed his fist on the table, shouting, "No, it's not a fucking joke, you child-molesting piece of shit! You sit there and smile about it one more time and I swear to God I will break every bone in your body. You think you can kung fu your way out of this room, tough guy? Go ahead and try it."

"No," Freddie said, mystified. "I don't think that at all. I really just don't understand."

"Understand this. Your ass is going down for three charges of rape, aggravated indecent assault, and every other goddamn sex crime on the books. They'll bury you at Graterford, and every orangutan in there is gonna use you as a cum Dumpster, get it?"

"No, actually, I don't."

"Did you rape those little girls?"

"No."

Bender slapped the table. "You raped those little girls, Freddie. You're a child-raping piece of shit, and you know you did it."

"Except, I didn't."

Harv's finger was like a gun, aimed between Freddie's eyes, "If you have one shred of decency in your entire body, you'll tell me what you did. Take this one chance to be a decent, God-fearing person, and spare those little girls any further humiliation." Harv's pointed finger trembled and his voice was shaking now. "Those little babies didn't deserve what you did to them. Now, you do the right thing, you asshole. Just once. Do the right thing."

Freddie's voice was very low and calm when he said, "I have no idea what you're talking about, Detective."

There was sudden movement on the screen, and the video camera went sideways and shut off at the sound of screaming.

The chief smiled slyly at Carrie and said, "We had, what you call, technical difficulties there for a second."

"I bet," Carrie said.

"Harv always had a soft spot for kids. He's a flaming jerk sometimes, but he gave this case his all." The tape came back on, and they saw Freddie sitting at the table, playing with the freshly torn shreds of his shirt collar. The case file was now bent and turned over, with reports and photographs scattered across the table. "Harv's problem was, he got too emotional over child sex cases. He used interviews as his chance to let out all that pent-up anger and frustration. Sometimes, caring too much can be as big a hindrance as not caring at all."

On the screen, a much thinner, much younger looking Bill Waylon came walking up to the table and said, "I apologize for that. It was unnecessary. You came in here like a gentleman, and we should have treated you that way."

"I thought I was coming in here trying to help you," Freddie said. "Instead, that guy assaulted me! Who do I talk to about pressing charges?"

"Let's slow down a second," Bill said. "We can deal with that later. First, let's take care of your situation.

Can you do me one favor? Can you let me send some-one else in here, just to ask you a few questions? Let me do that, and I promise we'll get you on your way."

"Is he going to assault me too?" Freddie snapped.

"No, I promise he won't. In fact, I don't think he'll be in here more than a few minutes. As far as I'm con-cerned, you didn't do anything and this has all just been a big misunderstanding. Can you spare a few more minutes for my guy?"

Freddie took a deep breath and said, "All right. I'd rather get this cleared up now anyway. Listen, thank you for being such a decent person. I was raised to re-spect police. I still might try to become a cop. It's something I've always thought about."

"I can tell," Bill said. "You've got the right stuff for it. Give me a second."

Bill exited the room and Freddie slumped forward, fluttering his lips as he looked down at the papers. There were hospital logs and evidence slips and a few photographs that he tried to get a better look at but did not want to appear too interested while the camera was watching.

Carrie looked at the chief and said, "That sounded pretty good to me, boss. That guy was eating out of your hand."

Bill shifted in his seat and tried not to look too proud, saying, "Yeah? I had some moves back in the day." The door closed in the interview room on the screen again, and Bill said, "But nothing close to what *he* had."

Freddie looked up at someone standing off camera and said, "Are you the one with the questions?"

"Just a few," a voice replied softly. A tall man came around the side of the camera, his hands adjusting the knobs along the side and saying, "Just give me a second to shut this thing off. I was never comfortable talking on camera. How about you?"

"Doesn't matter if the camera's on or not," Freddie said. "I'm telling the absolute truth, as God is my witness. I swear on my mother's soul, so I have no reason to fear what anyone hears me say."

"Well, I was hoping we could have a more private kind of conversation, if you don't mind." A hand jostled the camera, leaving it still activated. "There, the camera's off. Now it's just us. I'm glad you stayed here to talk to me. I don't often get to ask someone the things I want to ask you."

Carrie watched the man circle the table and slide into the bench across from Freddie. He was dressed in a white dress shirt and long black tie. He had short, unkempt hair and several days' worth of stubble. He swept down the length of the table, sending all of the case's paperwork into the air. "We don't need any of that," he said, with a wide smile that showed off his white teeth. "It's all nonsense anyway, isn't it?"

Freddie watched the reports flutter down toward the floor. "I already told them it wasn't true."

"Now, that's not what I meant and you know it. I mean all this carrying on over something so stupid. First off, there's a difference between children and young women. People who like babies and toddlers? Those people are sick, am I right?"

"Absolutely," Freddie agreed. "Totally sick."

"But for society to lump sexually mature young women into the 'children' category, that's just . . . I don't know, some Victorian fantasy about propriety. I mean, I started having sex when I was thirteen. I think the girl was eleven. Maybe even ten. Now, that's pretty young, but the fact is, a girl's body changes faster than a boy's and you know it."

"That . . . that's what they say, I guess," Freddie said.

"And let's face it, younger girls find older boys attractive, am I right? Especially ones that don't have any kind of man in their lives. In fact, up until not too long ago, it was perfectly normal for girls to be married and pregnant by the time they were fourteen. Hell, Romeo and Juliet were just kids, did you know that?"

"It's still that way in some parts of the world."

"Damn right," the man said. "Now, we can talk about how people in this country didn't have such a stick up their puritanical asses and we can talk about how nobody can fairly judge the relationship between a male and a female unless they are there, but really, it's just a game. They make up laws and put them in books, but what are they? Just words. And words are nothing compared to nature."

Carrie looked at Waylon. "Is this guy serious right now?"

"Just hang in there," Waylon said.

"I didn't have sex with those girls," Freddie muttered. "I was just trying to be a good role model to them."

"Sure, sure," the man said, holding up his hands over the table. "I've got to be honest, I don't give a shit if you did."

Freddie's eyebrows raised, but he didn't speak.

"But if you did, I just want to know how it was," he said, inching closer. "Was it fresh? Clean? Like a ripe peach on the outside and pink water ice on the inside?"

A thick drop of sweat slid down the side of Freddie's face.

"I bet it tasted like springtime, too," the man said, smiling wistfully.

Carrie pressed stop on the player, holding up her hands in surrender. Cold sweat trickled like ice down the length of her back. "I can't deal with this, Bill. I want to go back in time and punch this lunatic in the face. First, the lunatic who raped the kid, and then the lunatic who is sitting there with a shit-eating-grin talking about it."

"Perfectly understandable, kiddo," Waylon said, moving to get up from the table. "Do me a favor, let's forget this whole conversation ever took place. Have a good shift."

He reached to eject the video tape, and Carrie stopped him, saying, "Wait." She took a deep breath. "I'm just having a hard time listening to this, that's all. I wasn't expecting him to say those things."

"What you're having is a normal, human reaction to something that is absolutely the most vile thing on the planet." Waylon pointed at her face, at her flushed cheeks and enflamed eyes. "See how upset you are right now? Your voice is quivering with anger and horror. Can you hear it when you speak? I can. So can anyone you're talking to, including the suspect you're trying to convince to confess."

"He . . . he called the little girl's *thing* . . . Jesus, Bill. It's disgusting."

"That's right. Makes you sick to even thing about," Waylon said. "Know who it doesn't make sick? People like Freddie. And if you want to talk to people like him and get them to open up to you, you need to go into some real deep, dark places. It means being strong enough, committed enough, to engage them on their level. It is not a job for everyone."

"Did you do that?" Carrie said. She couldn't fathom sweet old Bill ever uttering anything so awful. "Talk like that, I mean?"

"No," Waylon said. "I never could."

"That's a good thing. That means you're a normal person, right?"

"It just means I was too weak," he said. "Keep watching."

Carrie pressed play, folding her arms as the tape began again.

"I met this girl last year," the interviewer said. "Goddamn, she was good. Pretty little thing. Fourteen. Maybe thirteen, but developed, you know?" he said, cupping his hands in front of his chest. "You know what the best thing was? Where I met her."

Freddie's eyes shifted back and forth from the man to the door, and he said, "W-where did you meet her?"

"Right here," the man said, glancing over his shoulder to make sure no one else was listening. "On the job. She had some kind of troubled home life and needed help, so I kindly offered to keep tabs on her, you know what I'm saying? Take her out to the mall. Buy her some makeup and underwear. It got so she couldn't keep her hands off me. God, she was sexy. I had a naked picture of her in my locker, but I had to get rid of it, or else I'd show it to you." He made a circle with his thumb and forefinger, saying, "Nice pink nipples. Perfectly silver dollar-sized, just like this. Those the kind you like?" Freddie's breath quickened. He reached down to adjust the front of his pants under the table, hidden from the man but in clear view of the camera. He swallowed hard, staring at the circle.

"I was looking at the pictures of these fine young things, and that one with the long black hair, with the freckles?"

"Judy," Freddie whispered.

"Yeah, Judy." He leaned sideways, picked up a picture that was lying on the floor, and held it up, showing the camera a little girl in a middle school class photo. Her butterfly headband was low on her forehead and she smiled at the camera, showing off her braces. "She has that look in her eye. I need to know, man. Tell me."

"Tell you what?" Freddie asked.

The man held up Judy's photograph to his face and inhaled, grinning as he put the picture back down. "Tell me about her."

Freddie stared at him, the knees of both legs bouncing up and down at the heel so furiously that the table was shaking.

"Come on, man, I need to know," the man said. "Was it good? It had to be good. My God, just look at her."

"It . . . it was her first time."

"How'd you do? You give it to her nice and hard? Make her squeal a little or a lot?"

"I had trouble holding back. It was over pretty fast."

The man looked down at the picture again, "Well, who could blame you? What about the other two? Which one was better or worse?"

"Judy," he said, leaning toward the older girl's photograph. "I couldn't get the younger one to myself long enough to make it work."

"Well, they can't all be home runs. You spend *any* time with her? Get any oral at least?"

"A little."

"How was that?"

"Not that great," Freddie said. "She has an overbite. Bit me pretty good down there one time."

"Well," the man said, grinning, "I sure am glad we talked. I feel better. How about you?"

"It's not that often you get to talk to someone who understands. Especially a cop."

The man slid the little girl's photograph back off the table. "Tell me about it."

"So can I go now?" Freddie said.

"Hang on one second, let me get Bill." The man got up from the table and opened the door, calling out, "Bill, can you come in here?"

Bill walked in holding a pair of handcuffs behind his back. "Do I even need to ask?"

The man put his hand on Freddie's shoulder, then pointed to the camera and said, "He gave up all three. You might want to turn that off before Harv comes in. But don't let him listen to the tape yet or we'll be cleaning blood off the ceiling for days."

The screen went black, and the chief stopped the tape again. He looked over at Carrie and saw her sitting motionless, eyes wide and fixed on the screen. "Pretty awful, yeah?" Waylon said.

Carrie could not respond.

"So here's what you don't know," Waylon said. "We had no physical evidence in any of those cases. Just the little girls' initial statements, and they were starting to crack from the mental pressure of having to testify. The youngest one, Mary? She started throwing up every time anyone even mentioned the investigation. On the night we did this interview, she was rushed to the emergency room for dehydration." Waylon leaned back in his seat. "If we hadn't gotten a confession, the DA was refusing to prosecute just to spare the children the trauma of having to face their accuser. This interview was do-or-die. As awful as it is to watch, as awful as it is to even contemplate, what you just saw is an act of heroism."

"It's heroism talking about how much you enjoy having sex with children?" Carrie scowled.

"No." Waylon shook his head. He scratched his scalp, trying to find the right words. "You know how in war, there's the guys you see on TV, wearing their nice, clean uniforms? Those are the guys we watch on the news and let lead the parades. That's the way we want to imagine our soldiers."

"Okay," she said.

"Well, there are also guys you don't hear about. The ones behind enemy lines, crawling through sewage lines just to sneak up on some poor bastard and kill him while he's sitting on the toilet. There's people doing necessary things that we don't want to know anything about. Things that violate all the ideas we have about what's proper, yet that's what it takes to win. If you really want to be a detective, you need to understand that."

She looked at the TV screen, not speaking.

"See, to get a confession sometimes means putting the well-being of the victims over your own mental health. Jacob used to always say that it felt like he was unlocking areas of his mind that weren't meant to be unlocked. Going places that you never come all the way back from. A kind of darkness, was how he put it. Looking back, maybe he was right. I guess the darkness won. It's like that quote about the abyss."

"What quote?"

"When you look into the abyss, it looks back into you." Bill ejected the tape from the machine and slid it back into the envelope, saying, "I've known a lot of cops over the years, kiddo. A lot of investigators. Everyone from federal agents to big-city homicide detectives, and Jacob Rein was the best. Anybody who says different better not say it around me. I get that he did a terrible thing, and he paid a heavy price for that. But more than a few little kids got safe because of what that man was willing to do when it was his time to do it."

Carrie watched him get up from his seat and head down the hall toward his office. She looked at the black TV screen, seeing her own reflection staring back at her in the dark glass.

4

That day the calls trickled in. It was the kind of shift that dragged on. Sometimes Carrie got so bored she scanned the state police channels, listening to their dispatcher fire off jobs nonstop. Domestics, car crashes, retail thefts, one after the other in rapid succession. She dreamed of that kind of police work, going job to job with barely enough time to write the paper on each one. The days would fly by then. Instead, her slow twelve-hour shift felt like a prison sentence. Hard, monotonous labor for twelve hours, paroled for twelve, and then right back the next day to do it all over again.

She ran a speed trap on the 423 Highway, keeping her car parked close enough to the road to let drivers see her and slow down in time. Most did. Only the real idiots flew past, somehow missing the marked police unit with full decals and lightbar and the uniformed officer behind its wheel holding an Accutrak. At each car stop, she walked up to the car and asked for their license and registration, and the rest was up to them.

Cops, cops' family members, military veterans, prosecuting attorneys, and nurses didn't get tickets. Nobody she knew on a first-name basis got a ticket, which tended to be a lot of people in such a small area. They all received written warnings the first time just to let them know it wasn't a game and there was an official record.

Old people, and anyone who looked as if they were struggling, they just got a verbal warning. A "slow down and drive safe, you speed demon, these young folks can't keep up with you," or something cute like that.

Everybody else got a citation. But it was up to them, what kind and how many. She had a mental scale of how much attitude she would tolerate from someone before issuing another citation, kind of like a mental thermostat. Most people had some sort of attitude when they got pulled over, that was just normal. But they cooled out as she went through her spiel, and by the time she was done, they thanked her for keeping the roads safe.

Assholes who ran their mouths were talking themselves into more citations with every word that fell out of their faces. Fines and points on their licenses racked up with every curse and every ignorant comment about her gender, her police department, and cops in general, ringing out in her mind like winning amounts on a slot machine.

She heard the next car's engine coming her way before she could see it. It was moving so fast that it hit the first white line of her speed trap before she could press the Accutrak's button. It was a black blur across the highway, doing at least 100. Carrie's heart pounded against her ribs as she peeled out after it, throwing gravel and dirt in every direction, kicking on the over-heads and wailer. "Thirty-Four-Four, I'm attempting to stop a vehicle, high rate of speed," she called out on the radio, shouting over the siren.

The car pulled ahead of her—a black Nissan, tinted windows, after-market exhaust—and she jammed the gas pedal down.

Drug dealer, she thought. Active warrants. Maybe an escaped prisoner. A wanted homicide suspect.

These possibilities raced across her mind like quicksilver, flooding her arms and legs with adrenaline. The dispatcher asked for her location, and it was all Carrie could do to spit out, "North on 423, black Nissan," in between multiple short, sharp breaths.

The chief's voice crackled over the radio, "Thirty-Four-C to Thirty-Four-Four, are you in pursuit?"

"Negative, sir," Carrie panted. "Just trying to catch up."

Pursuits were nearly forbidden except in the most extreme situations, and Carrie knew it. Police departments around the country had been sued enough times for chasing people and causing multiple innocent victims to be crushed, run over, and blown up that their insurance companies had stricken them from the rulebooks.

Telephone poles whipped past in a blur. Oncoming cars slowed and pulled over at the sight of her Crown Vic screaming up the highway. They were heading into a long stretch of road through Hansen Woods, with nothing but trees and fishing streams on either side.

She tightened her grip on the steering wheel, feeling it vibrate under the strain and speed. Other cops were calling over the radio, saying they were en route to back her up, their voices charged with excitement at something, anything, finally happening. She knew this was dangerous. Cops in pursuit tended to be over-loaded with adrenaline when it ended, and invariably wound up kicking the living shit out of the suspect. It was the kind of thing that made national headlines and lived forever on the Internet.

She could see the Nissan ahead of her, now close enough to make out the tag, and she grabbed the microphone, calling out, "PA, Echo-Delta-Gulf . . ." but her voice faded as the car's brake lights flashed once, twice, and the car suddenly pulled over. "I-It's stopping," she said, feeling a strange sense of calm flooding through her, washing up through her hands and into her arms, sliding down her chest and pooling deep in the pit of her stomach.

The road was narrow here, without any shoulder. Just two lanes, and nothing but trees as far as she could see. No houses. No people. The sun streamed through the clustered foliage all around them, giving everything a soft, golden light.

She picked up the radio and said, "We're stopped," then reached down and unsnapped her holster, putting her hand on her gun's grip.

Water trickled out of the Nissan's fat exhaust pipe, and she could hear its engine rumbling. The rear windshield was opaque in the shadows of the woods. She drew her pistol and kept it low as she slid out of the police car, shutting the door quietly so it didn't give her away.

"Driver!" she shouted. "Put both of your hands through the window and keep them there."

A pair of hands came out through the window.

She circled to the left, trying to get a look inside the car. The windows were too dark to see through. Any hidden occupants had a perfect shot at her. She doubled back to her vehicle, keeping the gun in both hands as she went around the passenger side, coming up to the rear right bumper. She slapped the fender and said, "Roll down the passenger window."

It came down and she moved sideways, eyes zeroed in on the car door, waiting for it to pop open. Movement inside the rear compartment made her twitch and touch the pistol's trigger, feeling the smooth curve with the tip of her finger. She could see something in the side mirror's glass and said, "Passenger, put your hands out the window! Do it now!"

The car rocked, followed by the unclicking of a seat belt, and then a pair of tiny, sticky hands slid through the open window. A little girl poked her head out, her long, curly hair draped over the door. "Hello, police. I have to go potty."

The sound that came out of Carrie was something like a punctured football as she lowered her gun. "Officer?" the man called from the driver's seat. "Can we make this fast? I'm trying to get my little girl home before she has an accident."

Carrie holstered her gun and walked up to the passenger window, feeling sweat pouring down her sides, soaking through her bra and bulletproof vest. She smiled at the little girl and said, "Go ahead and get back in your seat, honey."

"Okay," the little girl said.

The dad ducked down to see Carrie and said, "I guess I was speeding?"

"Yeah, just a little," she said.

"Sorry about that, she was screaming. We're just starting potty training."

"Go."

"And then my wife called."

"Go, I said!" Carrie wiped her forehead and felt her hand come away wet. She smacked the roof of the car with her hand. "Get going before I change my mind, and slow down."

He looked at her in confusion, as if he was about to continue arguing, but then he thought better of it, rolled up his window, and stepped on the gas. Carrie watched the Nissan take off down the highway, just as the sound of sirens appeared over the distance. Four police cars, coming her way, fast. The dispatcher had been calling to check her status since she'd gotten out of the car, and Carrie had forgotten to turn on her portable radio.

In the old days, people had to come to the police station to report crimes. There was a two-way telephone mounted to the wall outside the station for when someone needed help after hours and the clerk had already gone home. The telephone went directly to the county's only dispatcher, and it was hit or miss if they were awake, or sober enough, to answer it.

In those days, people did for themselves, Carrie figured as she headed back toward town. Now, they can't drive past a cat crossing the street without calling 911. Back then, there was no guarantee the police were coming anytime soon, so folks tended to sort things out themselves. Probably much more efficiently, too, she thought.

In the very old days, before police had radios in their cars, there was a tall pole near the station's entrance, with a blue lightbulb at the very top. When someone needed help, they flicked on the light and had to wait for the cop working in that area to drive by and see it.

They probably had a better chance of seeing Jesus walking up the street than seeing a cop when one was needed, she thought. Criminals knew it too. If you broke into somebody's house, you weren't getting chased off by the sound of a burglar alarm, you were getting a chest full of buckshot. Done and done. Efficient. Old school.

As she passed the station, she saw someone standing by the station door and flicked on her blinker to turn into the parking lot. She looked at her radio, making sure it was on. Dispatch had not called. She stopped her car at the edge of the driveway and looked at her phone. No missed phone calls. She lowered her sunglasses to get a better look. A woman, early fifties, holding a large purse. Large enough to have a gun, Carrie thought. In her first year on the job, a state trooper at Blooming Grove barracks had been ambushed by a maniac with a sniper rifle.

Carrie unsnapped her holster, getting her weapon ready to draw, if needed. Some of the best advice she'd ever heard about policing was, "Treat everybody like a million bucks, and have a plan to kill them."

Carrie looked the woman over, thinking, *If she comes out with a gun when I park my car, I'm going to bail out the driver's side door, get low for cover, duck around the rear fender, and come up shooting.*

She pulled in, watching the woman just stand there, holding her purse. Carrie got out of her car and shut the door, keeping the car between her and the woman. "Can I help you?"

"I'd like to report a missing person," the woman said.

Carrie moved around the police car, keeping an eye

on the woman, assessing her demeanor and posture. "Who's missing?" she said.

"My daughter. She went out last night and never came home."

"How old is she?"

"Twenty-two."

Carrie stopped walking and pulled a small notepad out of her uniform shirt pocket. "Name?"

"Denise Lawson. You probably know her."

Everybody assumed all cops knew the people who dealt regularly with any other cops. "Nope. What's your name?" Carrie said, still writing.

"Marianne Lawson." The woman dug into her purse, filing through papers stuffed inside. "I brought a recent photograph of her, and wrote down her height and weight and all the other information you might need. Can you track her on Facebook? I heard you can track a person that way."

Carrie stood there, looking at the woman, not writing. "Is your daughter suicidal?"

"No," Marianne said.

"Is she suffering any other mental disorders?"

"No," Marianne said, seemingly confused by the question. She went back to her purse. "I have the photo right here. Just give me a moment."

"Ma'am," Carrie said.

"Here it is," the woman said, pulling a picture out of her purse.

Carrie looked at the photograph, seeing the pretty, young dark-haired woman smiling back at her. She wasn't impressed. At twenty-two, Carrie had already been out of her father's house for years, worked two jobs, put herself through the police academy, and gotten hired as a full-time police officer. It was hard for her to pity some little miss thing who lived with her parents and couldn't be bothered to come home at night. "Ma'am."

"Yes?"

"I can't put your daughter in as a missing person."

"Sorry?"

"I can't put her in as a missing person. It's not against the law for an adult to not come home if they don't want to, and they have the right to not be bothered by the police about it. Best I can do is take a report that she hasn't shown up, but I'm sure she's fine. Just hang in there."

"No," Marianne said. "No, you don't understand. She would never not call. Not after everything we've been through."

"I'm sure there's a very good explanation for it when she turns up."

"Look at this," Marianne said, thrusting her phone toward Carrie. "She updates Facebook constantly, but nothing since last night. Scroll through her history and you'll see!"

"I can't get on Facebook at work, but I believe you," Carrie said, dropping her notebook back in her pocket, not looking.

Marianne's hands were clenched around the purse straps so tight her knuckles were white. "What am I supposed to do? I need your help. We have to find her."

Carrie smiled as kindly as she could manage. "Listen, it's going to be all right. These things happen all the time. What you could do is start calling all the local county prisons."

"Why?" Marianne said. "She's never gotten in any trouble before."

"Well," Carrie said. "That's where I normally find

people. They go out for the night, get drunk, get in a fight, get arrested, and wind up in jail. Then they can't remember anybody's phone number because all their numbers are stored in their phones, and they have to wait to bail out."

Marianne's eyes flared. "Why would you tell me to call the jails and not the hospitals?"

"Because hospitals call any family members they can find when there's an emergency so they can get paid," Carrie said. "Jails don't."

"Well, she's not in jail," Marianne said, her voice little more than a whisper, as if spoken from far away. "She isn't like that. She's been behaving herself for a while now. Long enough that she wouldn't be in jail."

"Well, that's good," Carrie said. "Then you have nothing to worry about. Listen, I'll write up this report and you let me know if she turns up, okay?"

"Okay," Marianne mumbled. "Please keep an eye out for her."

Carrie pulled open the police car door, repeating, "All right." She backed out of the station lot and drove away, saying, "Behaving herself for a while now, huh? Keep living in that dream world, lady. People like you are why people like me will always have a job."

She left her vest and shirt and gun belt in her locker at the end of her shift. She dropped her gun into her off-duty holster and headed out of the station, feeling cool air on her bare arms. Her white T-shirt was clinging to her, and she pulled it away from her body, letting her skin breathe. She walked to her car and opened the door, standing behind it as she made sure no one else was in the parking lot, then reached up inside her shirt with both hands, grabbing the underside of her sports bra and pulling it forward. She sighed with relief at freeing her breasts, shaking them back and forth, wanting nothing more than to take the damned thing off. The bare refrigerator in her apartment loomed in her thoughts, though, and she did not feel like walking through the supermarket with her nipples poking through her wet, white T-shirt.

She drove down the gravel roads of Old Town, a place built for coal miners back in the early 1900s. Those coal mines had been dug out for decades, and now all that was left were cheap houses and bars. She slowed past Tailfeathers, looking to see if Molly's car had been moved yet. Instead, there was a marked police unit in the parking lot, with a muscular, uniformed officer leaning against the driver's side door, scribbling into a notepad. It was Sergeant Dave Kenderdine, who headed up the Task Force, she realized, and she turned into the lot and waved to him. "Hey, Sarge," she said, rolling down her window. "You all right?"

"No, not really," he said. "You know Hawthorne from the Task Force?"

"Was he there the other night?"

"No. He was here the other night," Kenderdine said, pointing at the bar's front door. "In a marked police car, which our department lets him take home but does not allow him to take out drinking."

"Oh no," Carrie said.

"Oh yes. And it gets better. Not only does he bring said police car to go out drinking, he leaves it unlocked, because in his mind, who is going to mess with the police, right?"

"Christ," she said.

"It is not until today that he opens up the trunk and realizes he is missing some equipment."

"Not his gun, I hope."

"No, but only because his dumb-ass took it inside the bar. Looks like they got one of his flashbangs, though."

"What an idiot. What's going to happen to him?"

"If he worked for your chief? He'd have his ass in a sling so tight he wouldn't be able to get a job selling toothbrushes. He's my boss's cousin, though, so with my luck he'll probably get promoted to lieutenant."

"Is there anything I can do?" Carrie asked.

"No," Kenderdine said. "I just came out here to see if the thieving pricks ditched the stuff somewhere. I expect we'll hear about a bad guy in a police uniform holding up gas stations in the next few days, though. Won't that be fun?"

Carrie turned down the next street, entering a long corridor of poorly kept townhomes. The first one on the corner had been condemned for over a year, after its roof collapsed. The house still sat there, caved in, its insides exposed like a dissected animal. An old woman smoked on the porch connected to the ruined house; the only thing separating her house from the condemned property was a line of knotted caution tape.

Gravel crunched beneath her car tires as she searched for a place to park. She pulled behind a large station wagon with rusted bumpers. It was fall, and the house still had Christmas lights strewn across the porch from the year before. A thin, older woman opened the door for her, her short hair the color of bright silver. She wore large hoop earrings that made her ears sag. Her makeup was piled on to fill in the deep ravines etched across her face, and she inhaled on her cigarette as she saw Carrie but was kind enough to blow the smoke out the side of her mouth. "Hey, baby doll, what are you doing here?"

Carrie smiled and kissed the woman on the cheek. "Hi, Penny. Just wanted to swing by and see you guys."

"Well, come on in. Molly's upstairs in her room with Nubs. The older one wasn't feeling too well today."

"I bet," Carrie said. "I got an interesting phone call."

"Oh, stop," Penny said. "She doesn't go out that often anymore and you know it."

"You're right," Carrie said, happy to acquiesce. From the time she was thirteen years old and had first walked through Penny's front door, when there was no good reason to, Penny had treated her like family.

"How's that father of yours? Is he good?"

"He's still drinking."

Penny's face wrinkled, puckering up on the left side as if she was chewing a piece of tough meat. She patted Carrie on the face and said, "The toughest part about growing up is that you realize your parents are just as screwed up and confused as you are." She wagged her finger in the air near Carrie's face and added, "But Rosendo did right by you, young lady. So don't go around talking about him like he's some kind of disappointment."

"Yes, ma'am," Carrie said.

"Don't call me ma'am. You make me sound old."

"It's not me making you sound old. It's those things

you keep smoking. You're starting to sound like a drag queen with a chest cold."

Penny rolled her eyes. "Oh, listen to the high-and-mighty police officer! I guess you get to point out what everybody else is doing wrong now."

"Very funny," Carrie said. "You know, speaking of my dad, I always said he just needed a good woman in his life. He's still got all his hair, you know," she added.

"You've been trying to hook us up since you were a kid, baby doll. You're never gonna quit, are you?"

"Just imagine how great it would be. All of us under the same roof. Just like one of those movies where everyone winds up one big, happy family."

"Yeah, a horror movie," Penny said, laughing so hard that she began to cough up nicotine phlegm. Carrie headed for the staircase, dodging the toys piled at the edges of every step. She recognized ones that she'd bought, seeing that they were well played with, and congratulated herself on being the greatest aunt in all of human history.

Before she could even knock on the closed bedroom door, two voices called out, "Come in!"

Carrie opened the door and found a large clump in the center of the bed, hiding two bodies entangled under thick blankets. There were strands of wheat-colored hair sticking out from the top, splayed out across the pillow. Carrie crept across the floor, cackling in her best evil witch voice, "I know someone's in here. Where is the pretty little one? Where could she be?"

A little girl's giggle escaped from under the blanket, high-pitched and excited. Carrie cried out, "There she is!" and dove onto the bed, tearing back the blankets to reveal Nubs hiding in her mother's arms. The child squealed with delight as Carrie kissed her and tickled her tiny ribs and sides. When both of them ran out of breath, she raised her head to Molly and said, "What are you doing in bed, slacker?"

"I don't feel good," Molly moaned.

"That's called being hungover."

"It's called shut up and go get me a cup of coffee."

"Loser."

"Bitch."

"Hey!" Carrie snapped, looking down at Nubs.

Nubs frowned. "I'm not allowed to say any of Mommy's bad words."

"And neither is she, or I'll put her right in jail."

Nubs turned toward her mom and poked her in the stomach, "No more bad words. You wouldn't like being in jail."

"You two are not allowed to gang up on me when I don't feel good," Molly said. She pressed a cold pack to her forehead and looked down at the television, smiling at the angelic face there.

"What is this crap—I mean, garbage?" Carrie said, correcting herself as Nubs's head whipped around.

"Shut it," Molly said. "It's the best movie ever!"

"Is this *The Notebook*?" Carrie groaned. "Nubs, quick, look away! It's already taken your mother, but I won't let it get you too!" She bent down and scooped Nubs up into her arms, pressing her head down into her chest.

"Mommy said it was your favorite book," Nubs called out with a muffled voice.

Carrie's eyes widened as she looked down at Molly. "How dare you! You know corruption of a minor is a crime in this state. You better watch yourself, lady."

Molly laughed so hard that she winced and pressed her hands to the sides of her head, moaning in pain.

"Come on," Carrie said, turning with Nubs still in her arms. "Let's go make this whiny baby some coffee, what do you say?"

Nubs said okay as Carrie opened the bedroom door and maneuvered them through it. Molly rolled over on the bed to watch them go and called out, "Aspirin, too, please."

"Anything else?"

"I have to pee."

Carrie looked back from the hallway, "Want me to bring you a bucket?" Nubs laughed out loud at that, and Carrie looked at her. "Maybe we can find some of your old diapers for her?"

"Neither one of you is funny," Molly said as she threw the blankets away from her, still pressing the cold pack to her head. "Neither one at all."

Nubs wrapped her legs around Carrie's sides and squeezed as they made their way down the steps. "I just started watching a new show. Do you want to watch it with me?"

"Sure," Carrie said as she moved Nubs's leg off the hard corrugated plastic handle sticking above her waistband. "Watch yourself on that, sweetie. Don't want you to get hurt."

"Is that your gun?"

"Yep. So don't touch it."

"Do you shoot people with it?"

"Nope."

"Will you ever shoot people with it?"

"I hope not," Carrie said. "Only if they're hurting someone else."

"Or you," Nubs said, putting her head against Carrie's chest.

"Or me," Carrie said, stroking the little girl's hair.

5

Ronald.

He told himself that was his name as he drove, repeating it over and over in his mind like a mantra. He turned into the Hansen Mall parking lot, driving past the security car parked near the entrance. It was made up to look like police car, with yellow lights across the top instead of blue and red. In the rearview mirror, it looked just like the real thing, and he stored that away for future memory in case he needed it.

But not as Ronald, he reminded himself. Ronald from Houma, Louisiana. That day, he'd eaten a pound of crawfish layered in Cajun spices and listened to zydeco music, loud. Accordions blared through the speakers on his truck's dashboard as he found a parking spot, drawing looks from the people walking up the sidewalk. He tipped his hat to them and said, "Good morning," like a good Southern boy should.

The man calling himself Ronald parked his truck near the Macy's entrance and shut the door, taking a minute to thumb the shoulder straps on his overalls. He walked toward the entrance, humming an accordion line, thinking about alligators and shrimp boats and nutria, holding clear images of the bayou in his mind and telling himself that was home. Corn bread and cold beer, that was all a body craved.

Well, he thought, not *all* it craved.

He opened the door to Macy's, holding it for a family who walked past without saying thank you. He smiled anyway, knowing it was the decline of American social values doing us all in but taking it upon himself to shore up the line. He headed for the makeup section, where busy women flitted from passerby to passerby, offering free samples and makeovers. The women were overly done up, wearing thick layers of foundation like masks that threatened to slide off their faces if they turned their heads too quickly. He ignored them and they ignored him.

He moved down the aisles of glass cabinets until he found an empty black chair next to the MAC section and sat. It was only a few moments until he was seen. "I'm sorry, sugar, but you can't sit there. We have chairs you can sit in if you're waiting for someone," a voice said from behind him.

Ronald turned around in the chair, seeing the makeup artist who'd spoken, a tall, well-built man wearing bright red lipstick and deep eye shadow. ANTOINE was printed on the name tag pinned to his smock, and Ronald said, "Actually, I'm here alone, friend. I was wondering, can y'all do that to me?"

"Do what?" Antoine said.

"Make me look like you?"

Antoine stepped back, pressing his hand under his chin. "You want me to put your face on, sweetie? For real?"

"For real," he repeated.

Antoine spun his chair around to face a brightly lit

mirror and said, "Well, all right, then! You came to the right place, honey. It is Friday, and we are all ready to party! Going somewhere special tonight?"

"I have to meet someone," he said, watching as Antoine selected a bright pink lipstick from the assortment in the workstation and brought it close to him. Antoine tilted his head back, humming as he worked. Ronald felt the lipstick's softness press against his lips, and his eyes widened as he watched the lines of his mouth change color in the mirror's reflection.

People stared at his face as he walked through the mall. He told himself he did not mind, that *Ronald* would not mind. He caught glimpses of his new face in the shop windows and mirrored walls, delighted at the fullness of his lashes and the soft redness of his cheeks. The dark-skinned woman working in the clothing store looked up as he walked in, taking in his loose-fitting overalls and workboots and brightly colored face with thick mascara eyelashes, and said, "Can I help you?"

"I need to find something to wear," he said, trying to use Ronald's new voice, one fitting for his new face, imagining it should be high-pitched and soft. "For a special night."

She regarded him, looking at his size and shape, touching the side of her brow in thought. "Hmm, I think we have something back here that might work," she said, turning with one finger held in the air like a beacon for him to follow.

He watched her walking, noting that her waist was skinny but her backside was full and rounded to perfection. Her hair was tied in a tight bun, and she wore a long, flowing skirt with sandals that revealed most of her feet. Just a few days earlier, she would have meant something entirely different to him. Would that he'd met her when he'd been Ed, but now it was too late. He would have taken his time with her, running his hands up and down her body and licking the droplets of sweat beading on that wonderful chocolate skin. He wondered what she tasted like. Cocoa butter? He had taken black women before, doing things with needles and knives and red-hot irons to their dark nipples and thick bush pussies that made their pink tongues stick straight out as they screamed and screamed and screamed and oh how they screamed.

"Stop!" he said aloud.

The salesgirl's head whipped around in fright. She nearly stumbled into him, and Ronald fought the urge to pounce on top of her like a leopard, but he steeled himself and resisted. These were not Ronald's thoughts. Ronald just wants a pretty new shirt for his pretty new face, and that's all. "That one, pick from that rack right there," he said. "I'm sorry I yelled, sugar, they just looked perfect to me right away."

She laughed nervously. "I get excited too. That's why I got this job, for the discount. Okay, let me see what I can find."

He stood with his head lowered, focusing on the thick plush carpet, cursing himself for being so weak. She took his hand and slid something soft and silky across his palm, asking him how good it felt. He looked down and saw a lavender shirt lying across his wrist. "It's lovely."

"Do you want to try it on?"

He told her that he did. She led him to the dressing

room and pulled back the curtain. Stepping inside, he lowered the straps on his overalls and stripped off his T-shirt, careful not to smear his face.

"Do you want me to look for pants too? Maybe a skirt?" the woman called through the curtain.

He slid his arms through the shirt's delicate sleeves and fastened the buttons. It had frilly cuffs at the wrists and glittering pearl buttons that ended at the center of his chest. He stopped and admired Ronald in the mirror. "I don't need anything else," he said. He had too many things to carry in his pockets.

Heels were impractical, but he stopped at the shoe store anyway, holding his newly purchased purse by the crook of his fingers and posing with his hips jutted to the side. He enjoyed making comments about the shoes as he looked at them, sucking on his teeth in contempt of their lack of style, or whistling with delight when he saw ones he thought Ronald would like.

He decided against wearing sandals or flats or any other kind of women's shoe, because they looked as if they would come off too easily if he needed to run. He'd seen it happen firsthand. Women always tried to run and their shoes went flinging off, making them stumble, making them easy prey.

Quarter-length hiking boots, he'd learned after much trial and error, were the best. Rugged enough to withstand the elements, with thick-enough soles in the event he needed to kick in a door or a car window but comfortable enough to run in.

Boots were one of the few constants he allowed himself when choosing a new persona from the list. Sometimes his only improvement on the old formulas.

Once he'd reached the top and there was no one left but him, his ways and methods a testament for all time to be studied by everyone who came after, they would know two things. His true name, and what boots to wear.

The speakers inside Club Transmission ran along the wall behind the deejay's booth, stacked all the way to the ceiling. The deejay danced while he spun the records. He wore nothing but a sequined thong and angel's wings, sparkling in the rotating lights above him as if he'd been showered in glitter. The man stood at the bar, looking down over the crowded dance floor. Wigs and shaved heads, long hair that whipped back and forth. Neon fingernails flashed in the lights reflected from the metal rings and bolts of leather bondage gear.

They were like creatures of the abyss, Ronald thought. Squirming in one entangled, gelatinous mass, the intestines of a god who's laid down in this place and ripped himself open to release a horde of brightly colored demons.

He turned to the bar with his drink, a concoction of sweet liquors and twirling plastic sticks, barely touching it to his lips. He needed to be careful with how much he drank. It would do no good to have his senses dulled. He did not need to relax, and he did not need courage. It was merely a prop, an affectation to blend in. He swayed to the music, searching the faces of the men standing around him.

He noticed that the other queens, the ones wearing heavy makeup, despised him the same way they despised one another. They seemed catty, making overly grand gestures and talking loudly, making sure everyone around them heard their oh-so-witty remarks and gritty cynicism. He did not like them. Ronald did not like them. He swept the long blond hair of his wig aside and kept looking.

"You're new here," the muscular bartender said, taking his time wiping the counter in front of Ronald with his white cloth.

Ronald arched his eyebrow at him and drawled, "Why yes, yes I am."

"Where is that accent from? Somewhere down South?"

Ronald smiled. "Houma, Lousiana. You got an ear for accents, I reckon."

"Welcome to Shithole, Pennsylvania. I'm Zack." The bartender extended his hand.

Ronald admired the thick veins in his arms and the separation of the muscles along his forearm as he reached forward and said, "You can call me Dominique."

Zack continued to make small talk. Ronald said, "Oh?" as often as he could without seeming impolite, but in reality he was not interested in Zack. The bartender was far too physically strong for what Ronald had in mind. He waited for Zack to get called away by other customers and turned in his seat to continue searching, looking over the preppy-looking college types and mustached leatherboys and the heavyset, rough-looking bikers. He ignored all of them when they caught him looking. They were not what he wanted.

He waded through the crowd, ignoring unknown hands that slid against his groin and cupped his buttocks, until he saw exactly what he wanted sitting alone at a table at the other side of the room.

A middle-aged man with hair thin enough that his scalp showed under the lights. His glasses reflected blue and green as he turned to look at Ronald. The plain tan fabric of his jacket absorbed the flashing lights and laser pointers swirling all around them, like a plain projector screen showing a movie, every empty space filled with movement and color. Everything about the man was awkward and out of place. He wore jogging pants with a bright white stripe down the sides and old sneakers. He looked like the janitor in high school that spied on the girls' locker room, trying to tap his hand in time to the music but failing, able to summon the courage to come to a place like this but not enough to commit to it. Ronald smiled as he made eye contact with the man. Lonely. Desperate. Filled with self-loathing.

Perfect.

"Hello," Ronald said as he sat down, positioning his hands on his drink and pursing his pink lips to take a true, real sip.

The man swallowed hard, staring down into his pint of beer.

"Can't you say hello to me?" Ronald asked.

The man still had not looked up. "Hi. How are you."

"I'm fine," Ronald purred. "You don't see that very often in a place like this."

"What's that?"

"A real man like you, drinking a real drink like a beer." Ronald smirked. "All I see is a bunch of fake bitches with foo-foo drinks, how about you?"

"Actually, I don't come to places like this that often. Ever, really."

Ronald looked down at the worn wedding ring on the man's finger, and he leaned close to say, "Places like this are among the very few in the world where you can be whoever you are in the small, tiny space of this one particular moment." He raised his glass and took another drink, feeling the slow, warming rush down his throat as it settled him deep within. "I once heard that each of us has three selves. There's our public self that we show to the world. Our private self that we show only to the people close to us. And our secret self." He turned and looked at the man seated next to him. "Do you know what I'm talking about, by any chance?"

The man took another slight sip of his beer, barely touching it with his lips.

Ronald moved to offer his hand, and brushed the beer glass as he turned. It was warm to the touch. Whoever he was, he'd been nursing the beer longer than Ronald had been holding his own drink. He turned his hand over as he offered it, holding his fingers straight, and said, "I'm Dominique."

The man took Ronald's hand as if he were unsure of what to do. He grasped it as if he meant to shake it, but then lowered his mouth to the back of Ronald's knuckles and kissed them. "Jim," he said.

Ronald leaned back on his stool and dropped his hand over Jim's thigh, pulling it beside his own leg. He squeezed it through the thin nylon material and worked upward until he brushed the soft nuggets between Jim's legs with the tips of his fingers. Jim inhaled as Ronald found the length of his penis and stroked it through his pants.

"Do you want to take a little walk with me?" Ronald whispered in his ear.

Jim shivered and said, "Yes. Very much so."

Ronald picked up his glass and swallowed the rest down. Jim left his almost-full beer on the bar and threw down several bills, turning on his stool to leave. His erect penis stood out beneath the nylon fabric, but it did not matter. He grabbed Ronald's hand and pulled him from the stool, leading him through the crowd. The thing in his pants had taken over, and now that little general was leading them both into battle. Ronald threw back his head and laughed as he ran after Jim, raising his free hand high into the air and waving it in time to the jungle rhythm and emergency siren wailing along with it.

Outside, they raced through the parking lot. Jim was like a child, eager to get away from the club. Ronald had to run with one hand holding on to him and the other clamped down on his right pocket. The knife's clip slid back and forth against his palm, holding down the coil of steel wire and folded bandana packed beneath it. He kept a backup knife on the inside of his right boot, but there was no way to check if that was still there.

It was cheap anyway, as were all his knives—five-dollar Chinese blades that were perfectly suitable but easily broken apart and tossed down sewer drains and into trash bins. Anyway, he doubted he would need it. Everything was going according to Ronald's plan, as he knew it would. As it always did. That was the benefit of using the methods and templates of the old masters. All one had to do was commit.

"There's my van," Jim said, pulling him toward the large Ford parked at the very rear of the lot. It was backed into a spot, with nothing but dark woods behind it.

Ronald turned and saw his own vehicle—a white construction van—parked nearby, but he decided he did not need it. There would be nothing to clean up this way. No worry about getting stopped on the way home by some cop asking about the suspicious stains on his seats. All he needed was a large-enough work space and the time and privacy required. If anything, Jim's van was parked even farther back than his own, and so long as it wasn't filled with tools and crates, it would work just as well. He already had all that he needed in his pocket.

"Is there enough room in the back?" Ronald huffed. "I have something special for you."

"Plenty," Jim said, laughing as they both fell against the back doors. He draped his arm across the spare tire casing and tried to catch his breath. "So," he said, eyes fixing on Ronald. "What do we do now?"

Ronald pulled open the van's back doors and looked in, checking to make sure they'd have enough room. It *was* perfect. Nothing but a few tools, a thin layer of shag carpet, and a black curtain drawn across the width of the cabin, behind the two front seats. Total privacy. The wrench and pliers in the van would even come in handy. "Now," Ronald said, "you're mine."

Jim growled softly as Ronald pulled him close, and their lips crushed together. Ronald felt Jim's stubble scrape his face and the soft, wet intrusion of his tongue, and he pushed Jim back so that he was sitting on the floor of the van. His erection was sticking out beneath his loose pants, and Ronald grabbed it with his left hand, jerking it up and down.

"Suck it," Jim hissed. "I want to feel your mouth."

Ronald lowered himself to his knees on the parking lot pavement, feeling the cool metal of the van's bumper against his chest as he leaned forward. He tugged down the front of Jim's waistband and unveiled his rigid, purple penis. He took its thickness in his hand.

"Suck it," Jim demanded.

The man calling himself Ronald knew that he must. That was part of the scenario. That was what Ronald did, he knew it, and there was no turning back now. He closed his eyes and opened his mouth, feeling Jim's warm penis entering past his lips. It was like sucking on a large thumb. A small trickle of salty fluid spilled out across his tongue as he squeezed his lips.

"That's good," Jim moaned, grabbing a handful of Ronald's wig and squeezing. "Deeper."

Ronald reached up with his left hand to stretch out the dangling sack between Jim's legs. This would be the first to go. One swift slice and it would fall free into his fingers.

With his right hand, he reached for his pocket, moving back his purple shirt and working his fingers around the hilt of his knife.

It was time.

Jim's grip around his hair tightened, and he snarled, "I said suck it deeper, faggot."

Ronald looked up in time to see the wrench in Jim's hand whistling through the air toward the side of his head. He felt the impact of metal against his skull, knocking him backward against the pavement. The last thing he saw was Jim standing over him, still holding the wrench, exposed penis glistening in the moonlight.

He became aware of the voice speaking to him inside the van and the bright, pulsing pain on the side of his face. He could see only from one eye as he looked up, spotting his wrists bound together with rope, which was lassoed around the front seat of the van. He was bent forward, and he realized, to his horror, that his pants were pulled down to his ankles. Something was stuffed in his mouth. It tasted and smelled like an old sock.

Jim's hand patted him on the small of the back. "Now, what were you planning on doing with these, faggot?"

Ronald turned his head enough to see Jim flick his knife open with an expert twirl of the wrist. The steel coil and bandana were scattered on the floor behind them, too far out of reach for his bound hands. "You planned on using these on me?" Jim sneered. "You wanted to tie me up and rob me, huh?"

"No!" Ronald spat through the cloth in his mouth.

Jim lunged with the knife, stopping the tip of the blade just inches from Ronald's face. "You know what lying little faggots get, don't you? Coming around to where decent folks live, making them do all sorts of disgusting things. You couldn't wait to get on your knees for me, could you?"

Ronald felt Jim's rough hands peel apart his buttocks and spread him wide. A warm trickle of saliva spilled down across his exposed anus, and Ronald's eyes widened. "I'm going to give you what all faggots get."

Ronald grunted at the first intrusion bored through his body, being burned and stretched and split deep within until he could not help but scream. Tears of shock and outrage spilled down the sides of his face as he struggled against the rope holding him, but it was no use. Jim slammed into him again and again, like an animal, shouting, "Take it, you fucking homo! Take it!"

They were sliding back and forth on the carpet under the force of Jim's thrusts, until the black curtain was only a few feet away. His wrists burned and dripped blood, but there was no way for him to snap the rope binding them or to lift the lasso free from around the driver's seat.

The pounding grew faster and more frenzied, and Ronald's head dropped against the carpet. Using all of his might to pull himself forward, he managed to create enough slack in the rope to get his hands down between his knees. He grabbed at where his pants were pooled at his ankles. It still wasn't enough.

He strained with all his might to pull himself forward, feeling the rope cutting through the flesh of his wrists, and Jim said, "Get back here!"

The hands on his waist gripped tight as Jim slammed against him, tearing him open. His eyes rolled back into his head and he tried to focus. Everything was becoming blurry. Darkness swirled around the edges of his vision, threatening to swallow him whole. "No!" he shouted through the gag. He wiggled his hands down far enough to reach the top of his boot, feeling the warm metal clip of the knife hidden there.

"I'm cumming," Jim gasped, bucking against him a final time before slithering out. "Oh my God. You filthy . . . trash," Jim huffed, slumping back against the door of his van and wiping his face. "Look what you made me do." As he panted and tried to catch his breath, he looked up in time to see Ronald spin around with a ferocious snarl and the knife coming directly at him.

The man emerged from the van two hours later, when it became pointless to continue. The mass of flesh and organs scattered all around him was no longer even quivering. He popped the back door open and slid out into the parking lot, stopping to make sure no one was watching. Music still pumped through the walls of the club, echoing toward the woods. He was covered with blood and pieces of flesh and hair, but it was still dark, and no one noticed as he hurried across the lot to his own van. He got in and started it, spinning around the lot to back up into the spot beside Jim's. Blood spilled out of the van's open back doors, onto the pavement.

There was no hiding the body, or the vehicle, at that point. Still, precautions must be taken. He looked at his face in the rearview mirror and winced at the massive lump over his ear where he'd been struck with the wrench.

He opened the back doors of his van and looked over the crates and toolboxes stacked along the side. He slid on a pair or rubber gloves and grabbed one of the two-gallon pump sprayers strapped there, filled with two parts bleach and one part water, then walked around the back of Jim's van, spraying every surface that he'd come in contact with. He sprayed the exterior and interior of the van, even the ceiling, until it was dripping with bleach and blood.

The next item he needed was a small glass jar located on the bottom shelf in his stack. It had small holes poked in the lid, and he rattled it, stirring the dozens of black flies within. He checked Jim's van to make sure all of the windows were up as he walked around the back and closed the first rear door. He set the jar on the sopping wet rug and quickly unscrewed the lid, then closed the second rear door as the small cloud of flies rose into the air. He could hear them buzzing around inside as he stripped out of his soaking wet clothes and stuffed them into a large trash bag. Inside his shelves he found a complete change of clothes and packages of baby wipes, which he ran all over his body to clean himself as much as he could.

He threw the towels and gloves into the trash bag and tied it, then slid into the front seat of his van. He grabbed the baseball cap sitting on his passenger seat and pulled it on as low as he could stand, wincing at the pain spreading across his face, as he drove out of the parking lot and entered the dark freeway. He rolled down the windows and let the cool air wash over him. Desiccated raccoons and deer and rancid-smelling skunks littered the highway on either side, filling the night with the scent of copper and carrion. He inhaled deeply.

6

Carrie's Sunday ritual was to buy a newspaper and park somewhere remote flipping through it, looking at all the coupons of things she wanted to buy but couldn't afford yet. It would not be long, though. She was coming into her fourth year on the job and would soon be at top pay. She'd eked out a living on the pittance they paid rookies, then made do with the only slightly less pitiful salary they paid second-year officers, and started being able to pay her bills each month on time with her third-year salary. But the fourth year was when it all became worth it. Top salary, and an extra week's vacation, just for sticking with it long enough.

That morning she filled her thermos with the remaining coffee in the station's pot, then got in her car, waving to the cars driving past her on the off chance they waved back. She'd almost made it to the gas station to buy her paper when the radio crackled, the dispatcher calling, "County to Thirty-Four-Four."

She picked up the microphone. "Four, go ahead."

"Meet your complainant at Club Transmission, eight

hundred block of Cardinal Way for a parking violation."

"En route," she said, hanging the mic. She pulled
into the gas station lot and turned her car around, heading the opposite way.

Mr. Darren was a large man whose bright red suspenders always accented whatever shirts he wore.
White, short-sleeved button-down shirt with a tie? Red
suspenders. Tattered blue T-shirt with a pocket over the
left breast? Same suspenders. He was prone to make
frequent complaints to police regarding the properties
he owned all over town, and in all the times Carrie had
dealt with him, she'd never seen him without them. As
she pulled into the gravel parking lot of Club Transmission, Darren thumbed his suspenders as he waited
for her by the front door.

She drove her patrol car up alongside the entrance
and said, "Morning, Mr. Darren."

"Hiya, Carrie. Can you get that van out of here for
me? I want it towed."

Carrie turned to see the van parked at the far end of
the lot, backed into one of the spaces in the last row.
"Unfortunately, this is private property," she said. "If
you want it towed, you'll have to call them yourself."

"And pay for it myself." He scowled.

"Yeah, at least until the owner comes to pick it up.
How long's it been here?"

Darren squinted at the van. "We were closed yesterday, so at least since Friday. I figured somebody got
lucky and went home with his new friend, if you catch

my meaning. I was hoping they'd come get it out of here by now."

Carrie tapped the steering wheel with her thumbs, rolling the situation around in her mind. Any other time, she'd have said good-bye and driven off, but Mr. Darren was a well-known businessman with good connections throughout the township. There were certain people whom it paid to go the extra mile for, and he was one of them. Besides, she liked that he never asked. He just stood there, thumbing his suspenders, waiting.

"Tell you what. I'll go run the tag and see if I can find the owner."

He patted the side of her car and said, "Thank you so much, young lady. I will be sure to let Chief Waylon know you helped me out."

"That works," she said, dropping the car into drive. She cruised across the lot toward the van and got out, looking it over as she circled. She saw a black speck on the passenger window, and then another, and they were moving.

Flies?

The van seemed to buzz from within, as if its speakers were thrumming with static feedback. As she rounded the van's rear corner, she saw deep crimson droplets on the grass. The droplets grew bigger as she approached the rear doors, forming a dried puddle beneath the bumper.

It's paint, she told herself, then stopped and looked at it again. Red dye? Leftover Jell-O shots the bartender dumped in the grass. Has to be.

She bent down and peered closer, deciding it could possibly be blood, maybe from a deer. She looked out at the highway, thinking how the van might have come around the corner, struck a deer, and pulled into the lot.

The driver, probably too freaked out to drive after that, had called for a ride. There were deer carcasses littered up and down the highway. It happened all the time.

She reached for the van's back door and wrapped her fingers around the metal handle, giving it a quick twist and pulling, telling herself it was nothing even as the black cloud of flies burst in her face, sending her leaping backward, swatting.

The stink of rotting meat and offal filled her nose and mouth. Her eyes burned from bleach fumes and methane gas, but she forced herself to look. Even as her mind struggled to calibrate the immensity of horror spread out before her, she forced herself, with burning eyes, with clenched teeth, to look. And it could never be unseen.

"You seriously touched the handle with your bare hand?" Harv Bender asked for the third time. "A key piece of evidence at the scene of a homicide, with your bare hand? Please tell me you're joking."

Carrie stood at the center of the crucible while activity swirled all around her. Paramedics stood off to the side, leaning against their ambulance, not speaking. They'd come running after she reported finding a body, racing down the highway with lights and siren. Their tires squealed as they rounded the corner into the parking lot. They parked and jumped out, carrying their medical bags and oxygen tank and defibrillator. She watched them hurry past her. They stopped at the van's open doors, staring in mute horror at the contents inside.

Someone had strung yellow caution tape around the van at Harv's direction, and he was talking on the phone with the on-call district attorney, loud enough for everyone to hear. "We haven't touched a thing. Well, except for the back door. The cop who took the call finger-banged the back door all up before we could process it." His eyes flicked toward her, and he turned away, saying, "I have no idea why. I'll make it work, though. Somehow."

A dark Crown Victoria turned into the parking lot, and Carrie's heart sank. She could barely look up as Bill Waylon parked behind the long line of police cars and walked toward her. Carrie leaned back on her police car, knowing what had to be done.

"What do we got?" Waylon said.

She turned to him and said, "I screwed up, Chief."

His face shifted in surprise. "How?"

"I touched the back door," she said, flapping her arms in frustration. "I screwed up the crime scene. My first homicide, and I screwed up the crime scene."

He looked at her, and then at the van. "This came out as an abandoned car, right?"

"Yeah."

"Could you see inside it when you got here?"

"No. But I could see something red on the pavement. I should have known better. I just wasn't—"

"What?" he said. "Expecting to find a body in the back?"

"Exactly."

"There's a wise old expression that goes, Experience is something you get five seconds after you need it. We'll work it out. Grab your camera. Let's get to work. Did you get a positive ID on the decedent yet?"

Carrie glanced nervously over her shoulder. "I told them I didn't touch anything else."

"I don't care what you told them. *I'm* asking."

She leaned close to him. "There was a wallet with a driver's license inside it. It came back to the owner. The tattoos on the dead guy's arms match the ones in his mugshots."

"You couldn't just tell from his face?"

When she didn't respond, Waylon walked around the van and peered inside the rear, looking over the open doors and blood smeared across the back bumper. He saw where blood splotches had dried on the pavement and trickled down into the grass, trampled by dozens of boots from all the cops who wanted to get a look. Word had spread about the body, and cops from five surrounding jurisdictions were doing nothing but standing around. Waylon snapped his fingers at two of them and said, "You and you, expand this crime scene tape twenty feet in every direction. Everybody else, get back and stop stepping all over my evidence." He reached in his pocket for his phone and tossed it to Carrie, saying, "Find Eddie Schikel's number and call him. I want him and his crime scene wagon here ASAP. If his boss asks, I'm paying the overtime."

Harv Bender strolled to Waylon's side, his voice sliding like oil when he said, "Hey, Bill."

Waylon looked to see the officers stringing crime scene tape around the van's new perimeter and made sure everyone was moving back. He called out, "Double that. I want a nice clear field for the crime scene team to work in. Everybody back up!"

"Listen, I just talked to the on-duty DA, and he said to sit tight while he figures out if we need a search warrant," Harv said.

"We don't need one."

Harv rolled his shoulders back, like a boxer warming up for a fight. "Yeah, why don't we just go ahead and wait a few extra minutes on them before we call in any of your buddies from out of county. Regardless, we have our own crime scene people, and it looks bad if we go outside our own, you know what I mean?"

Waylon turned to him. "We do not need a search warrant, because the owner of the van is dead, Harv. He has no right to privacy. That's basic police work 101."

"I'm just telling you what the person with the law degree said, Bill."

"And I'm telling you we don't need one," Waylon shot back. "Now I realize your nose is buried so deep in the district attorney's ass that when you sneeze he whistles, but let's get one thing clear. This is my township, and I make the calls, is that clear? I think I'll rely on my thirty-five years of doing this instead of some dipshit fresh out of law school and a deputy chief detective who never cleared a single homicide we didn't hand him."

Harv backed away from Waylon, looking around to see who had been listening. "Handed me? Yeah, right," he said. "You wish! Hey, try not to let any more of your people put their hands all over the crime scene, okay, Bill? Great job in training them, by the way."

Carrie came up beside her chief and handed him his phone. "Schikel says he'll be here in forty-five minutes. He said forget the overtime. Something about a set of testicles being worth a hundred crime scenes?"

Waylon ignored her comment. "When he gets here, have him print you. We'll send your prints up to the lab along with whatever else we find. That way they can eliminate you and the victim."

"Aren't my prints already on file?" she asked.

"I don't have time to wait for some state police mail

clerk to dig them out of a filing cabinet. I want a one-to-one comparison done ASAP that eliminates you and searches for a suspect match."

Carrie told him she'd take care of it as soon as Schikel arrived and then stood with him looking at the van. "Hey, what did he mean about the set of testicles, Chief? Was he talking about Krissing? There was always talk that you and Rein castrated him when you arrested him."

"Jury ruled otherwise. It was just a freak accident," Waylon said.

"Oh, of course. I know that," she said, not wanting to sound accusatorial. "Hell, not that anybody would have blamed you."

"Let's focus on the situation at hand, okay?" he said, heading back to his car. "See if you can manage not to touch anything else, if that's not too much trouble."

She watched him walk toward the cops stringing up the crime scene tape, telling them to move it back even farther, into the woods. The stink of bleach and decomposition was almost more than she could stand, but she forced herself to breathe it, refusing to show any more weakness. When the time came for someone to go into the van, she was volunteering.

"I would like to buy an *I*, please," the Tyvek-suit clad man said from inside the van, his voice mechanical through his mask's respirator. "I've got an *E* and an *A*, but has anyone seen an *I* that I can buy?" He chuckled, ducking down to look under the seats.

Carrie leaned in and looked at the ceiling, trying to see through the misty shield of her mask, wishing she could wipe away the layer of fog that appeared every time she breathed. "What's that?" she said, pointing at an object stuck in the far corner, where the sidewalls met the roof.

Eddie Schikel turned and looked, duckwalking through a pile of intestines to reach into the rear corner of the van's ceiling and pluck the small lump stuck there. He pried it loose from where it had dried and turned it over in his gloved hands, saying, "Hey, you found my eye!" He turned toward her and held the smashed orb up to her face. "Here's looking at you, kid."

Carrie half grinned as she took it from him with one hand and opened the thick, red biohazard bag with the other.

"Make note that the optic nerve is cut clean through," Schikel said. "Looks like tool impressions on both sides of the eyeball."

Carrie looked down at the ruined lump of flesh in her hand, fascinated by what she was seeing. There were lined grooves in the white meat surrounding the green and black discs of the dead man's eye, as if someone had squeezed the white flesh of a hard-boiled egg with a pair of pliers. The dangling nerves were severed in a straight line. "Did he pull the victim's eye out with one of these tools and cut it free?" she said.

"Yep," Schikel said.

"Why would he do that? To keep it like a trophy? If he wanted it so bad, why didn't he take it with him?"

"Maybe he thought the eyes were staring at him? Some kind of crazy schizophrenic shit, or something. I don't know." Schikel looked around the cabin at the gore surrounding him and said, "If I had to lay money on it, though, I'd say he wasn't taking trophies. He was just ripping this poor bastard's eyeballs out."

Carrie dropped the eyeball into the bag and sealed it, saying, "Along with everything else, apparently."

"Whatever he could get his hands on. I'm going to need more bags. Can you tell Bill to grab them out of my truck?"

"Sure," she said, stepping away from the van. She took deep breaths as she walked farther from it, able to tell the difference between clean air and the chemical horror inside the van, even through the respirator. She found Waylon standing at the edge of crime scene tape and said, "We need more red bags."

"What sizes?" he said.

"Anything you can find," she said. "I'm not sure what he's taking and what he's leaving for the coroner. I think he wants anything that's been cut, or yanked out. The coroner's getting whatever's left."

He looked at her, leaning down to see her face through the mask. "You need a break, kiddo? I can have someone else suit up."

"I'm fine," she snapped.

"No, you're not fine. You're in there looking at a mutilated dead body on a Sunday afternoon when most girls your age are out at the mall, getting their nails done, or whatever. I'm not asking if you're fine, I'm asking if I need to order you to take a break."

"I'm good, Chief. I've got this," she said. "I'm working the case. This is what detectives do, right?"

"Sometimes," he said, backing away from her toward the crime scene van. "Most of the time we sat around staring at buildings, trying not to fall asleep. Listen, I'm pulling you out if you start to get wobbly."

"Would you be saying that if I were a guy?" she called out. "Instead of some silly girl that was supposed to be getting her nails done or some shit?"

"No," he said, considering her question. "But then, if you were a guy, I wouldn't care if you felt okay or not, either. Kind of like reverse-reverse discrimination, I guess."

"Probably because you think of me as the daughter you never had."

"I have two daughters."

"But not like me," Carrie said, smiling through her mask.

"Well then," he said, "maybe there is a God."

The individual bags had all been set inside cardboard evidence boxes and labeled with the body parts stuffed inside them. Some, Bill Waylon could make out. R EAR, L EAR, TONGUE, TEETH, ASSORTED INTES- TINES, and so on. He stopped when he saw one group of boxes, squinting at the writing on them. "Penis tip?" he said, looking at Eddie Schikel. "Just the tip?"

"Yep," Schikel said, wiping a towel across the back of his neck. He picked up a bottle of water, poured it over the towel, and draped it across the top of his head, relieved at how good it felt. "Stem of penis down to the circumcision scar," he said, pointing at the first bag, then pointed at the next two and said, "Root of penis, base of penis. I'm not sure about the exact medical terms for each and every section of a guy's cock. That was the best I could come up with."

Waylon ran his fingers through his gray hair, feeling queasy. He looked over his shoulder to make sure they were alone, then said, "Jesus. I've heard of somebody cutting off a dude's dick before, but whacking it into pieces?"

"Sliced it up like a cucumber, Bill. I'm traumatized. I won't be able to go near a vegetable tray for a long time."

Bill turned and looked over his shoulder at Carrie. She'd stripped down to her sports bra and pulled the Tyvek suit down to her waist, trying to evaporate the layer of sweat covering her body. She was guzzling a tall bottle of water, pretending not to notice the leering looks from the cops standing behind the perimeter. "How'd the kid do?"

"She did good," Schikel said. "Even when she looked like she was going to puke in her mask, she stayed put."

"Good. I'm going to need all the help I can get on this. God knows the county isn't worth a squirt of piss anymore."

They stood there, surrounded by bags and boxes containing pieces of a dead man, Schikel giving his friend time to absorb it all. He looked past the chief toward Harv Bender. Two more men in suits had arrived and were circling the perimeter like sharks following the scent of blood.

He glanced at Bender, then said, "I'm going to have to hand this over to those idiots. I just wanted to delay it a bit and remind them of their place, is all. Hope you don't mind."

"Who do they have that's good up there now?"

"Nobody. Not anymore," Waylon said.

Schikel wiped his arms down with the towel. "Have you talked to him recently, Bill? Any word on where he is?"

Waylon looked off into the distance.

"I was thinking that maybe if you asked, he'd be willing to take a look at this for you. For old time's sake."

"He wouldn't," Waylon said. "And I wouldn't ask." He looked at the boxes once more, then turned toward the county detectives and called out, "You guys going to stand around all day, or do you feel like getting some work done?"

7

At night is when it hits.

Police see things beyond normal the human experience, and they function as they are trained. For older, more seasoned officers, it is rarely something new. Brain matter smeared across a basement floor. A charred corpse. A dead child. A man charging forward with a knife, intent on killing anyone that interferes. The older cops deal with it as it happens, years of conditioning kicking in like gears on a machine, carrying them through. Younger cops, who've never seen true horror before, are bolstered by social reinforcement. The group makes them strong. Lets them know it's just part of the job. Nothing to get freaked out about.

But at night, lying there next to his wife, a grayhaired patrolman of fifteen years will stare at the ceiling, thinking about the marbled flesh of a young drug addict's body that he'd seen earlier. In his mind, comparisons to his own children will form like spiderwebs, stringing it all together, hurling him into the dark waters of sleep, defenseless.

A cop with only a few years on the job will dream

about being attacked, needing to pull out his gun and shoot, only to watch in horror as the bullets tumble uselessly out of the barrel and fall to the ground. Or the trigger is too heavy to pull, no matter how hard he grabs it with both hands and squeezes, trying desperately to get it to shoot, but it is too late.

Carrie knew all these things as she rolled from side to side, flipping her pillow so many times that neither side felt cool. The ends of her hair were tipped with sweat. She kicked free of the blankets and draped her bare legs over the pile of them, trying to cool down.

She was not afraid of bad dreams. She was not afraid of anything at all, really. At least, nothing brought about by seeing the mutilated remains of another human being. She stared at the wall across from her bed, the dark portal of the open bathroom door, the blank wall she'd never bothered to hang anything on, and she only felt empty.

Dehumanized. That was the thing. She had helped place another human being's assorted body parts inside a series of bags, labeled and marked, set out in an assembly line, or rather a disassembly line, to be catalogued and photographed.

That living person inside the van, whatever he had been, whoever he had been, whatever his hopes and dreams and loves and hates, had been made up of nothing more than the contents of those bags. The killer had been a mechanic, breaking his victim's body down into spare parts. A mad child who comes upon a completed Lego structure and tears it down to individual pieces.

Carrie felt her heart beating in her chest, pulsating all the way up through the vein in her neck, and knew her own parts were also only working together in unison. That someone could simply come along with a sharp-enough knife and extract them, until whatever she was ceased to exist; this weighed heavily on her too.

She quit the bed and padded across her bedroom toward the bathroom. The toilet seat was cool and familiar under her bare bottom as she looked back at the empty bed, glad to be away from it. She wandered into the living room, unable to decide what to do. It was too early to get up for work. Too late to call anyone to talk. She didn't want to eat. Not interested in watching TV.

She saw her work bag sitting on the kitchen chair and stopped, looking down at her clipboard and legal guide. Underneath them was a brown manila envelope with her name on it and a handwritten note from the chief clipped to the front of it.

> *Talking to you earlier made me think of this. I used to say that quote about the abyss all the time, but one day Jacob told me people only use it to sound like they have some deeper understanding of evil. What he said about it always stayed with me. The abyss doesn't just gaze at you like some passive onlooker, he said. It wants what it sees. Its tentacles snare you and drag you down into its cold, hard darkness, forever. Absolute black. This is the last thing Jacob Rein ever did as a cop. By the time the jury vindicated us, he'd already killed that little girl and then nothing was ever the same.*
> *—Bill*

She found a DVD inside the envelope, marked Court Record 4 – Civil Rights Violation Hearing. She slid it into her player and sat back on the couch, drawing a blanket over her legs as she turned on the television, filling the room with bright blue light. She pressed play on the remote, and the screen went dark.

The camera panned inside a courtroom—a large federal room, complete with old wooden benches and a carved, ornate judge's desk. The men and women sitting on the jury were dressed in garish clothes, some of them with thick glasses and bizarre haircuts. A heavy-set attorney stood up from the plaintiff's side. Sweat stained his collar as he folded his arms across his chest and said, "Detective Rein, is it your sworn testimony before this court that the injuries to my client were, as you described, caused by your rubber glove getting caught?"

Carrie recognized the same man she'd seen in the interrogation video, this time dressed in black suit and perfectly knotted tie. Jacob Rein turned toward the jurors seated across from him and said, "Actually, the injury was caused not so much by the glove but by me pulling my hand away too quickly."

Several men on the jury winced. The attorney came around the front of his table. "I'm sorry, Detective, but can you back up for a moment? How exactly did your glove come to be in that specific location of my client's anatomy again?"

Someone stood up from the defendant's table and called out, "Objection, your honor."

The camera passed a younger-looking Bill Waylon, gazing up at his attorney, who said, "This question has been asked and answered. Clearly, they are just trying to inflame the jury."

"The specifics as to what Detective Rein and Detective Waylon are swearing to are at the heart of the matter, your honor," Sweat Ring shot back. "I am seeking clarification only."

The judge folded his hands on the bench. "You may continue."

"So, Detective, how did your hand wind up inside of Mr. Krissing?" the attorney said.

"Just my finger was," Rein said calmly. "Not my entire hand."

"Fine. Just your finger then?"

"As I said before," Rein said, "Detective Waylon fired at the suspect and inadvertently hit him in what was immediately evident as a vital area."

"How did you know that?"

"The suspect clutched his groin, and blood sprayed between his fingers. I determined Mr. Krissing had been shot in the femoral artery."

The attorney turned toward Waylon and said, "Your partner shot Mr. Krissing in the genitals, is that not correct, sir?"

The faces on the jury were twisted in discomfort. Rein turned toward them and said, "Yes, he did."

"As vengeance?" the attorney said.

Rein turned to them again and said, "No."

The attorney shot up his hand with the fury of a Baptist minister and shouted, "Walter Krissing molested, mutilated, and killed how many children, Detective Rein?"

Rein turned to the jury and said, "Krissing was a prolific killer and molester of children. There were ten confirmed homicides that we know of. There were other victims along the way whom he raped or assaulted to varying extents. There are likely others we've never heard of."

"And just how many of those horrible, god-awful cases did you work personally, Detective?"

"All of them."

"Is it fair to say you wanted to see Mr. Krissing suffer for his crimes?"

The defense attorney called out, "Objection!"

"Sustained," the judge said.

"Withdrawn. Detective Rein," the attorney said, "when you realized your partner had shot Mr. Krissing in the privates, what did you do?"

Rein turned toward the jury and said, "In the interest of effecting an arrest on Krissing and successfully prosecuting him for his crimes, I attempted immediate lifesaving measures."

"And how, exactly, did you do that?"

"I put on a rubber glove and slid my right index finger inside the gaping hole between Mr. Krissing's legs, sir. I was attempting to stop the flow of blood from the wound."

"Inside of his scrotum?" the attorney said.

"That's correct."

There was visible discomfort from the people seated around the courtroom. The judge wrapped his fingers around his wooden gavel as a warning.

"And did you stop the bleeding, Detective?" the attorney continued.

"I was not sure," Rein said.

"Why were you not sure?"

Rein turned to the jury and said, "It was very difficult, because at the time, Mr. Krissing was writhing around."

"In pain?"

"I believe so."

"Was he screaming?"

"Very much so."

Several men on the jury smiled then, looking at Rein with visible approval. Rein tilted his head at them in recognition. "Your honor!" the attorney squawked. "Please direct the detective to stop playing to the jury! He is attempting to influence them with his testimony!"

In the background, just out of focus, Carrie could see Bill Waylon smirk.

The plaintiff's attorney collected himself and said, "Can you please tell us what made you remove your hand from Mr. Krissing before the ambulance got there?"

Rein appeared to struggle to frame his words correctly. "Well," he said, "the tip of the glove felt stuck. Pinched, I guess, is what you would call it. In all of Krissing's thrashing around, the elastic somehow got caught. He flopped one way, and I heard something snap, real loud."

"Oh Jesus," the man holding the camera muttered.

The judge cleared his throat and dabbed a white handkerchief across his forehead. "I believe we get the idea. Are there any more questions for the witness?"

"Just one, Your Honor. Detective, what did you do when you realized what had happened?"

"I looked down and saw what was wrapped up in my glove," Rein said.

"And then?"

"I believe the appropriate term is, recoiled in horror."

They attorney's face puffed with outrage. "Do you honestly expect the men and women in this court to believe that you ripped out a human being's testicles because your rubber glove got caught?"

Rein turned toward the jury and calmly said, "That's what happened."

Carrie paused the recording and got out of her seat, walking toward the TV where the frozen image of former detective Jacob Rein was staring back at her. There was victory in his eyes, and it was well deserved. The jury would break soon and render a verdict clearing both Rein and Waylon of any wrongdoing. She touched his face and drew her finger across the deep lines around his mouth, along the furrow of his brow.

She turned off the television and crawled back into bed. The bathroom door was still open, filled with darkness that spread across the blank wall, forming its own abyss. In her mind, the images of human body parts stuffed into bags were still lined up, a road leading to the brink of the precipice. As sleep descended, she felt darkness swirling around her bed, snapping at her hungrily, venomous drool spilling from its many fangs, but it did not matter. She thought of Jacob Rein's face on the television screen and knew that he was deep inside the void, and that he'd been waiting for her.

II
BLACK MILK

8

It was still early when Molly felt the covers move aside, exposing her body to the cold morning air. She groaned and turned over. "Go back to bed, Nubs. Mommy needs to sleep more."

Instead, soft, fleecy pajamas brushed against her sides, her daughter's cold feet seeking out any part of her body that wasn't covered. She squirmed and moved away, making room. Nubs leaned back against the pillows, holding her iPad up as she swiped, moving cartoon farm animals around the screen. "Just keep the sound down, okay?" Molly said, rolling away toward the other side of the bed. "Wake me up in a little bit and I'll make breakfast."

"All right," Nubs said.

"Did you go potty before you came in here?"

"No. I didn't need to."

"Are you sure?"

The little girl ignored her, only interested in the cartoon playing on the screen.

Molly turned her head and tickled Nubs's side. "Hey, I'm just making sure you don't pee on me. You got any pee in there?"

"Keep poking me and find out." The little girl giggled.

"Very funny." Molly rolled over and closed her eyes.

By ten she was out of bed and dressed, sliding on sweatpants and a T-shirt, no shower. She pulled her hair into a ponytail and did the same for Nubs, trying to keep the little girl's long blond curls out of the milk in the cereal bowl. She yawned as the coffee machine vibrated to life, and said, "What do you want to do today, Nubs?"

Nubs ignored her, too busy spooning heaps of Lucky Charms into her mouth as she stared at the iPad screen. Molly grabbed a handful of curtain and felt the warmth radiating through the glass window in the kitchen. It looked sunny and fine outside. "You want to go to the park?"

"Sure," Nubs said, never looking up.

"Then I guess you'd better turn off your game and finish eating so we can go," Molly said, watching as Nubs kept swiping. She poured coffee into a large Disney mug and picked up her phone to find Carrie's number.

"Hey," the voice on the other end said.

"You want to go to the park with me and the brat?" Molly said. "It's my last week of unemployment, and I can spring for ice cream as long as we split it."

"I'm not a brat," Nubs called out.

"Plus, we can check out all the hot, sweaty dudes jogging past the playground," Molly said.

"I can't. I'm still working on that murder we had last weekend. I have an appointment at the coroner's office this afternoon."

"Screw that nonsense. The guy's dead, right?"

"Uh, yeah. That's what normally happens in a murder."

"Well then, he can wait! What's the rush? Take the day off and come hang out with us. You've been working too much."

"Hey, it's a Thursday. Why isn't Nubs in school?" Carrie's voice held a tinge of unstated accusation. "Did you go out last night or something?"

"It's an in-service day, thanks, Officer. I couldn't find a babysitter, so I figured the job hunt could wait a day while I spend some time with my little girl, if that's all right with you. And I called you to see if you cared enough about her to do the same."

"Oh, spare me the drama, bitch. You know I'd love to, but I'm swamped."

"All right," Molly said. "It's okay, really. I hear children are adaptable. She probably won't even remember what you look like soon. You'll just be that weird old lady Mom used to bring around every once in a while."

"Har har har. Not funny."

Molly smiled and said, "Careful out there."

"Always. I will stop by and see you guys over the weekend."

Molly hung up the phone, muttering, "Sure you will." She looked over her shoulder at Nubs and said, "You done yet? Chop chop!"

On the other end of the line, Carrie hung up the phone and tossed it onto her bed, then snapped her dress pants clasp shut. She tore the tags off her new short-sleeved blouse and made quick work of the buttons, then tucked it in. She looped her new brown belt around her waist and stopped at the right side, letting it hang as she picked up her gun and matching brown belt and shining leather holster. The kind that wouldn't bite into her ribs and stayed flat against her body, out of sight. Also new.

Not that she'd ever tell anyone, but she'd picked out exactly the kind of outfit that female detectives wore on TV. Much to her surprise, none of the stylish pants she could find had loops big enough to fit a belt strong enough and thick enough to hold her gun. She'd settled for a thinner belt that she hoped would not snap in half, but it looked good, so it was worth risking the embarrassment.

Once her outfit was assembled, she clipped her badge to the left side of her waist and stopped to look in the mirror. "Badass," she said aloud, liking the way the badge and gun jutted out around the curve of her hips. She turned sideways, admiring how the dress pants hugged the curve of her backside. "Carrie Santero, Detective," she said, laughing at herself as she headed for the door. She needed to be at the station in half an hour to get to the coroner's office. It was the first follow-up of her first major investigation, and she didn't want to be late.

The sliding board was covered in small puddles from overnight rain, but Nubs didn't care. She scampered up the bars along the jungle gym's side and swung over the top bar, sliding back down as fast as she could, only to jump up and do it again. Molly yawned as she watched Nubs running past and said, "If I could run around half as much as you, I'd never have to diet."

Nubs scampered up the side of a large wobbling duck in the center of the playground. Molly helped her get seated, making sure she didn't fall off as she rocked back and forth. The duck's metal spring bent as far back as it could, until Nubs's long hair swept the rubber mats on the ground. "All right, that's enough," Molly said, gripping her daughter under the arm and hoisting her off the duck.

"Why?" Nubs hollered, kicking in the air.

"Because Mommy doesn't want to have a heart attack. Let me see you climb the jungle gym."

As Nubs ran past her toward the nearest rope ladder, Molly turned around, looking for the nearest bench. Instead, she saw a man sitting nearby, staring at her.

The woods behind him were thin with the golden and red leaves that had not fallen, giving her a clear view of the gravel parking lot beyond. She saw her car, and several others, most of them fitted with bike racks by the owners, who came to ride the woodland trails. At the far end of the parking lot was a large white van, backed in. Maybe a township employee here to do maintenance on the restrooms, she reasoned. Or a local contractor enjoying his lunch in peace.

Several joggers were in the area. She'd seen them running along the track when she pulled in, heads lowered, sports headphones tucked into their ears, blocking out the rest of the world as their legs pumped.

The man waved, realizing he'd scared her, then turned away. In the sunlight, she saw a deep bruise across the side of his face that he'd attempted to cover with make-up. He cupped his hands around his knees as he sat. Molly checked to see where Nubs was. She'd gone back to the sliding board again. He isn't bad looking,

Molly thought. He looks okay. Kind of boring. God knows I could do with boring for once.

"Hi there," she said, walking toward the benches.

"Hello," he said. "I'm sorry I startled you. I'm supposed to meet someone here, and I was looking to see if you were her."

"Nah," she said. "I wasn't startled."

"Oh, I'm glad."

He turned at the sound of a car coming into the lot, looking at it expectantly. It was just an older couple. They got out of the car and headed down the trail, his eyes following until they vanished from view. "Isn't that beautiful to see?" he said.

Molly prided herself at being able to read people. She took the time to read him then. His jeans were dark and stylish, and his suede boots were new and unscuffed. He wore a button-down shirt that had been pressed and creased along the sleeves. His hair was thin, despite his age, which she placed at early thirties. Just a few years older than she was. Gentle looking. Vulnerable. With large eyes and soft brown hair that made him look like a mouse. Molly found herself wondering where he'd gotten his bruise.

"So, what's her name?" Molly said.

"Sorry?"

"Her name. The one you're waiting for."

"We haven't actually met yet," he said. "It's an online dating thing. I guess that sounds pretty weird to someone like you."

"What does that mean?" She laughed, knowing what he meant.

"You know. Someone so pretty. You must think people who have to meet online are freaks or something."

"I've dated guys online before. Plenty of times. But you have to be careful. A lot of people are just completely crazy."

"I bet," he said. He looked back at the parking lot. "I guess she isn't coming. I can't blame her. It was a dumb idea to tell her to meet me at the park anyway."

"I don't think so. I think it was kind of sweet." She leaned forward to look at his bruise and said, "What happened? Were you in a car accident or something?"

"A drunk driver hit me Saturday night. It looked a lot worse when I was in the hospital, believe me."

"I believe you," Molly said. "That sounds awful. So did you really like this girl, or what?"

"I honestly don't even know what she looks like in person. It's just so complicated nowadays with all this modern technology."

"I hear you," Molly said. "It's not like the old days when you grew up in a small town and married your best-looking cousin."

He laughed. "No, it certainly isn't."

"I'm Molly," she said, extending her hand. She pointed at the swing set and said, "That little monster is Nubs."

He took her hand and squeezed it lightly. His skin was soft and warm, and he leaned closer to her and said, "My name is Robert Rhoades."

9

The Vieira county coroner's office was converted from a 1940s schoolhouse. It was made from fine, redbrick walls that someone had covered over with snot-yellow polyurethane siding. The paneling was cracked and rotted around the front door, revealing hints of the true exterior beneath, and Carrie found herself wanting to stick her fingers into the crumbling slots and tear them away.

Bill Waylon held the door open for her, and she thanked him and stepped into the front lobby, overwhelmed by the stench. The air was putrid, made worse by the scent of dozens of sickly sweet plug-in air fresheners. Powerful floor-unit fans were stationed in the hallway, the industrial strength ones used by fire departments to suck smoke out of homes, aimed at them both.

"What the hell, Chief?" Carrie gagged, pressing the fabric of her shirt against her mouth.

"It's a morgue, kiddo. What did you expect?"

"Nice combo of air freshener and rotting meat. It smells like somebody took a dump under a Christmas tree."

Waylon's nose twitched with disgust, but he was too proud to show it. "You'll get used to it."

The walls were painted faded lime, still decorated with large pushpin boards. Long ago, the boards had been filled with drawings by the kids in class. Sketches lovingly done in crayon for their teachers, rewarded with glittering stars and encouraging notes.

The corridors were now representative of all life, Carrie thought. You keep walking down the same hallway long enough and all the things that remind you of your childhood and innocence empty out and fill with the stink of decay.

She watched the chief turn into the next classroom, and she followed him in. Nothing was changed about the room from when it had been filled with third graders. A line of cubbyholes still waited for their books and lunchboxes. The walls were lined with cabinets, where the teacher had kept her supplies. The windows were hand-cranked. Even the chalkboard at the front of the class remained. The only difference was that the desks and chairs had been removed, and in their place were three metal gurneys.

"Is this where they do the autopsies?" Carrie said, looking around.

"No, they do them in the cafeteria. The old walk-in freezer is where they store the bodies."

"Trippy," Carrie said. "That would probably explain most of the school lunches I ate as a kid. So where's the coroner?"

"He better be here. We had a meeting scheduled."

A voice from the back of the room called out, "Coroner's not gonna make it. Something about an old lady doing the ol' coronary face-plant into her beef stew at the old folks' home." Eddie Schikel leaned against the doorway, holding a thick file under his arm. "Apparently, it caused quite a scene. They thought all the other old fogies were gonna start dropping on the spot."

Carrie laughed, and Waylon shot a look at her, one of his eyebrows cocked. "My mom's in one of those places," he said.

"Sorry, Chief," she said.

Waylon leaned back against the antiquated metal air-conditioning unit that ran the length of the room and folded his arms. "I'd have thought my homicide a little more important than a routine medical call. Why does everybody in this county have to be a clown?"

"Come on, Bill," Schikel said, making his way in. "This guy's not even a doctor. He's a funeral director who contributed enough money to the right people to get elected. Why do we need him here? He'd just get in the way."

Waylon moved toward the middle table as Schikel opened his file and flipped through the pages. "First things first. I called in a favor, and Philly's crime lab did a quick check of our blood samples from inside the van."

"Tell me there's good news."

"Well, if by good news you mean did we get a DNA profile for the suspect, the answer is categorically 'no.' We didn't get shit."

Waylon muttered a curse and lowered his head.

"How's that possible?" Carrie said. "There was blood everywhere. Some of it had to be his. In the academy they told us that most people using a knife tend to cut themselves in the process."

"That is an excellent observation, young lady," Schikel said. "Unfortunately, the suspect contaminated it."

"Contaminated it? With what?"

"Bleach. He saturated the entire scene with enough bleach to ruin our chances of getting a decent profile on him."

"Goddamn it," Waylon snapped.

Carrie's eyes lit up. "Wait. Can you tell what kind of bleach he's using? What brand, I mean?"

Schikel stared at her in mystification. "Sorry?"

"Acme, Super Fresh, Giant . . . don't they all have their own brands of bleach or something?" Carrie said. "Can't crime labs identify exactly what brand of bleach he's using? Then, maybe we can get the store to provide us with some kind of customer profile, right? All the stores track their customers' purchases. That's how all these big companies know exactly what coupons to send us. I think we might be onto something here. We narrow it down to one local store, run a behavioral profile on the customer list. Boom! One in custody. News at eleven!"

"Do me a favor," Waylon said. "Stop talking."

Schikel removed a plastic bag from the file and held it up, showing them several long strands of hair. "We found these stuck to the victim's hands. He must have ripped them out of the doer's wig at some point. You know what that means."

Waylon rolled his eyes. "It means some lucky S.O.B. gets to go hang out at Club Transmission and talk to everyone wearing a blond wig, which is most likely going to be a bunch of dudes. And given my options as far as reliable investigators, that lucky S.O.B. is me."

Schikel laughed and clapped him on the arm. "Look on the bright side, Chief. You might find out something new about yourself. Open up a whole world of possibilities."

"Go f—forget yourself, Eddie."

Carrie laughed aloud, and Schikel looked at them both in confusion. "What the hell does that mean?"

"This isn't like TV, Carrie," Waylon explained as they drove back to the station. "There's no magical database in any supermarket that's going to help us. I've seen thousands of surveillance photos from super-markets over the years, and you know how many were ever solved off the picture? Zero. You know why? Be-cause supermarkets don't give a damn about customers ripping them off. They just jack up the price of milk and potatoes for the week and pass along the cost to you and me."

He turned to look at her, concerned he was hurting her feelings. Instead, Carrie was tapping her fingers rhythmically on the windowsill. "I got it, Chief. Makes sense now that you say it. It's just TV these days, they make it all seem so simple."

"It messed us up when those shows started getting popular. Juries couldn't understand why we all didn't have laptops that scanned DNA databases and magi-cally produced suspects' driver's licenses. The worst thing about those shows is they taught the average per-son about forensics. Now we've got maniacs spraying bleach all over the place to defeat us."

Carrie pursed her lips and said, "This is cool."

Waylon looked sideways at her. " What exactly is so cool about it?"

"The whole thing. Being part of it. Finally getting the chance to do something real. I mean, thank you so much for keeping me in the loop on this. I always wanted to work these kinds of cases. Give me all the crimes scenes and dead bodies you can handle. You want to hear something crazy? I don't mind it. I want to be up to my knees in blood and guts, getting the evidence we need to put this bastard away forever. I hope he does it again tonight!"

Waylon's foot slammed on the brake, sending the car fishtailing to the right. The sound of screeching tires and smoked rubber filled the woods around them as the car bounced to a stop. The chief's face puffed wide as he spat, "What in the *fuck* are you talking about?"

Carrie had never heard him curse before. Not seriously curse. She pushed back in her seat, looking at his large, outstretched finger as he shouted, "You *hope he does it again*? You think this is some kind of game, young lady? I worked fifteen years in this shit, up to my ass in bugs and worms crawling out of the eye sockets of dead fucking children, okay? Fifteen years of my life that are the biggest nightmare you can imagine, and the reason I came up here was to get away from all that!"

"I'm—I'm sorry, Chief. I didn't mean anything by it. I was just talking."

He ran his hand through his hair, his bulk settling into the seat. "Listen, I get it. I was young once too. But when you get to be my age, you reach the point you just don't want to see this kind of thing again. I've had enough of it for one lifetime."

"I understand," she said. "So let me take care of all that. You tell me what to do and I'll go do it. The interviews, the follow-ups, anything else. I'll do a good job, I swear it."

"I know you will, kiddo," he said. "But at the end of the day, it's my responsibility, and I can't just pass that off on you." He concentrated on the road, then squinted and said, "But I will let you help. Maybe you can go talk to the ladies, or whatever they are, at that nightclub and find out who was wearing a blond wig."

Carrie pumped her fist and said, "Yes!" The chief's stare made her clear her throat and add, "I mean, sounds like a plan. No problem."

Carrie folded her hands, trying to keep from showing how excited she was. It was a forty-five-minute ride back to the station. She was determined to do her best to stay quiet and enjoy the thick, green foliage stretching along the road. She felt her phone vibrate, and she slid it out of her pocket. A text message from Molly read *Image: Received.*

She opened the message and waited for the picture to download, watching the bars on her antenna flicker as they wound through the hills of the county's backwater. The image clarified, leaving Carrie's face contorted in disgust. "What the hell is she doing now?"

Molly was in a plain black dress and black heels that Carrie had never seen before, and both of her hands were raised defensively, as if she was backing away from the camera. She was posed with her right foot turned to show off the length of her leg and the shoe's heel. Her hair was pulled back, so it looked like it had been cut short, and her face was twisted in mock terror. Even more strange, the picture was set on a wooden farming platform, with crisscross beams and open slats that revealed the bright blue sky and open green hills behind her. It was a place Carrie had never seen. Since when did Molly start doing macabre photo shoots at places they never went to? And who the hell had taken it anyway?

She looked at Molly's swollen cheeks and knew what happened after the picture was taken. Both she and Nubs must have burst out laughing. It was typical of her, coming up with some new and elaborate way of guilt-tripping her for not spending time with them.

Carrie rolled her eyes and laughed. Molly was a crazy bitch, but she was Carrie's crazy bitch, even if she did have a seriously deranged sense of humor. She picked up her phone and typed, *Nice picture. You should use that for your online dating profile to warn people what kind of a nutjob you really are.* The message swirled, not sending. She decided to try again later, when she had a better signal.

10

The house was dark, except for lights flickering in its front window. From her car, Carrie could see her father stretched out in his recliner, staring at the television. He had a couch but never used it, preferring the deep sink of his chair, lowered so far back he had to spread his hairy feet to see the TV screen.

In one hand, the remote control, and in the other, his favorite companion—a tall, plastic green cup. Carrie knew what was in the cup. It was the same thing that had been in the cup since her mother left. That was a lie they both agreed to let be true. If it was ever brought up, Rosendo Santero claimed he never touched a drop until the day his wife abandoned him and their little girl, leaving him to face the pressures of raising a daughter all by himself. In reality, Carrie knew, he'd always been a drunk.

In grade school she'd drawn a picture of her family. She drew a colorful sky and bright, smiling sun. In the picture, her mother was sitting in the car, waving to them, and Carrie was standing next to her father holding his hand. Her teacher picked up the picture and saw Rosendo's other hand was holding a beer.

Her mother did not leave for another two years, but somehow Carrie had known it was coming. The blond-haired, blue-eyed beauty named Beth Anne Richards was a free thing. Beth Anne had never even taken her husband's name. She never wore a wedding ring. Or a bra, for that matter. She'd talked so often about touring with the Grateful Dead before she met Rosendo, Carrie thought she'd been part of the band. When she left, Carrie made up her mind that her mother was simply back out on tour and would return once it was over.

Rosendo was not a mean drunk. Never abusive. When he drank it was the only time he seemed happy. One night when she mentioned Beth Anne being on tour, her father sat next to her and put his arm around her, hugging her close. "My sweet little angel, your mama was never part of any band. She was what you call a groupie. A fan. She followed them around and lived in a tent, or slept in strange cars, waiting for them to play their music. I only tell you this because I don't want you to think she is going to come home. She isn't. From here on out, it is just you and me. The two amigos." Rosendo had bent over and kissed her on top of the head, expecting her to cry. She didn't.

Carrie had absorbed the information like a heavyweight boxer takes an uppercut to the rib cage. It hurt like hell, but years of training taught you how to take the hit. You just brushed it off and kept going. After that night, Beth Anne never appeared in any of Carrie's drawings again. Luckily, the year her mother moved out was the same year a foul-mouthed, short-haired blond girl wearing ripped jeans and Converse All-Stars moved into town. She and Molly became instant friends, and for all the trouble they got into together, it was Molly's mother, Penny, who took her to get her hair done and instructed her father what kind of tampons to buy.

Sometimes, Molly and Carrie would stay up late, plotting ways to get Rosendo and Penny together. Rosendo wasn't a bad-looking man. The alcohol had given him a pronounced stomach, but he still had a strong, firm chin and smooth olive skin. Women always commented how much they loved his accent, still bearing the slightest touch of his Cuban youth. Penny had even seemed interested for a while, until it became clear that Rosendo had simply given up on that aspect of life. He'd cut it out of his being and thrown it away.

Looking back, Carrie knew that Rosendo had not said his wife was never coming back for his daughter's benefit. He was saying it to force himself to believe it, but they both knew he didn't, and never would.

Carrie let herself into the house, calling out, "Papi, it's me."

"Oh," he said, sounding happy. "Come in, come in. Are you hungry?"

She opened the refrigerator and frowned. The shelves held nothing but blocks of half-eaten cheese, a bag of sliced pepperoni, and several tomatoes. The bottom two shelves were stacked with beer. "It's not like you have anything to eat anyway, so I guess not," she said.

He waved for her to come into the living room. "I will order anything you want. Just tell me. You want a pizza?"

"Are you hungry?" She looked him over like a school nurse inspecting the dirty kid in class. His skin was sallow, and his cheeks sagged under dark circles. "It doesn't look like you're eating much."

He patted his stomach and said, "I eat all day. Nothing but health food." He shifted in his chair to turn toward her, careful not to spill his drink. "So what brings you by? Everything okay in the police world? You shoot anybody today?"

"Not today." She looked down at her pocket, buzzing and lighting up with an incoming call, but ignored it.

"You need to get that?"

"Nope," Carrie said, keeping her eyes fixed on Rosendo.

"Is it a boy?" he said, eyes sparkling.

That made her laugh. "Not likely. Unless it's someone from work."

"You stay away from those police officers," Rosendo said. "I know all about men in uniform. We called them pigs back when I was young, because that is how they act. Trust me."

"People call us pigs now too, Papi," she said.

"These people today," he said, waving his hand. "They are just crazies. You remember what I tell you. Shoot first, ask questions later. They see you are a police officer and all they do is try to kill you. This place is worse than Cuba now, even back during the bad times. So listen to me, okay? You see anyone that looks dangerous, you just pull out your gun and take care of business. If anyone asks why you did it, you tell them I said to. No problem."

"Okay," Carrie said, chuckling.

"Good. Now, how about some pizza?"

"I'm okay, really. I had a long day and have to be back in tomorrow, but I wanted to stop in and check on you."

"I'm good. I don't see you enough, though. You working too much. Take tomorrow off. Tell them I said so."

"All right, I'll tell them you said so," she said, getting up from the couch. She leaned over her father and wrapped her arms around him, kissing him on the side of his face. "You need to shave."

"I need a haircut, too. You think you can bring your scissors over tomorrow? Otherwise I have to pay the girl twenty dollars, and she don't cut it as good as you."

"I just told you I have to work tomorrow."

"Oh, right, right," he said, descending into the fog once more. "Okay, but soon, then."

She kissed him top of the head again and said she promised.

Her phone was buzzing again by the time she walked to her car. She pulled it out of her pocket, hoping to see Chief Waylon's name on the call screen. She wanted to hear there'd been a shooting, or a big burglary, or something that needed her to come back to work. The thought of returning alone to her quiet apartment seemed depressing. She wanted the kind of action that comes from putting together leads and chasing down a suspect, not an evening of folding laundry and putting it back in the basket, unable to muster enough interest to put it away. She looked at her phone and groaned when she saw Penny's contact picture on her screen. Another call with no promise of action. "Hey, you. What's up?"

Penny's voice was anxious and angry. "Is Molly with you?"

"No."

"Goddamn it. I've been trying to call her all evening. She was supposed to take me to get my hair done."

"Do you want me to swing by and get you?"

"No. I already canceled."

"Where's Nubs?"

"With Molly," Penny said. "When's the last time you talked to her? Did she say where she was headed?"

Carrie closed her eyes in thought. "She was taking Nubs to the park today."

"Well, it's already eight o'clock and that little girl has school tomorrow. She better get back and put her to bed, or else."

"Listen, let me call around for her," Carrie said. "I'll figure out what's going on."

Typical, Carrie thought as she slid into her car. Typical and irresponsible. This is the shit I'm talking about. Sure, Molly is a caring mom, but where's she going in her life? What kind of example is she setting for Nubs? She doesn't have a job, she lives with her mom, and her and Nubs still sleep in the same room, in the same bed. Whenever I try to encourage her to come up with some sort of plan, it turns into a fight. If it wasn't for the baby, I'd give up on her and be done. Really, really done.

She scrolled to the last text message from Molly and opened up the bizarre photograph once more, studying it in greater detail. Molly was posed with her hands up, looking at the lens like she was trying to appear scared. Since Nubs wasn't in the picture, it was easy to assume the child had been the photographer. Carrie pictured Molly telling Nubs they were going to play a prank on Aunt Carrie and it was going to be epic. Pathetic was more like it, she thought. It was one thing to involve meth-snorting frat boys in her shenanigans, but now she was dragging the kid into it too?

In the furthest depths of her being, Carrie had always imagined that Molly got pregnant for the attention. Now it was her excuse for not doing anything else.

Stop fucking around and call me, Carrie wrote. *No more pictures. Your mom is scared shitless and I have work tomorrow.*

By the time she arrived home, she'd sent text messages to everyone in her phone and reached out to everyone on Facebook who knew Molly, copying and pasting the same message over and over. Had they heard from her? When they did, she told them to let her know right away. After the last message was sent, she called Penny. "Anything yet?"

"No, not yet."

The older woman was starting to sound worried, and it chilled her. Penny had lived more and seen more than all her girls combined, and it wasn't easy listening to her get rattled. "Everything is going to be fine," Carrie reassured her. "I reached out to everybody we know. She will pop up somewhere."

"If she didn't have Nubs, I'd agree with you," Penny said. "But she's never done this before. Not with the baby."

"Is she seeing anyone?" Carrie said. "Any chance she met a guy and they're over his house or something?"

"Not that she mentioned."

Carrie paused, unsure of how to phrase the words on the tip of her tongue. "Penny," she started, then backed off, searching for the right words. "She's been going out a lot lately. Have you seen anything . . . bad?"

"What do you mean bad?"

"I mean anything that will help me find her."

"Oh, for God's sake," Penny snapped. "No, Carrie. I didn't find any crack pipes or heroin needles, if that's what you mean."

"Look, I'm just trying to help."

"I know, I know, baby," Penny said. "You probably hear about this kind of thing all the time. The worst part is, I keep hearing car doors slam and seeing headlights come down the street, thinking it's them. But it isn't."

"They'll turn up," Carrie said. "Let me know as soon as you hear something and I'll do the same."

Carrie only had two kinds of dreams. The first involved searching for something she needed and not being able to find it. Her dream would be wonderful, involving a night out in the city, or being invited to a party, but then she could not remember where she parked her car, or could not find one missing shoe. She'd spend the rest of the dream scrambling around, desperate to find whatever was missing, until she awoke.

The second kind of dream was about someone she needed to say something to. Someone she was trying to forget, an old boyfriend who'd broken her heart or a particularly awful person at work. She'd berate them as they stood there making flimsy excuses, but nothing was ever resolved, because none of it was real. Those dreams were so potent, she'd spend the rest of the next day dwelling on it. The person who appeared most frequently was her mother.

Beth Anne Richards still wandered the corridors of Carrie's mind, for all her efforts to forget the woman. Sometimes, Carrie dreamed she was on duty and pulling over a car. When she walked up to greet the driver, she'd see an older, sadder-looking version of herself and know it was her mother.

Sometimes, she dreamed about finding the skeletal remains of a thirty-year-old woman someone had left buried in the woods, and she would find the photograph of a young, smiling child in the woman's belongings and recognize herself.

That night she was so tired, she began dreaming the moment she closed her eyes, only to wake up several minutes later to check her phone for any calls or texts. As she reached the part of her dream where she was digging through her closet fruitlessly searching for a matching high-heeled shoe, the loud song of her phone's ringtone sounded. Carrie bolted upright in the darkness and slammed the phone to her ear. "Is she back?"

Someone was screaming on the other end, a high-pitched scream interrupted only by sputtering curses. "Is this Carrie? Officer Santero?"

"Yes," she mumbled. The name on the screen said *Sgt. Kenderdine, Hansen Twp PD.*

"It's Dave Kenderdine, from the task force. Listen, I'm over here at the Michaels residence, and a woman named Penny is freaking out. She said she knows you and demanded I get you on the phone. I wouldn't have bothered you, but she's really losing it."

"Why is she freaking out?" Carrie said, sitting up. "What happened?"

He started to reply, but his voice was drowned out by Penny's cries of "My babies! My baby girls! Go find her, you useless piece of shit!"

"Ma'am! Do not touch me, do you understand?" Kenderdine barked, away from the phone. "I know you're upset, but do not put another finger on me or I will put you on the ground." His voice was calm again as he came back, saying, "I was checking the park after hours and I found a car registered to someone named Molly Michaels at this address," Kenderdine said. "When I came here to ask about the car, this lady started going nuts. Is this Molly person missing or something?"

The voice on the phone was still speaking, and the woman's voice behind him still screaming, as Carrie leaped from her bed and stumbled through the darkness, snatching whatever clothes she could find.

11

As Carrie parked her car, Penny raced down her front steps, flapping her hands in the air, shouting, "There! There she is! Maybe you'll listen to her, you prick!"

Several neighbors stood on their front porches, smoking and hunched forward to get a better view. They eyed Carrie as she hurried past them, none of them bothering to ask what was wrong. They were content to watch the spectacle unfold.

Penny latched on to Carrie's arm as soon as she drew close. "Please, please tell this idiot that my daughter and granddaughter are missing and we need to put out an alert right now. What do you call those things? Amber Alerts? That's what we need. Tell him!"

Sgt. Kenderdine lowered his voice to say, "It's my understanding Molly is an adult. You already know what I'm going to say, right?"

Penny's face quivered with anger even as her eyes swelled with tears. "You're not going to tell me the same thing, Carrie. Are you? Please tell me you're not."

"Listen to me," Carrie said, trying to find her mental footing. "Go sit down on the steps and give me a minute to talk things over with the sergeant, okay? I will figure out what's going on. Go have a cigarette. I've got this."

Penny jabbed a finger in the air at Kenderdine as she walked past. "All because this asshole is too lazy to do his damned job!"

Carrie followed the sergeant around the side of his car. "I'm sorry, Dave. She's just upset."

"I get it," he said. "What's up with your friend Molly? Does she bug out like this a lot?"

"Not like this, not with her daughter. I can't imagine she would just leave without telling someone."

"I tried telling the old lady we can't put her in as a missing person. We can't put the kid in as missing, because she's with her mother. My hands are tied here, Carrie. It sucks, but they really are."

"I know, I know. I just had the same conversation with someone earlier on," Carrie said, looking at the front steps where Penny was sitting, sucking a cigarette down to the filter. Her neighbors from either side had come over to her, pretending to console her by rubbing her back but actually just being nosey. Penny's eyes were fixed hard on Carrie.

"How did the car look?" Carrie said.

"Fine to me. A little messy inside, but nothing unusual for someone with kids."

"Shit. Shit, shit, shit, shit, shit," Carrie said. "What the hell is going on here?"

"Listen. I'll put a general broadcast message out that we're looking for those two. Not an alert or anything. Just a stop and ID or something, okay? I'll check all the local spots and see if anyone has seen her."

"Thanks, Sarge," she said. "I'm going to go search the park, see if I can come up with something. Do you have a flashlight I can borrow?"

"Sure. There's a spare in my trunk."

She hoisted the trunk's lid up and reached inside for the long metal flashlight. It was heavy and good, stuffed with D-cell batteries. The kind that cops had used in the old days to cave in people's foreheads. So help me God, Molly, she thought, smacking the metal against her palm. If this is another stupid escapade of yours, I'm going to use this on you.

The park was quiet and dark, the metal gate rattling back and forth in the wind as Carrie exited her car and closed the door. She left the flashlight off, preferring to move in darkness. Her right side felt empty without the weight of her duty weapon. She'd run out of the door so fast, she'd forgotten her gun.

Gravel crunched under her sneakers as she walked across the parking lot, keeping a constant vigil on the dark woods surrounding her. Molly's car was at the far end of the lot, a ten-year-old four-door with a taped-up rear taillight and stickers across the back window that read 90.2 COUNTRY ROCK and KEEP HONKING, I'M RE-LOADING.

"Why do you have that on your car?"

Molly just rolled her eyes. "So people know not to mess with me."

"Yeah, but when they find out you don't really have a gun it's going to be bad, real fast. And with Nubs in the car, it's almost like you're asking for trouble."

"Would you listen to yourself right now? Jesus, you sound like Coppy McCoperson all the damned time! I

knew you when you were smoking reefer in the back of the record shop, bitch, so don't sit there and try to be something you aren't."

Carrie jabbed her finger into Molly's side, poking her so hard in the ribs, she yelped. A hand came flying around the back of Carrie's head, and Carrie swatted the nearest thing she could reach: Molly's swollen right boob. "Shit! You hit my tit! What the fuck?" Molly shouted, backing up and clutching her chest.

"Language!" Penny shouted from the kitchen.

"Well, it's not my fault they're all ginormous now because you had a kid," Carrie hissed.

"Don't worry, yours will grow in someday, flattop."

Carrie looked down at her chest and frowned. "They're not small. They're just not all saggy and gross like yours."

"If I had milk I would so seriously whip one out and squirt you right now."

A pot clanged against the sink in the kitchen and Penny called out, "Not in my damned house, you wouldn't!" She emerged, staring at them, her pink sweatshirt pulled up to her elbows, a cigarette dangling from the side of her mouth. "It was bad enough I had to listen to this when you two were fourteen and one got tits and the other didn't, but now you're grown up and I've had it! Can you knock it off for once, please? I'm trying to make dinner, and you're going to wake up the goddamned baby."

Molly waved the air in front of her and gagged, saying, "I hope the food doesn't smell like an ashtray. Can you put that out? It would be nice for the kid to at least wait 'til she's five to get cancer from secondhand smoke."

"I left the windows open. She'll be fine. I smoked around you your whole life."

Carrie rolled her eyes. "Oh shit. Then I'm calling

Children and Youth tomorrow. Lord, we need to save this child."

Molly draped her arm over Carrie's shoulder and said, "You better listen to her, old lady. She's the law."

Carrie winked and said in her best Texan accent, "That's right. The law. And this here's my deputy."

"Much obliged, Sheriff," Molly said.

"Anytime, partner."

Penny gave them both a look and said, "Don't gang up on me, bitches. I'll cut you both."

Carrie aimed the flashlight at Molly's car and turned it on, checking the doors and locks. Everything was intact. The steering wheel and column had not been tampered with and neither had the ignition. Everything looked normal, except for the fact that it was sitting in the middle of a park in the dead of night.

"Fine," Carrie told herself. At least we know she and Nubs arrived here in one piece.

She looked around the outside of the car, checking for signs of struggle, or even blood. There was nothing. The gravel around the car was undisturbed.

That's good news too, she thought. If people had tried to snatch her or Nubs as they got back in the car, there would have been chunks of human flesh everywhere from Molly scratching their faces off. Even if they got her, it would not have been an easy battle.

"Think, Carrie, think," she told herself. "What do you know? Think like a detective."

She knew Molly and Nubs had not come home. She knew it was past Nubs's bedtime and Molly was generally pretty good with things like that. She knew their car was in a public place, after hours, with no explanation. There was no indication of a struggle. No evidence of a crime.

On the other hand, she thought, there was plenty of evidence that Molly was being an asshole. She loved getting attention. She loved busting Carrie's balls for not spending more time with them. She loved getting Carrie's goat with phony pictures and stories.

In her mind, she pictured Molly yelling at her. "Oh my God, you idiot! I sent you a picture just the other day. How did you not know this was a freaking joke?"

Any experienced cop was going to hear all of that, nod politely, and walk away.

She moved past the car toward the playground, seeing the swing set and monkey bars ahead, in the clearing. The swings rocked back and forth in the breeze, like something from a poltergeist movie. Carrie ignored them, sweeping the tree line with her flashlight, searching for any signs of disturbance in the woods. She saw no broken branches. No discarded shoes or clothing. She cursed under her breath, turning around as she searched.

"Molly!" she cried out, throwing her head back. "Nubs!" she bellowed, so loud and long that her voice cracked like dry wood. "Answer me," she whispered. "Please."

Carrie had not prayed since she was a little girl. She'd stopped when she heard her father do it and realized her prayer would not be answered. Rosendo would get drunk in his chair, then stumble into his room late at night, shut his door, bury his face into his pillow, and cry out, "Please, please God, I beg you. Bring her back to me. Please. In the name of sweet Jesus, and the Virgin, and all the Saints, I pray to you."

He'd done his best to hide it, but Carrie had heard every word and his long-drawn-out sobs afterward. In her mind, prayers had always been for the weak.

Standing in the park, she lowered her head and closed her eyes. "God, I've never asked you for anything, but I'm asking you now. Please let them be okay. Please give me a sign and help me find them and let them be okay." She paused, then added, "In the name of Jesus, the Virgin, and the Saints, I pray to you."

She kept her head lowered, listening. She heard nothing but the swings rocking on their chains. "Fine, then," she said, as she clicked the flashlight back on and headed into the woods to hunt anew. "I'll do this myself."

12

Bill Waylon folded his hands behind his head and remained motionless, eyes closed, as he listened, taking in every detail. "Tell me again. One more time."

Carrie sorted her thoughts. "She called me in the morning and asked me if I wanted to go to the park. She said Nubs had the day off. She said something about wanting to watch the joggers run past."

"I got all that," Waylon said. "Did the kid really have the day off from school?"

"I checked the calendar online. It was just like Molly said."

"And as far as you know she's had no contact with anyone since that phone call?"

"Not directly. I even called all the prisons this morning. Nothing."

"And we know she left in her car, because it was found at the park," Waylon said. "What we don't know is how she left it there. Or why."

"Or where she went."

"And there was nothing in the woods, you said?" he asked.

"Nothing. I searched for two hours, then I went

back this morning when it was light out and searched again."

A thought jolted his mind hard enough to knock him out of his meditative state, and he looked across the desk at her, squinting through one open eye. "What was that part you said about 'not directly'?"

She'd been dreading having to explain this part to anyone. It all sounded so stupid. "Molly sent me this weird picture yesterday. I don't know. She's always doing stuff like this to guilt me into spending more time with her. It's bizarre. I'm almost embarrassed by this whole thing because I feel like it's one of her gags and she's going to laugh her ass off when she finds out we all freaked out."

Waylon leaned forward against his desk and held out his hand. "Show me the picture."

Carrie brought up the text message as she said, "It came in as we were leaving the coroner's office." She handed her phone across the desk.

"Was she going to a party or something?" he asked, looking at the screen. "She's awfully dressed up to go to the park."

"No, and I've never seen that dress or those shoes before, either. I don't even know where the hell she took that picture. We don't know anyone with a farm." She reached to take the phone, but Waylon did not move. He continued to stare at it, rubbing his fingers through the long whiskers of his mustache. "Hmm," he said.

"What?" Carrie asked. "You see something?"

"I don't know. It looks familiar to me, but I can't say from where."

"Oh, that's just great," Carrie said as she slammed back against the chair. "I can't put out an Amber Alert because Nubs is with her mom. I can't put out a missing person report on Molly because she's not suicidal. Now the closest thing I have to an actual detective is telling me, Oh, I think I recognize it but I'm not sure. Well, that's not good enough, Bill! I'm telling you right now, if I don't find out what happened to that little girl, I'm going to lose my mind."

"Listen to me, kiddo. I know this whole thing means a lot to you, but sometimes we can't control what other people do. If your friend decided to run off, you just need to hope she has enough sense to call you. My advice is to let it go, for now."

"No!" Carrie shouted, slamming the desk with her hand. "You saw something in that picture, and I want to know what it was!"

"I'm not sure what it was."

"Then what can I do next?"

The gears of Waylon's mind seemed to be rotating against one another like some antiquated, enormous machine.

Carrie thought of something. "Just a few days ago I took another report of a missing girl. A twenty-two-year-old named Denise Lawson. She just never showed up, either. Maybe there's a connection."

"We see connections when we want to see connections," Waylon said.

"Or we see them because there's an actual connection."

"Listen, young people leave home all the time, Carrie. You know that. Let's be honest here. The only reason you're interested in this is because she's your friend. If you took this same exact call on the street, you'd think nothing of it and move on. And guess what? You'd probably be right."

"Maybe this isn't a street cop type of situation, Bill."

"You want to call one of your new friends up at the County, is that it?" he said, sounding wounded. "My word's not good enough for you all of a sudden?"

"What I need is a real detective," she said. "Someone who understands all of this."

"Well, there's no one like that around here, Carrie."

"There used to be," she said. "The best. You said so yourself."

When Waylon looked down, averting his eyes from her, Carrie cursed and got up from her seat, slamming the door open so hard it rattled the closet full of old uniforms behind it. She was halfway down the hall before she heard Waylon's voice, beaten and weary. "I don't know where he is. He went into hiding after he got out of prison. He didn't want me to be able to find him."

She stopped, turned, and looked up as he came to the door, slumping against the frame, the weight of his years imprinted on his face like deep weathering. He lowered his head and said, "But I know who we can ask."

The mechanical voice on the car's mobile data terminal laptop said, "Stay on this route for seventy-six miles. You will arrive in Harrisburg, Pennsylvania, by ten thirty-six A.M." Waylon glanced down at the computer screen and checked his route, making sure he was going the right way.

"Can't you just use the GPS on your phone like a normal human being?" Carrie asked.

"These phones are going to be the ruin of society, you trust me. The more we rely on them, the more the government takes over our lives. No, thank you. I'll use the GPS on this thing, and the NSA can stuff it."

Carrie rolled her eyes as she opened the case file sitting on her lap and read through the papers assembled there. "You put a report together on your friend already?" Waylon asked.

"No, this isn't for Molly. Almost two weeks ago a woman came to the station to report her daughter was missing. Denise Lawson," Carrie said, lifting a driver's license photo out from behind the report. Carrie shook her head. "Young, brunette, pretty. Her mom said she didn't come home and nobody had heard from her. You know what I told her?"

Waylon didn't have to look away from the road to know her eyes were boring into the side of his face.

"I told her there was nothing I could do."

"Look, it's not your fault that the State Police don't let us enter capable adults into the system, kiddo. If you're an adult in this country, you have the right to walk away and not be bothered by the government. Does it go wrong sometimes? Sure. But think how many abused women were able to escape their husbands because the police weren't allowed to stop them."

"I should have looked into it."

"You're looking into it now."

Carrie looked out the window at the road signs whizzing past. "Where are we going in Harrisburg?"

"To the district attorney's office."

"Who's there? Someone who knows Rein?"

Waylon ignored the question. "If you see a Dunkin' Donuts, holler. I need coffee bad."

Cornfields and trees stretched as far as she could see. "I think there's a Starbucks up ahead," she said, pointing downrange.

"Can't stand Starbucks," he said. "It tastes burnt to me. I'm a Dunkin' man, all the way. You ever had a Krispy Kreme?"

"I don't think so," she said.

Waylon whistled and said, "You are missing out. They've got this red light in their window that says 'Hot and Fresh Donuts' or something, and when it's turned on, that means the original glazed are just coming out of the oven. They've got this conveyor belt that if you walk into the store, they sometimes just hand you one for nothing, just for walking in. And the second you put that thing in your mouth, it just melts. I'm serious. It melts into warm, sugary goo. You could eat those things until you get diabetes."

"If I ever see one, I'll keep that in mind," she said.

"But the coffee sucks. Tastes like somebody took Starbucks already-burnt coffee and burnt it up all over again."

"Conversations like this are why people think all cops do is eat donuts, you know," Carrie said.

"You know where that comes from?"

"No, but I'm sure you'll tell me." She sighed.

"Back in the old days, you didn't have 7-Eleven or Wawa or any of that sort open overnight. Everything shut down after nine p.m. Except the donut shops. So that's where all the old-timers used to go to get coffee. They were just looking to find a way to stay awake, and protecting the only businesses open at three in the morning, so people would always see cop cars parked there and assumed it was for the donuts. You ever seen a cop eat a donut on duty?"

"No," she said. "I guess I haven't."

"And you never will. Gets all over your uniform and makes a hell of a mess. Cops drink coffee. They don't eat donuts. That whole thing is bull."

She laughed and said, "Unless it's a Krispy Kreme."

"A hot and fresh Krispy Kreme original glazed is the exception to the rule. When the red light is on, that's not a donut. That's what they call a transcendental experience."

They drove the next ten miles in silence, Waylon tapping the steering wheel. They'd given up on trying to listen to the radio, as the stations seemed to change every ten minutes. The only thing they could get was low-fi, static-filled gospel music, and neither one of them was in the mood.

Carrie watched him drum with his thumbs and said, "Are you nervous about whoever we're going to see?"

"I'm excited, actually. Haven't seen him in a while. I keep up on him in the paper and on Facebook, you know how that goes. He's always taking pictures with different good-looking women. I mean, *really* good-looking women," he stressed.

"I get it, you dirty old man," Carrie said, smiling.

"Older than dirt. Not dead."

They walked out of the parking garage and looked up at the Dauphin County Courthouse, a bizarre, boxy building. It looked like an art deco version of an ancient Greek temple, with squared-off pylons that stretched up the length of the building on the front and the sides. She followed Waylon to the front desk. He held up his badge and said, "We're both carrying."

The desk officer, an overweight, white-haired man

with hearing aids in both ears, placed two plastic bins in front of them and said, "Put all your weapons in here. You'll get them when you come out."

Carrie slid her pistol out of its holster and laid it flat inside the container. The desk officer slid each container into a small storage bin and locked it, handing each of them a key. "Go around the side. The elevator is on your right." As they walked away, his hearing aids emitted a high-pitched squeal, and he dug into his ears to adjust them.

"Makes you feel safe, doesn't it?" Carrie said as they waited for the elevator. "Hopefully the bad guys don't figure out that all they need to do is rub two nickels together to disable the guard."

Waylon looked at the people standing around them and leaned toward her, whispering, "We're in someone else's backyard right now. Understand?"

"Yes, sir."

When they reached the district attorney's floor, Carrie followed Waylon, who smiled politely at the secretary behind the bulletproof glass and said, "Bill Waylon, here to see Jacob Thome."

As the secretary lifted her phone to call into the back offices, Carrie glanced at her chief and said, "Thome?"

He ignored her, watching through the glass as a young attorney, no older than Carrie, came hurrying down the hall and called out, "Uncle Bill!"

Waylon smiled as the office door opened and the man propped it open with his foot to give the chief a warm embrace. "Why didn't you tell me you were coming?"

"I wanted it to be a surprise," Waylon said.

"Come on in, I want everybody to meet you."

Waylon cocked his thumb back at Carrie and said, "Jacob, this is Officer Carrie Santero. She works for me."

Thome shot his hand out toward her and squeezed firmly, his smile radiating through his firm and squared-off jaw. "Nice to meet you, Officer Santero."

His eyes were fixed on hers and she was held by them, finding them familiar but unsure why. "I . . . Hi, how are you?" she said.

She fell in beside Waylon as they made their way down the hall, and he leaned toward her ear and said, "See why he gets those good-looking women? He's not married, you know."

"Oh, shut up." Carrie groaned.

Thome held up his hands as they entered the main room and called out, "Everybody, I want you to meet somebody!" The attorneys and secretaries stopped working and looked up at them. "This, is my uncle Bill Waylon. He's chief of police out in Coyote Township, but back in the day he was a county detective with my dad. Together, they caught Krissing the Child Killer." Thome put his arm around Waylon, whose face flushed with embarrassment, and he said, "This man right here is a goddamn hero."

Thome's desk was piled high with cases and law books. Three frames hung on his wall. One was his law degree from Temple University, the second was a photo of his mother and him at his Temple graduation ceremony, and the third was a small photograph of Thome as a child standing next to a man, both of them holding a large fish and smiling proudly. Carrie leaned forward to get a better view and realized the man in the picture was Jacob Rein.

"He made me use my mother's maiden name," Thome said as he went around the desk and sat down. "Told me I'd never get hired anywhere otherwise. I understand why he thought that, but looking back I regret that decision." He looked at Waylon and said, "I have no reason to be ashamed of him being my dad."

"I'm sure he's real proud of you either way, Jacob." Waylon looked around the office and said, "You seem to be making out pretty good here. How many trials you had so far?"

"Ten in two years," he said. "We're running understaffed, so we try to slide everything through with pleas, but I've been able to get in on some important cases."

"I read about that rape case you handled with the two defendants. Shame the jury wouldn't go for Felony 1."

"Can you believe that?" Thome said. "They got hung up on the fact that the victim went to the one guy's house to have sex with him, but not the other. They set that girl up, though. Those guys deserved to go to prison forever."

"Juries are tricky. Told you that a long time ago. It's hard for the average person to conceive of what kind of animals some people are. They try to find the good in everybody. In my experience, if you've got three charges of all varying degrees of penalty, they'll usually pick the one in the middle. Just to be fair."

"I'll get them next time."

"That you will," Waylon said.

"So what brings you guys out here? Some kind of training seminar?"

"Not exactly. I need to speak to your father." Before Thome could say anything, Waylon held up his hand and said, "Now, I know he doesn't want that, but it's important. Real, real important. You know I wouldn't ask if it wasn't."

"What's it about?" Thome said.

"We've got a few missing girls and a bad murder, Jacob. I'm not too proud to say I don't understand exactly what I'm seeing, and I'm hoping he can help me."

Thome scrunched up the side of his mouth as he weighed his thoughts. "You know, I think he'd love to see you, Uncle Bill. It might be good for him."

They watched Thome turn to his computer and bring up his address book, searching for the address listed under the word *Dad*. Carrie pursed her lips to keep from smiling in victory, but when she turned to look at Waylon, there was no delight in his face, only a look of deep concern.

13

"I'm going to tell you the truth about what happened to Jacob Rein," Waylon said.

He'd been quiet ever since they reached the highway, following directions from the GPS on his laptop. "It's important for you to understand why he might not be that happy to see us. It's not what you'll read in the papers, or what most people think, but it's true. I know this because I was there."

Carrie watched him sip his coffee as she steered, knowing she was about to be taken into a confidence not easily shared. She kept quiet, waiting for Waylon to continue.

"At the end of the Krissing case, we were both burnt out. We'd seen too many things. Dead bodies are one thing. Dead kids are another," he said. "And dead kids, killed for nothing more than the pleasure of a sadistic human being, in a sadistic way, well, that changes a man. Every detective, if he does the job long enough, comes to realize our bodies are just sacks of meat. Organic machines made up of nothing more than systems of working parts. When you see a dead body, it's not

scary or creepy, it's just the same as looking at a to-
taled car. Whatever it was before, it isn't there anymore. But when you see a dead kid, any dead kid, and
you realize that all the light they brought into the world
is gone, it's different. All their laughter. All their joy.
All their potential. All the love they felt, and were
given, when that gets taken away . . . it's like some kind
of light went out in the universe. It was as if I could hear
their laughter fading as they ran off into the darkness,
never to be heard from again. That's what Krissing was
doing. He was stealing our light." Waylon flinched
under the weight of the images momentarily flooding
his mind. He fended them off and said, "So after it was
done, and Krissing was arrested, we got put on trial for
violating his civil rights. His attorneys claimed we
used excessive force and said we castrated him, and
they were coming after our badges, our pensions, everything. They were trying to put us in prison for a long,
long time. Looking back, I'm not surprised the jury
found in our favor. Everybody knew what Krissing had
done. I guess they figured that even if we did castrate
him on purpose, it was deserved."

"I would have," Carrie said.

"Would have what?"

"Cut his nuts off on purpose."

"They weren't cut off," Waylon replied. "They were
accidentally removed by a very, very, complicated and
unfortunate mishap with the elastic from my partner's
rubber glove." Waylon's face did not give an inch
when he said this, but his right eye twitched.

*Blood squirted out from between the screaming man's
legs. He was kicking and thrashing on the floor like a
stuck pig, bucking on the cold cement and shrieking.*

Smoke twisted up from Waylon's pistol and he shouted, "You like that, you sick fuck? How's that feel? That was for every one of those fucking kids."

Jacob Rein had been standing by Waylon's side the entire time, watching the old man sink down on his knees to beg for mercy. Instead of mercy, Waylon raised his gun and fired a shot at Krissing's crotch. While Krissing writhed, Rein calmly said, "You're going to bleed out unless we do something, Walter."

Rein raised his hand and moved Waylon's gun aside, walking past Waylon, who bellowed, "Leave him be, Jacob. Let him bleed! I want him to scream!"

Rein reached into his back pocket and dug out a black rubber glove, fitting it onto his hand. "You're hit in the femoral artery, Walter," Rein said. "I'm going to have to get in there and pinch it off. It's going to be a little uncomfortable."

"I swear to God, Jacob, you help him, I will shoot you next."

Rein turned and looked up at his partner, his face having morphed into something Waylon had never seen before. Eyes blank, the blood drained from his face, like something laying on the slab in the morgue. Rein reached forward, fingers digging into the bullet hole torn through Krissing's pants, then opened the gaping wound enough to make the old man flop and scream. "Hold still, Walter," Rein said, holding Krissing down with his other hand as he continued to dig. He used all his effort to pin Krissing at the hips and keep him from bucking as he found what he was looking for and began to twist and pull. "There it is."

Rein reached into his left pocket and removed a curved metal tool Waylon had never seen before. He flicked it open with one hand, revealing the talon-shaped blade at its tip as he reached between Krissing's legs.

The old man's eyes rolled back into his head as he convulsed on the floor, slamming it back against the cement of his basement, clotted white foam spilling out of his mouth as his words turned to gibberish. When Rein stood up, he was holding two clumps of dripping wet meat, no bigger than skinned chicken nuggets. He tossed Krissing's severed testicles down onto the old man's face and said, "Oh no. Something must have gone wrong with my glove."

"On the night they cleared us of all charges, we went out to celebrate. Just him and me. Neither one of us had been sleeping much, with all the stress. I was having bad dreams and living like a zombie at home. My wife was talking about moving out with the kids, because all I did was sit in front of the television and ignore them. I was just shutting down inside. I'd seen too much. It was like I was broken and couldn't figure out how to put myself back together. Now, luckily, I eventually got help. I can't imagine what would have happened to me if I hadn't had them to go home to during all that."

Rein sat next to him, slumped forward, staring hollow-eyed at the dirty mirror behind the bar, face drawn, pale, sickly looking. Waylon's was no better. Waylon swallowed the rest of his beer. "You want another?"

His partner looked at the last inch of amber drink in his mug and said, "No, one's enough for me. I feel like I could pass out right here."

"That's good though," Waylon said. "We could both use some sleep."

Rein rubbed his eyes, trying to keep them open. He pushed the mug away, leaving beer still in it. Waylon raised an eyebrow. A fundamental rule of drinking had just been broken. When a man orders a drink, he finishes it. He watched Rein put the mug next to his empty shot glass and say, "I'm going home."

Waylon turned on his stool to watch Rein stumble, recover, and head for the door. They'd had only one shot of Jack before their beers. "Hey, you all right?"

"I'm fine. It's all hitting me at once," Rein said as he backed into the door, popping it open and saying, "I think I just need to get to bed."

"No problem, you big pussy," Waylon said, smiling as he picked up Rein's beer and finished it for him. That's what friends did. They kept one another from breaking the fundamental rules. Rein backed away, the door creaking closed after him.

Waylon squeezed the steering wheel tightly with both hands, working it back and forth until the leather covering stretched. "I had a few more beers and called it a night. I remember going out to my car and sitting there, letting it warm up, listening to the radio, when my cell phone rang. It was a number I didn't recognize."

"Detective Waylon?"

Waylon frowned, thinking he was being called into work. "Yeah. What is it now?"

"Your partner, Jacob Rein, has been in an accident. It doesn't look good."

As the officer gave him the location, Waylon dropped the phone without ending the call, tires spinning on the bar's gravel parking lot. He flew past stop signs and red lights, not bothering to slow down, ignoring the honks and shouts from the other drivers he raced past.

He saw red and blue lights flashing from the intersection ahead and slammed on his brakes, getting out of the car without remembering to put it in park, jumping back in his seat and slamming the transmission forward without braking, and jumping out again. "Where is he?" Waylon shouted as he ran up, blinded by the sea of lights.

Rein's SUV had smashed into the side of another car, a small four-door that was crumpled inward, behind the driver's seat. A man was spinning around in circles by the smaller car, being held back by a police officer, crying out, "How is she? How is she? I want to see my little girl!"

Metal around the car's rear twisted and groaned as a team of firefighters cut through the frame, showering the night with sparks. "There she is, we've got her," the fire captain said, pushing his men out of the way to climb inside the ruined car.

Through the broken windshield, Waylon could see the little girl's curly blond hair matted with blood. He watched the fire captain reach forward and tilt her head, checking for a pulse, and saw the man's helmet drop forward as he lowered his head.

"No . . . no!" the father screamed, his words tangling into long strings of incoherent sobbing. Two of the firefighters continued to work to extract the girl's body as the others stood back, watching in mute horror.

Only a few feet from the crash, Waylon saw Jacob Rein, his hands cuffed tight, getting stuffed into the back of a squad car.

"He was under the legal limit," Waylon said, "but that didn't matter much. The family was out for blood, and Jacob didn't put up any kind of fight. He accepted a plea for involuntary manslaughter against his attorney's advice, our union rep's advice, and he sure as hell wasn't listening to me." Waylon smacked his thumb against the steering wheel with a hard whack, his voice rising. "He could have beaten that case. I studied that accident report, and the girl's father was just as responsible. That asshole had the stop sign, but he was in such a damned rush to get home, he tried to beat oncoming traffic. Jacob's fatal mistake was that he told the officers on scene that he must've fallen asleep. He said he closed his eyes for a second, and when he opened them, they'd already crashed. It could've happened to anyone. It could have happened to me. If he'd just kept his mouth shut, none of this shit would've happened."

Waylon slumped back in his seat, his voice growing quiet again. "He never asked for special treatment or protection from the other prisoners. In the end, he did sixteen months on a four-year sentence. I went to pick him up at the prison, you know, like you see in the movies? He never asked me to, but I figured he didn't have anyone else to ask, so I went. He walked right past me like he didn't even know me. I tried to stop him, but he kept going. Haven't seen him since. Not even at his own son's graduation from law school."

"But why didn't he fight it?" Carrie said. "Why would anyone in their right mind want to go to prison?"

"Honestly? I think he wanted to be punished."

"For what happened with Old Man Krissing?" Carrie said.

"For that. Maybe more than that." Waylon turned to look out the window, seeing fewer trees than they had before. Now it was trailers, decorated with cheap American flags and Confederate flags, parked on dirt lots. People sat alongside their trailers on mismatched folding chairs, drinking beer as they stared back at him. Waylon looked back at the road and said, "I always suspected it was for all those times he went into those dark places and opened up doors that shouldn't be opened. Who knows what he let inside?"

14

Migrant workers poured off the back of the land-scape trucks assembled throughout the gravel lot, their yellow T-shirts ringed with dirt, layers of sweat coating their forearms and faces. They hurried toward the foreman, lining up as he passed out thin white envelopes to them one at a time. The boss never bothered to learn their names and did not care if he ever saw them again.

Dust swirled up around the trucks, sticking to the lawn mowers, weed whackers, and pole saws piled in trailers behind each one. Far behind the brown-skinned workers lined up to get paid stood a white man, resting against a propane tank. He was in no rush to get in line and let the others jostle for position while he stood back, wiping his long brown hair out of his sweaty face. His thick beard was tangled with clumps of dirt. Both were streaked with gray, but he wore it handsomely, Carrie thought. To her surprise, he was staring back at her.

"That's him," Waylon said, pointing. "The one in the back. At least I think so."

The man was still staring at her. "You mean fat Jim Morrison?"

"He's not fat," Waylon said. "You think he's fat? He's skinnier than I am."

Carrie cocked an eyebrow and said, "That's not saying much, boss. Anyway, I meant like in the movie when he goes to Paris and grows his hair all out and tries to stop being sexy."

"Fat," Waylon grunted, letting himself out the car. "You stay here."

Waylon made his way around the front of the car, standing where he could be seen. He took off his sunglasses and squinted in the hard sun, uncovering his face so there would be no mistake. He watched his former partner move forward to take his thin envelope and turn to start walking, his long hair blowing in the wind.

It was true what she just said, Waylon thought. Rein had a little gut now, but he had a hardness to him also, musculature around his arms and shoulders that had not been there before. It wasn't the kind of strength you got working out at the gym, though. It came from swinging hammers and working shovels. Real-world strong, Waylon's father had called it. Waylon was older than Rein by more than ten years, but during the time they'd been apart he'd sat behind a desk, feeling his musculature dissolve into a puddled mass that jiggled when he walked and puffed out over his belt when he sat. Rein's face was leaner than it had ever been, the hard points of his eyes and nose giving him an almost feral appearance.

Rein was only a few feet away when he stopped, seeing Waylon. The two of them squared off across the blowing dust without moving, and Rein said, "Well?"

"Jacob," Waylon said.

"Is everyone all right?"

Waylon knew what he meant. If someone in Rein's family had died, it would probably have fallen to Waylon to track him down and break the bad news. "Yeah. They're all fine, far as I know. I just needed to come talk to you."

Rein looked past him at the pretty young woman sitting in the car. "Jacob Junior tell you where to find me?"

"Yeah, he told me. Said you might even be glad to see me. That true?"

"No."

"I didn't think so," Waylon said. "I came anyway."

"You're still a master of the obvious, Bill."

"We've got a few missing girls and a dead body," Waylon said. "I was hoping maybe you'd talk things over with me. Kick it around and see if we can get some direction on it."

Rein turned toward the trucks parked behind him. "All I do now is cut grass, Bill. That's about the extent of my direction these days."

"Is that right?" Waylon said, toeing the dirt with the tip of his boot. "I just thought, you know, for old time's sake you'd give it a listen."

"You wouldn't want my help. Trust me."

Waylon watched Rein walk past him, going wide to avoid having to shake hands. He raised his head and said, "I never bothered you, all these years, Jacob. I left you in peace. Now I'm coming to you as a friend and asking for help. You really gonna just turn your back on me again?"

Rein looked back at him, holding up his white envelope. "You see this? Twenty bucks, cash. We worked from six this morning until whatever time it is right now. I couldn't even tell you. Twenty bucks. That's what my help is worth. You're a chief of police now,

Bill. Get back in your car and go act like one." He stuffed the envelope in his back pocket and kept walking.

Carrie came out of the car, staring at Waylon in disbelief. "What the hell was that? Go after him!"

"And say what?"

Carrie slammed the passenger door shut and hurried after Rein. "Hey! Hey, excuse me. Mister Rein? Wait a second, *sir.* I need to speak with you a second, *sir.*"

Cops have a special way of saying *sir* that substitutes for the words *asshole* and *shitbag* that Rein recognized. He turned around. "You're one of Bill's people?"

"That's right."

He peered into her eyes, seeing through her mirrored sunglasses, taking in her tight-fitting dress pants and the shiny police badge on her hip. The gun and holster were also brand-new, all of it matching. Her stylish button-down shirt fit tight around her slender waist, showing off her physique. She'd even taken the time to do her hair that morning. "How long have you been on the job?"

"Long enough to be the lead on this case. Now, I need to show you something," she said as she reached into her pocket for her phone.

"You're the lead investigator on a homicide?"

"That's right." Carrie held up her phone in the harsh light and raised her glasses, scrolling through her text messages to find Molly's as she continued talking, "I want to ask you if you recognize this." When she looked up to show Rein, all she saw was the back of his head, halfway down the driveway. "Hey! Where are you going?" When he didn't stop, she took off running after him, waving her phone in the air. "I have a picture I need you to see! Wait!"

Rein spun around on her, his face contorted in anger. "You know, it's one thing to show up at my work and try to drag me into something I want no part of, but it's a whole other thing to do it so sloppily. Your lack of expertise is embarrassing me, and I cut grass for a living! You want my help? Fine. Here it is." He got up close to her, so close she could see the jagged red veins in his eyes. When she didn't back away, he said, "That's right. Really get in there. Sink yourself in. Show them you aren't afraid. Now, here's what Bill should have taught you, but I'm not surprised he didn't because he was never that good at any of this in first place. You ready? Right now is when you show someone a picture, so you can see their reaction. That way, if I'd recognized it, you'd know it before I said a single word. You understand? Maybe the next time you interview someone, you'll keep that in mind instead of being too busy screwing with your damned phone!"

"Yes, sir," Carrie said, not moving.

"Good," Rein said, disengaging from her. "Now get back in the car and go home. Turn your case over to somebody who knows what they're doing before you make a mess of it."

Carrie was too angry to speak as he walked away, but she closed her eyes and thought of Nubs and Molly, forcing herself to swallow her pride. "Wait," she called out. "Listen, you're right. I have absolutely no idea what I'm doing. I've never done anything like this before, and to be totally honest with you, there isn't anybody else I can turn it over to."

Rein did not stop walking. "That's not my problem."

"I get it. But the little girl and her mother who are missing? They're like family to me. I just need you to tell me if they're in trouble or not. Please. I'm not going to ask you for anything else. If it was just my friend that would be one thing, but her daughter is the sweetest, most perfect little kid you could ever meet."

Rein stopped, his back still turned to her. "How old?"

"Six. Her name's Natalie. We call her Nubs. Molly took her to the playground yesterday, and they haven't been heard from since. The thing is, she sent me this weird photo later on, and Bill said it looked familiar but he can't place it. Can you take a look at it?"

Rein held out his hand for her to hand over her phone. He raised it and turned away from the sun, using his body to shade the screen as he maneuvered it around, trying to get a better view.

"Is it a joke?" Carrie said. "Tell me it's a joke. She's done this kind of thing before, and I keep thinking she's pulling some crazy prank on me for not spending more time with her. If that's the case, I'm going to kill her for wasting your time, I promise."

From across the parking lot, a soft breeze blew clouds of dust and dirt across the tops of his shoes, creating a low, soft whisper in Rein's ears as he stared at the screen. The girl was talking to him, babbling about something, but he could not hear her. He looked up from the phone. "How long after she went missing did you get this?"

"Why? Do you see something? What did she send it to me for?"

"When did you get it, I said."

"Yesterday. In the early evening. She took Nubs to the park earlier in the day. What is going on, Rein?"

He looked back down at the picture, examining it, seeing it was still daylight in the photograph, searching for any tiny details he could make out. The sun was hidden, but he could tell from the shadows that it was taken in the late afternoon.

"Oh my God, it's no joke, is it?" Carrie gasped.

Bits of dust blew into his eyes and he blinked them away, wiping his sweaty hair out of his face. "How many are missing altogether?"

Carrie forced herself to focus, despite the rising panic in her chest. "Another young woman, about the same age," she said. "Denise Lawson. Now Molly and Nubs. And we had a guy get killed in the parking lot at a gay club, and it was really, really bad, I mean, forget that part. It probably doesn't have anything to do with it. Right?" She stopped herself. "Look, I'm sorry we just showed up like this, but I'm desperate!"

Rein watched her. "What makes you think the parking lot murder isn't involved with the others?"

"I don't know! Christ, I don't know anything. Listen, Molly likes to pull pranks, okay? She likes to do things like this to screw with me, but she's never dragged Nubs into it before and it's never felt like this. I need help. Can you help me?"

He dropped the phone in her hand, and Carrie wiped her face on her sleeve. She looked up to see Rein heading back toward Waylon's car and he said, "Let's talk."

Rein leaned back against Waylon's police car while Carrie showed her chief how to connect to the Internet. He scratched at his beard, picking clumps of dried dirt from its tangles and flicking them into the dusty driveway. The wind was rising, sending large plumes of earth off the tops of the trucks inside the parking lot. Carrie paced back and forth, holding her phone in her hand with the photograph of Molly on the screen as they waited for the computer to connect.

Waylon glanced at Rein. "I like the new look. They say beards are in these days."

"They're damn itchy, I can tell you that much. I see your mustache came in," Rein said. "I guess rubbing all that Rogaine on your lip worked. Sam Elliott would be proud."

"All right, it's connected," Waylon said, laughing. "What was that name you told me to look up, again?"

"Regina Kay Walters," Rein said. "Do an image search."

Waylon typed the name into the search bar. Carrie came around the car and stood behind him, gripping the phone as Waylon started the search. Rein moved away from the car, knowing what they were about to see. He heard Waylon's breath catch and Carrie's muted cry of disbelief.

A teenage girl stared back at them from the computer screen, both of her hands raised in the air defensively, dressed in a black dress and tall black heels. Carrie held the photograph of Molly next to the computer screen, seeing that they were both standing in the exact same pose on an old wooden platform, surrounded by open farmland.

The plastic casing around Carrie's phone cracked as she squeezed it, her hands shaking with rage as her eyes darted from the computer to the image on her phone, two women, posed and dressed the same, two beautiful faces spoiled by the unmistakable mark of terror.

Rein looked down at his hands, seeing that the lines of his skin were crusted deep with dirt. His fingernails were black. He was scraped and raw from working with crude machines all day, earning his twenty dollars. "Bill, can I talk to you privately?"

Waylon followed him, but Carrie's voice called out, "I want to hear it."

"Just give me a minute, kiddo."

Hell was in her eyes when she looked at the men. Red hell, dragged up from the lowest depths of her being. "I want to hear it."

Dust blew across the driveway, collecting clumps of grass from the truck tires and lawn mower blades, scattering them across places where the grass would not grow. Small specks pelted Rein on the cheeks and in his eyes, but he would not raise his hand to shield them. "In 1990, Regina Kay Walters was kidnapped by a trucker named Robert Ben Rhoades. He made her put on that black dress and those heels, then he made her pose for that photograph you see there. She was fourteen years old."

"And then what happened?" Carrie said.

Rein looked at her with heavy, sad eyes. "He tortured her. Then he killed her."

15

Waylon slowed the car as he followed Rein's directions, going through a neighborhood two miles from his work. The sidewalks were littered with trash cans, most of them overflowing so much with debris that there were more discarded beer bottles and trash lying around them than inside them. Cats patrolled the piles of garbage, searching for hungry rodents to kill.

The stretch of row homes on both sides of the street was a mile long, with power cables dangling in unsecured loops from the roofs. At least twenty people hung out in each front yard, many of them wearing work clothes similar to Rein's. Waylon knew what he was looking at. Slum housing for undocumented workers. Homes that were designed to hold a family of four, converted into makeshift hostels.

Waylon had been in homes like that, where the owners had filled every room with mattresses and charged people fifty bucks a week to sleep there. They were crammed into the basement, the attic, the bathroom, the kitchen, some even paid to sleep on the steps. They were packed in like cattle. Normally, the slumlord wanted nothing to do with the property, so he picked one of the tenants to be the superintendent, letting him stay there for free as long as he collected the money from the others on time.

Rein tapped on the rear window of Waylon's car and said, "You can let me off here."

Waylon turned around in his seat. "You want to go grab a bite to eat first? Maybe get caught up?"

Rein grabbed the door handle and then let himself out. He stood beside the car as he looked up the street at the homes and the people he lived with. He walked around to the driver's side and leaned down as Waylon lowered the window. "What's your next step on this case?"

Waylon and Carrie looked at each other. Carrie leaned close to the window and said, "I was thinking we should go talk to the mother of the first missing girl. See if she can give us anything."

"Good," Rein said. "What then?"

"I have no idea, to be honest," she said.

"What about that murder?" Rein asked. "The one from the club."

Waylon stopped him. "There's no connection. Male victim, gay club, doesn't fit this at all. Just a coincidence."

"All those years working cases and you know what I learned about coincidences?" Rein asked. "There aren't any."

"All right," Waylon said. "We'll go to the club. You want to come with us and help with the interviews?"

"Not particularly."

Waylon extended his hand, not wanting to push the issue. "Partner, it was good to see you back in action, even just for a minute."

Rein took his hand and squeezed, his grip strong and rough. "It was good to see you too, Bill."

Waylon did not let go. "I don't want to wait another five years, man. I miss you. That's just me being for real with you. We don't have to talk about work at all. I just want to stay in touch."

Rein patted him on the shoulder and said, "I know." He stepped back from the car, giving in just a little bit, and said, "So, here or work is where I'm at. If you run into another roadblock on the case, come find me."

"You mean that?" Waylon said.

"Yeah. Not like you were ever any good at this kind of thing."

Waylon laughed as he shifted. "Yeah, right. Your back probably still hurts from carrying me all those years, I bet."

"Little bit," Rein said, touching his side. "Right here. But only when it rains."

It was dark by the time they arrived back at the station. Waylon had to nudge Carrie to open her eyes. "We're here," he said.

She sat up, rubbing her eyes with her palms. "Okay. What now?"

"Now we go home. Get some sleep."

"I can't," she said, grabbing for the case file. She searched through it, making sure all the papers were there. "We need to go interview Mrs. Lawson about her daughter. See if there's any way to connect her to the other jobs."

"Carrie," Waylon said, "we've been at this all day. I'm tired. I still have a police department to run, and I have an eight a.m. meeting with the traffic signal repair company. Let's call it a night."

"I can't call it a night! I don't give a shit about your meetings, there is a little girl missing and some maniac has her! What the hell happened to you? You used to be a county detective, Bill Waylon. Did you and Rein worry about traffic signals when you were chasing down Old Man Krissing?"

"No." Waylon leaned his head back against the seat. "We most certainly did not."

"Exactly. So let's go," she said, waving her hand for him to get going. "I'll get you the address in a second."

He watched her going through the files, then looked out the window at the station's dark parking lot. Only one police car was parked outside the front door, which meant one officer was on patrol and the other was sitting inside watching television. They never ran more than two cars. Never needed to. The parking lot's only source of light was a POLICE sign mounted above the front door. The sign was cracked and chipped, faded and old, but it was still lit, he thought, like it wasn't smart enough to give up just yet. "Listen, I'm not going out tonight. In fact, maybe this was a mistake anyway. Tomorrow I'm going to get ahold of the County detectives," he said. "They're equipped to deal with this kind of thing. Harv Bender can work the case, and who knows, maybe he'll come up with something."

"Oh bullshit," Carrie said, clapping the folder shut. "That's a cop-out and you know it. Bender won't do a goddamn thing about this."

"It's too much for us."

"Only because you won't show me how to do this!"

"Because I don't know how! Okay? I don't know how to just manufacture something out of nothing.

How to think like these monsters. Jacob wasn't kidding, Carrie. I never was worth a squirt of piss at this kind of case."

"You were a County detective, Bill."

"Jesus Christ!" He laughed. "So what? My old man was a big contributor to the Republican party and his friends got me into that job so I didn't have to write parking tickets for the rest of my career. I'd never been a criminal investigator. I was a street cop my whole career up 'til then. So there I am, a political hack surrounded by a bunch of other political hacks, and I realized none of us knew what the hell we were doing. You know how I got by? I took loser cases. Dead-end investigations nobody else wanted to touch because there wasn't a chance in hell of making an arrest, and I phoned it in. I did that for two years. And you know something? I would have been perfectly content to keep on doing that, until that pain in the you-know-what showed up. We all pretty much kept our heads down back in those days. Collecting our paychecks and going through the motions. Guys like me, Bender, and all the rest. And then this young guy shows up out of nowhere, and he's got way, *way* different ideas about police work. This dude is taking the whole thing too seriously, and it's making the rest of us look bad. Bender leads the charge to try to get him fired, and everybody pretty much goes along with it, including me. You know what changed my mind?"

Carrie told him that she didn't.

"The first time I saw a little girl with her hands tied behind her back and blood smeared down the front of her summer dress. This beautiful, perfect little angel, and some sick bastard kidnapped her and killed her.

Now, nobody wants to touch this case with a ten-foot pole, nobody in their right mind would take responsibility for an unsolvable child murder, but here comes new guy, volunteering. He starts working the case as if he has a chance at figuring out who did it. I laughed at him, telling him he was nuts, just like everyone else, but secretly I was waking up in a cold sweat every night. I'd sit crying in my daughter's room when I put her to bed, thinking about that little girl. Then one Saturday I can't take it anymore and I drive to the office and I find him there, and you know what I said?"

Waylon put his hands down on top of Rein's desk and said, "Everybody wants to see you fired because you're an arrogant son of a bitch who's trying to make the rest of us look bad."

Rein looked up from the folder spread open on his desk, surprised to see anyone else in the office on a Saturday. "I already know this."

"I'm one of the ones who said he hopes you get fired, Rein."

Waylon was soaking wet. Rein turned and looked out the window, realizing it was pouring rain outside. The sky was still dark and it would be noon in a few hours. Waylon's shoes were still leaking water, and his wet hair was dripping down onto his face, but he did not seem to care. Rein folded his hands across his stomach and said, "I know that, too. Is there something I can help you with, Bill, or did you have nothing better to do on your weekend than come bother me?"

Waylon looked down at the photograph on Rein's desk, seeing the smiling little girl in her school uniform. "She's the same age as my little one. It's not . . . it's not right what happened to her."

"The whole thing is a tragedy. Now, excuse me, but I have to get back to work."

"I know it's a tragedy," Waylon said, *"that's not the damned point."*

"What do you want, Bill? I'm working. If you need to talk to someone, go to a bar, or go to a shrink, but if you don't mind, I'm trying to find the person who did this."

"I want to work it. Goddamn it, I need to."

"Well, I'm sorry, but that's not possible," Rein said. *"I'm already into it. I can't just hand it over."*

"I want to help, okay? You tell me what you need, I'll get it. No questions asked, as long as we catch this scumbag."

Rein looked up at him. *"And you expect me to trust a partner who wants to get me fired?"*

"I didn't say we were partners. I just said I'd work this one with you, your way. After that, it's back to business as usual."

"You'll do whatever I ask."

"If it helps find the murderous son of a bitch, yeah."

"I need old cases pulled, evidence reexamined. Grunt work. Things most of you people seem to think is beneath you."

"I said I'd do it," Waylon snapped.

Rein slid his chair back to make room at his desk and said, *"Grab a notepad and pull up a chair."*

Waylon stroked his mustache, seeing the images of the dead girl in her summer dress in his mind as clearly as the day he'd looked at her small, stiff body. "After that, it was off to the races," he said. "Rein already had a suspect, it was just a matter of his connecting the dots."

"So, is that how you guys became friends, then?" Carrie said.

"Friends? No. I was still telling all the guys that the second we put handcuffs on the murderer, I was right back on their side. I never got a chance to do that, though. Thank God."

"What happened?"

"Krissing," he said, uttering the word as if something filthy was in his mouth. "It took us another four years to figure out what was going on, but from the first missing kid, Rein was on it. Sometimes I wonder which one brought the other one in, you know? Maybe kind attracts kind. Then I think that the gods are just cruel and crazy bastards and they put pieces in play that will give off the best show. A whole lot of awful stuff happened in that show, let me tell you. A whole lot. And now it's happening again and I'm just about as goddamn useless as I always was, except this time there's nobody to hide behind."

Carrie put her hand on his arm. "You're a good man, Chief. A good man, and a good cop. You aren't giving yourself enough credit."

He wiped his nose on the back of his hand and turned his head away from her to collect himself. "Yeah, well, that's how all that really went down. Look, you work this case as you see fit. Do what you can. But if there's any more bodies or missing people, I'm going to have to hand it off. If your friend and her daughter are in trouble, I can't risk us not doing everything we can to save them."

Carrie wrapped her arms around Waylon and squeezed. "Thank you, I won't let you down."

He watched her jump out of the car and run toward

the station's front door, silhouetted by the dim glow of the POLICE sign. She popped the door open and disappeared inside the station, letting the door slam shut behind her. The metal door frame rattled, and something inside the sign sizzled and popped. Waylon watched as the POLICE sign faded, and kept on watching it until it went dark.

16

The Lawsons' home seemed clean and well kept, at least from the living room. Family portraits lined the walls, the people in them smiling. There were five photos in all: two parents and their daughter, sometimes with a dog, sometimes without. The daughter was a baby in the first one—a smiling, tiny thing with thick black hair—and by the last, she'd developed into a bored-looking teenager with a shaved head and piercings.

Mrs. Lawson saw Carrie looking at the last photograph. "She went through a phase, that's all."

"I understand," Carrie said. "She wasn't the only one."

Gary Lawson sat next to his wife, keeping silent. Every so often, his eyes flicked up toward Carrie, then fell back down to the cup of coffee between his hands. He had something to say, she could tell, it just hadn't bubbled up yet.

"What sorts of things were you looking to find out about Denise?" the mother asked.

Carrie picked up her pen. "I'm guessing there has

been no contact since the time you came to the police station?"

"No, none," she said.

"And her phone?"

"I called the phone company, and they said it's shut off. We asked if they could ping it, you know, send it a signal and tell us what tower it bounces off of, but they couldn't. It was already off."

"That was a good idea, though," Carrie said, writing.

"My husband watches a lot of those CSI shows," Mrs. Lawson said.

Carrie looked up at the husband, smiling, and he stared back at her. "Did you speak to any of her friends? Anyone who might have seen her last?"

"I checked with everyone I could think of, and they checked with all their friends. No one has seen her."

"And what kind of crowd did she hang out with?" Carrie said. "Did you not like any of them? Did she have any trouble with ex-boyfriends?"

"No," Mrs. Lawson said. "Not anymore. Not living out here."

The father let out a grunt as his wife spoke, and she turned her head sharply at him. "Don't start, Gary," she said.

Carrie leaned forward to get their attention. "Listen, I know it's not easy, but I need you to be very, very specific with me about Denise. If there's anyone you can think of who might have something to do with this, or anything, please tell me."

"How about all the people in the rehabs I sent her to down in Florida?" Lawson said. "How about all the in-patient facilities and outpatient programs and AA meetings and NA meetings? How about all the pieces of shit who go to those meetings, just looking for people to hook up and get high with? How about them?"

Mrs. Lawson pressed the back of her fist against her mouth. Carrie looked at the husband and said, "I'm not sure what you're talking about. Was Denise into drugs? What kind of drugs?"

"What kind?" Lawson said. "Jesus, I thought you people at least had half a clue. She got kicked out of so many schools we had to homeschool her. The Easton cops came to our house so often to tell us they'd found her at a party or in the back of some dealer's car that I knew them by their first names. So we come out here, thinking it was going to be better for her. And guess what?"

"It was better for her!" Mrs. Lawson shouted. "She was doing good! She worked. She had friends. She was going back to school in the summer."

"Yeah, right," Lawson said. "We thought she was doing good, but we've had that trick played on us before. You ever known a junkie?"

"Of course, sir. I see them all the time."

"I mean, really known one. You got any in your family?"

"I'm more interested in your daughter, sir."

"Well, you go get one for a child, then tell me how it feels. Watch her change right before your very eyes. Watch all the light go out of her and leave nothing behind but some kind of shell you don't recognize. You do that, and you give her chance after chance after chance, praying to God Almighty that this time she means it. This time, she's gonna get better. And you watch your marriage fall apart so bad you and your wife can't even stand to be in the same room as each other."

"Gary," Mrs. Lawson begged. "Please, she's here trying to help us."

"I don't need help," Lawson said. "I'm beyond needing help. You know when my daughter died, Officer? She died the first second she put a needle full of heroin into her arm. Everything after that has just been a long funeral. You had the right idea back when you told my wife there was nothing you could do. Why don't you just keep on doing that, and we'll sit here and wait for someone to tell us where to go identify the body."

Carrie looked at the mother, who had lowered her head into her hands, and waited. It was clear the conversation was over. She stood up and gathered her things before placing a business card down on the table. "Thank you for your time. If you can think of anything else, please contact me."

She moved toward the door, her legs moving of their own accord. A thousand responses to the man's words raced through her mind, but nothing that would matter. She pulled the front door open, desperate to be away from those people and their despair. She'd come to them intent on helping to solve a crime, and the old man had done everything but chase her off the property with a stick.

Denise Lawson is still out there, Carrie told herself. *And so is Molly, and so is Nubs. Fuck anybody that says otherwise.*

An argument was brewing in the living room, Gary yelling at his wife, "I told you, it's nothing!" but someone was coming toward the door and turning the knob. Carrie turned around and waited as Mrs. Lawson came to her.

"I know it's probably nothing, but I wanted you to hear this," Mrs. Lawson said.

Carrie watched her pull her cell phone from her pocket and locate the app. "I'll take anything at this point, to be honest."

"That's what I thought. It came in a few days after Denise went missing, on a blocked number. I don't recognize the voice, but the whole thing sounded so bizarre that I saved it."

Carrie bent her head forward to listen as Mrs. Lawson raised the phone and pressed the play button. A disturbingly high-pitched, childlike voice came on: *"Hi, Mom. Just wanted to let you know, I got myself a new lampshade. It's so beautiful! And I also got this new bowl, and a lovely Halloween mask. I can't wait to wear it. If you ever see it, you'll scream."*

"What the hell was that?" Carrie said, looking down at the phone. "Play it again."

Mrs. Lawson pressed play, and both of them leaned close to listen. When it was finished, Mrs. Lawson said, "Gary's convinced it's a prank caller."

"Probably," Carrie said. "Some burnout who got high and started calling different numbers, saying random crap."

"Exactly," Mrs. Lawson said. She touched her phone's screen until it went black and slid it back into her pocket. "Just a bizarre coincidence, I guess."

Carrie thanked her and reminded her about the information on the card and how to reach her if anything else came up. Mrs. Lawson thanked her for coming by and apologized for her husband. Carrie told her not to worry about it and headed down the front steps toward her car as Mrs. Lawson stood on the porch, watching her go. It was late. She was tired. Emotionally and mentally drained. Ready for bed.

She got into her car and sat down without starting it. Penny had left her a dozen voice mails and text messages, asking for constant updates. There was nothing she could say. How would poor Penny react to the photograph of Regina Kay Walters, dressed up by a sex torturer? How would she feel knowing Molly had been dressed, posed, and photographed in the exact same way?

And Nubs, she thought weakly. Poor, sweet, little angel Nubs. Just where in the hell are you, baby girl?

The most bitterly ironic part of all was that the only person who seemed to have even the slightest idea of what was going on was a convicted felon. She pictured the detective she'd seen in the videos, compared him to the bearded landscaper she'd met that day, and could not reconcile that they were the same person. Carrie thought about his dirty face and arms and sweat-stained T-shirt, the way his voice rumbled when he uttered deep and insightful bullshit like, "There's no such thing as coincidences." She uttered the phrase aloud, spitefully, and leaned forward to turn the key in the ignition, seeing the porch was empty. Mrs. Lawson had given up staring at her and was at last heading back inside.

"Wait!" Carrie cried, throwing open the door. She ran up the sidewalk, shouting, "Hang on! Did you delete that message?"

"What?" Mrs. Lawson said, turning around in surprise. "I think so." She fished the phone back out of her pocket and checked, then said, "No, wait, it's still here. Why?"

"Something you said reminded me." Carrie panted, trying to catch her breath as she ran up to the porch.

* * *

The landscaping parking lot was alive with activity at six A.M. The men arrived before the sun, loading up their trailers and work trucks with shovels and hedge trimmers. They looked up at Carrie's car as she pulled into the lot, their dark faces already glistening with sweat. She jumped out of the car and ran from group to group, calling out, "Jacob? Jacob Rein?"

The workers laughed at one another, calling out, *"Inmigración!"* Some of the workers saw her and ran away, making the others laugh.

She spied a bearded man climbing onto the back of a stake-bodied truck at the far end of the lot. He slapped the side panel when he got seated, telling the driver to start moving.

"Wait!" Carrie shouted, running after the truck as it pulled away, waving her hands. "Wait! Rein, wait!"

The driver could see her in the mirror as he circled around, staring at her in confusion as she ran through the swirling dust from his tires. Carrie called out to Rein again, but he did not look up, and as the truck left the lot she did the only thing she could think of. She yanked her badge from her pocket, held it high, and shouted, "Immigration! Stop that truck, asshole!"

The truck's brake lights lit bright red as the front end squealed, stopping so hard the front end dipped, bouncing Rein a foot into the air from the truck bed. "What the hell are you doing, Marco?" he shouted through the window.

Carrie raced through the dust and grabbed the back of the truck gate with both hands, then hoisted herself up. "I need you to listen to something."

He stared at her. "Are you crazy?"

"Maybe," she said.

"We're leaving for a job right now. It will have to wait." He smacked the truck's back window and shouted, "Get moving. It's nothing."

Sweat was running down the driver's face, along with the two men crammed in beside him inside the truck's cabin. Carrie held up her badge and pointed at him through the window and said, "Like hell. You move this truck and all of you are going right back across the border. Try me!"

Rein's eyes widened as the men inside the truck and the workers all around them chattered in Spanish. He stood up in the truck bed and said, "That is way, way out of line, young lady."

"You know my boss. Call him and complain if you want."

"You think that's funny?" Rein stepped over the back of the truck and lowered himself down. "These men work sixteen-hour days and sleep ten to a room just to send enough money back home for their families to eat. Not cool, whatever your name is. Not cool at all."

He walked around the side of the truck and tapped on the window with his finger, talking to the driver in Spanish. "No, no," he said repeatedly. "*No Inmigración. Es bueno.*" He patted himself on the chest and explained he would handle it, then he pointed at the road and told them to go do their work.

The truck pulled away, the driver's eyes glued to Carrie. When he was sure she wasn't going to chase them, he slammed his foot on the gas pedal and took off down the dirt road, sending columns of dust flying in his wake.

Rein ran his fingers through his long hair before he

turned around. "This had better be important, Officer,"
he said.

"Carrie."

"What?"

"It's Carrie. Carrie Santero, to be exact."

"Santero? Really? And you come down here threatening these people with deportation?"

"I'd threaten Mother Teresa if it meant getting
somewhere on this case."

He leaned in, "Mother Teresa exploited the poor and
glorified people's suffering instead of actually helping
them, so that doesn't impress me."

"Are you a Catholic?"

"Not in the slightest."

"Then I don't give a shit what you have to say about
Mother Teresa."

"What do you want, Officer Santero?"

"A few days after my first girl went missing, the
mother received an odd voice mail. She thought it was a
misdial, just a coincidence," she said, trying not to
sound self-satisfied but failing. Rein only stood there,
hands tucked in his rear pants pockets, waiting for her
to get on with it. "I listened to it a few times, and I
think the caller is digitally altering his voice to sound
like a little kid. I want you to hear what he says. See if
it means anything to you."

Trucks were driving past them, one at a time now,
everyone eager to get away from the lot as soon as possible. Rein watched them leave. "If I don't work today,
I don't get paid," he said. "The rent is due."

"I will drive you to the job site, for God's sake,"
Carrie said. "Can you just listen to this?"

Rein let Carrie hold the cell phone up to his ear,

waiting as she pressed the play button. She leaned close to Rein to listen too, so close that his beard blew against her face, tickling her with its lengths. He smelled different than she'd expected. A mixture of lime oil and cloves, like bay rum.

She heard the message begin to play, the same one she'd listened to over and over in the car on the way there. *"Hi, Mom. Just wanted to let you know, I got myself a new lampshade. It's so beautiful! And I also got this new bowl, and a lovely Halloween mask. I can't wait to wear it. If you ever see it, you'll scream."* In every police show, there would be a clue of some sort in that audio recording. The sound of a speed bump that the team of elite forensic investigators could use their technological wizardry to pinpoint the exact location of a road, or the screech of an owl indigenous to one part of the country that told them where to look for the killer. The shows made it look so easy. No matter what the crime, it got solved in less than sixty minutes.

She looked at Rein, ready for him to dazzle her with investigative wizardry. Instead he stepped back and scratched his beard. "Play it again."

Carrie did as he asked, letting him take the phone and cup it with both hands to hear. He handed the phone back to her, then closed his eyes and pressed his fingers against his temples, rubbing them.

"What is it?" Carrie said. "Is it bad? It's bad, isn't it? Will it help us find the killer?"

Rein needed time to process what he'd heard. Carrie continued talking, pressing him for information, so he held up his hand and said, "Please. Be quiet. Just for five seconds."

"All right," she said. "Sorry."

Rein turned and looked at the empty lot, running

both hands through his hair to get it out of his face. He was the only worker left. He lowered his head and started for the large foreman's trailer with Carrie following close behind, staying quiet.

He climbed up the wooden stairs to the trailer's door and knocked, stepping back as it came open. The foreman looked down at Carrie, then over at him and said, "Why ain't you on your truck?"

"Something came up," Rein said.

"I needed four men at that site."

"I know," Rein said. "I talked to Marco, and he can handle it. If I can catch up to them, I will help them finish it out."

The foreman's eyes narrowed on Rein. "No work, no pay. You know the rules."

"I know."

The trailer's door slammed shut in Rein's face, and he lowered himself back down the stairs, walking past Carrie toward her car. "Can I talk now? What's going on?" she asked, hurrying after him.

"Ed Gein killed a woman in Wisconsin in 1957," he said over his shoulder. "When the cops tracked him down, he'd done things with her body."

"What kinds of things?"

"Made artwork out her. Lampshade out of her torso, used her skull as a soup bowl, and wore her peeled-off face as a mask."

"Oh my God—"

Rein ignored her and grabbed the passenger-side door. "We have to get moving. Now."

"Okay," she said, fishing her keys from her pocket. "Where are we going?"

"Robert Ben Rhoades and Ed Gein," Rein said. "Two serial killers with very specific methodologies, and someone is referencing them. Where does any young lunatic interested in killing people go first?"

Carrie thought it over. "The butcher shop?"

Rein rolled his eyes. "Just keep driving. I'll tell you where to turn."

"The video game store?" When Rein didn't respond, she added, "You know, getting conditioned to all that killing. I heard the military is using those first-person shooter games to train young soldiers to be killing machines."

"No."

"Well, I don't see why they'd need to go anywhere," she said. "All you need to do is sit at home and turn on the TV. There's stuff about serial killers on every other channel."

"That's the first almost right thing you said today."

"So I'm right?" she said.

"I said almost right."

"What good is being almost right?"

"For you? Let's take the small wins wherever we find them."

17

The automatic doors slid open at their approach. potted plants and large cardboard signs advertising local bingo night and book club meetings adorned either side of the entrance. Carrie looked at a line of women at the checkout counter holding armfuls of books, and said, "This is where young lunatics go when they want to learn about killing people? The library?"

"Yes, the library," he said. "Think about it. You're a young, poor, troubled white male driven by hormones and powerful sexual energy. You fantasize about hurting people. Killing them. Taking things out of them. Cutting holes in their bodies you can stick your penis inside of."

The group of women standing near the desk turned around, eyes wide, glaring at Rein. Carrie held up her hands. "Sorry! It's okay, honest."

Rein was oblivious to them, still talking over his shoulder. "Where can you go to learn? To feed your fascination? It has to be somewhere that doesn't look suspicious." His eyes scanned the computer desks, filled with young mothers searching help wanted ads, homeless people killing time, and older people fumbling with the mouse and keyboard. "Somewhere right out in the open."

"Wait," Carrie said. "Who said anything about being poor and white?" She looked at him with renewed admiration and said, "You developed one already?"

"One what?"

"That is so cool! How did you do it? I need to know. I read everything by Ressler, and I used to try doing it with burglars, but they just aren't complex enough, right? There's not enough methodology, normally, unless you're talking about a serial burglar. But God, the whole thing is so fascinating."

"What is?"

She looked at him in confusion. "You developed a profile on the suspect, right?"

Rein leaned forward. "Listen to me. Profiling is nonsense. Understand? Snake oil. Voodoo. It's the fictional equivalent of something we used to call common sense and deductive reasoning."

"So how do you know he's poor and white?"

He looked her up and down. "Did you grow up rich?"

She snickered. "Hardly."

"Were you poor?"

"We got by."

"Did you have food stamps?"

Her eyes lowered. "So what if we did? My dad was sick a lot."

"How often did you go to the doctor?"

"Only when it was serious. I broke my arm once and needed to get stitches another time. The rest of the times we toughed it out."

Rein snapped his fingers at her. "Exactly. Doctors

are expensive. Medicine is expensive. Now, let's say you're rich and you begin acting strange. You begin having vivid hallucinations or fantasize about women getting eaten alive by alligators, or you start having sex with dogs. What do your parents do?"

"They take you to the best doctor in town and get you help."

"The best doctors, the best medicines, the best hospitals, and if the kid never gets better, they put him in the best institution for the rest of his life, where he can never embarrass Daddy and Mommy at the country club. Right?"

"Right," Carrie agreed. "And if the kid comes from a poor family, they have to make do with whatever they can afford, which probably isn't much. Plus, he'd come to the library because it's free."

"Now you're thinking. So why is our suspect most likely white?"

"Because aren't all serial killers white?"

"Wrong. Most serial killers are white. Not all. Try again."

"Well," she said, "we live in a predominantly white area. If he's from here, he's most likely Caucasian."

"Better. You're getting close. But there's another more simplistic and brutal reason. A young, psychotic male will have multiple contacts with the police. If the cops come in contact with a psychotic black male enough times, you know what they do?"

Carrie looked around to see who was standing nearby them, uncomfortable with the conversation. People were staring. "I get it, okay? Point made."

"Who do cops kill, Carrie?"

"Stop."

"They kill young black males. All the time. Especially ones they have repeated contact with, and even more especially when they are dangerously deranged. And if the cops don't kill them, the courts put them in jail where nobody notices their deteriorating mental health. Common sense and deductive reasoning. The suspect we are looking for is most likely white."

"Fine," Carrie said, lowering her voice. "Can we just get started already?"

"All right. Our suspect wasn't just looking for books about murders. He was fascinated by the entire process. He came here looking for books on anatomy, wanting to see how all the organs looked inside the body, trying to decide which ones he wanted to eat, or which intestines he wanted to wear around his neck like a scarf."

A woman with a young child looked up from the nearby computer desk, glaring at Rein as he spoke.

Carrie cringed. "Will you please keep your voice down?"

"We need every medical book, true crime, police procedure, surgical, and obviously anything to do with serial killers. I want a list of everyone in the past fifteen years who took out those kinds of books on a regular basis. From there, we can check for poor white males, run their criminal histories, prior contacts, and mental health issues. It's not much, but it's a start."

"Let's do it like this," Carrie said, moving ahead of him. "You find every book you think applies and bring it to me. I will write down all the names and information." She looked past him at the librarians, seeing that they were scowling at Rein. She couldn't blame them. With his long hair and beard, he looked like a hobo. With his loud voice ranting about killing people, he sounded like a *dangerous* hobo. "Listen, you need to turn it down a notch in here with all the intestinal stuff, okay? They're going to kick us out."

"I'm working. This is how I work. You don't like how I do it, you can leave. Or better yet, I can leave. It's not like I need to be here. You came to me, remember?"

"I remember," she said. "I didn't take you for the type that likes to scare women and children, though."

His nostrils flared, but he said nothing. Instead, he backed away from her and turned, heading for the nearest aisle with his hands in his pockets, eyes down. A woman he passed pulled her daughter out of his way.

Someone had left a copy of *The Notebook* on the desk to be put back by the librarians, and Carrie saw it as she came to the last stack of books piled in front of her. She put it on the seat next to her, saying, "Lucky for you Molly isn't here. You'd probably be covered in snot and big baby tears by the third chapter." She looked down at the book and whispered, "I don't care what she says. You're still a crappy book."

"Screw you," Molly shouted. "The Notebook is my favorite! It's a beautiful love story. No wonder you hated it."

"I liked the part at the end where he forced himself on her after reading her that dumb letter," Carrie fired back. "There she is, lying on her bed, too riddled with dementia to get up and use the toilet on her own, and what does Mr. Beautiful Love Story do? Pulls off her diaper and humps the poor lady."

"She wasn't wearing a diaper!" Molly's voice cracked. "What's wrong with you?"

"Name one old person sitting in an old-age home with dementia that isn't wearing a diaper, you idiot."

"There is something seriously wrong with you, Carrie. I'm not kidding. Anybody who could read The Notebook and think those things is not a good person. You've got the devil in you. Demons out!" Molly said, reaching forward and smacking Carrie right between the eyes.

Carrie sat there, stunned, until both of them burst out laughing, clutching each other and laughing so hard they cried.

She used her cell phone camera to photograph the covers and library cards of the books Rein had collected, making sure she got all of the names scribbled on the cards in focus. She remembered filling out the same kind of cards herself as a kid. Nowadays, everyone was issued a library keycard with a bar code, and the librarians just scanned it at the desk, tracking whoever had their books via computer. God help you if you stole it.

The Pennsylvania Crimes Code listed several strange anomalies that mystified Carrie. For instance, aggravated assault was a Felony 1, the highest criminal charge below murder. A Felony 1 carried a penalty of up to twenty years in prison. However, it was almost impossible to get a conviction on aggravated assault.

Aggravated assault was written for whoever caused, or attempted to cause, serious bodily injury to another person. It sounded deceptively simple. The problem was that years of vigorous appeals had twisted and morphed the sentencing guidelines into something incomprehensible. It all boiled down to the use of the word "serious." Enough defense attorneys had argued enough times that practically no one could agree on just what constituted "serious" anymore.

In Carrie's previous trial, a man had stomped a woman on the head so hard it fractured her right orbital socket and almost dislocated her eyeball. "That sounds god-damn serious to me," Carrie had said while writing the criminal complaint that night. Unfortunately, by the time the trial came around six months later, the victim had healed. All that was left was a little tenderness around the woman's eye, a hospital report written in medical jargon, and photographs of the injury.

"Ladies and gentlemen of the jury," the public defender said. "I ask you. How serious could it have really been? Look at this beautiful young woman sitting here before you without a mark on her. She was drunk. My client was drunk. They had a fight. It got out of hand. But does my client deserve to spend twenty years of his young life in a state prison for something that did no lasting harm?"

Not guilty.

On the contrary, simple assault was much easier to establish and to prove. You had to show only that the defendant caused or attempted to cause someone bodily harm. The mystifying part was that the charge was a stunted Misdemeanor 2. It carried a maximum penalty of just two years in jail, which nobody ever served. Misdemeanor 2 convictions paroled out in a few weeks for good behavior and went right back home.

Those are the only two assault charges available in Pennsylvania, much like the rest of the country.

Aggravated assault at Felony 1 and simple assault at Misdemeanor 2. Everything else was a summary offense. A glorified traffic ticket.

Library theft was another one. The way the law read, if you stole anything from the library one time, it was a summary offense. For instance, she thought, if you stole *The Notebook* it was just a summary offense.

But if you were one of the people who liked it and

came back to steal *Message in a Bottle*, then it was a misdemeanor. And if, for some godforsaken reason, you liked that and were compelled to come back and steal *A Walk to Remember*, well, then it became a Felony 1, punishable by up to twenty years in prison. Any idiot who liked Nicholas Sparks enough to do that deserved to be in jail, as far as Carrie was concerned. The only authors worth going to jail for were named Cormac, Elmore, or JK, she thought. Not debatable.

Carrie picked *The Notebook* back up and pressed it against her chest, feeling warm in the pit of her being. Something was telling her everything was going to be all right. Someone was listening to her. Watching her work. Sending her messages to keep going. She'd prayed in the woods that night at the playground, and nothing had happened, but that was all right, she thought. Sometimes you needed to be tested and found worthy. She looked up at the ceiling, imagining that she was peering deep into the cosmos, and whispered, "Thank you."

At the other end of the table, Rein was looking through the books Carrie had sorted, double-checking their library cards. She called out to him and said, "You making sure I didn't miss anything?"

"No," he said, peering down at one of the cards before sliding it back in its sleeve and setting it aside.

"Oh," she said. "What are you looking for, then? I'll help you."

His large, dark eyes were bright and sharp despite the ragged, weathered look of his hairy face. He turned the pages on another book and checked the back. "If I find what I'm looking for, it's something I will have to handle personally."

18

The GPS announced their destination. Carrie peered over the steering wheel, seeing only a small metal sign for the Barnetta Police Department warning people that the parking lot was for official vehicles only. Rein was snoring as she turned in. "Wake up, old man. You took us to the wrong place."

He grunted as he sat up, rubbing his eyes, then opening them wide. "What?"

"This isn't the Barnetta library." She pointed at the police department's front door. "You must've punched in the wrong address. Look at this dump." It was even more run down than her own department's headquarters. The front door was rusted through its cracked green paint job. The windows were black and covered with so much film they looked like they'd been soaped over. She picked up the GPS and searched for the input screen. "Let's try this again. Where did you mean to go?"

Rein let himself out of the car and said, "Right here." He closed the door and tapped his hands on the roof. "Come on. We're losing daylight."

"Well, I guess somebody's all energized from his afternoon nap," she said. "I bet you're really missing your slippers and rocking chair right about now, huh?"

He pulled the station's front door open so hard that it knocked a cloud of red and green rust off the frame. "You have your badge, right?"

She tapped her back pocket. "Right here."

"You're going to need it."

The lobby was the size of a dining room table, with a locked door on one side and a thick bulletproof glass window at the other. An older woman with pinched lips looked at them through the police clerk's window. The plastic frames of her eyeglasses were thick, and fake pearls dangled from either side. They rattled as she sorted the papers on her desk. "We close in two minutes," she said before Carrie could speak. "If you need a copy of a report, you have to come back tomorrow."

"Show her your badge," Rein said.

Carrie dug out her wallet and flipped it open, revealing the silver shield inside. "I'm Officer Santero." She glanced at Rein, who was keeping his head down so that his long hair blocked the woman's view of his face. "And this is, um, we're here for . . ."

"Working a homicide."

"Working a homicide investigation," Carrie repeated.

The clerk folded her hands. "We haven't had any homicides in fifteen years. What do you need from us?"

Rein turned his back to the woman and lowered his voice. "Tell her you want to see all their records for contacts with Alan Lloyd."

Carrie repeated what he said and added, "Please."

The clerk turned an ear toward the window but did not get up from her chair. "What name was that, dear?"

derdeveloped. Probably doesn't work and has trouble fitting in with society."

Behind the station door, they could hear someone coming down the hallway, a pair of thick soled boots squeaking on the station's tile floor. They heard a man's voice ask, "What did they say they wanted?"

The clerk's response was muffled to keep them from hearing, but the man's reaction was loud. "You're kidding me. We'll see about this." The station's door flew open and a uniformed officer came barreling through, eyes wide and angry. "You want to tell me what the hell is going on? Who are you, lady? What are you looking me and my family up for?"

As Carrie moved to show him her badge, she saw the name embroidered across his shirt. *Lloyd.* He stopped cold when his eyes fell on Rein, his voice thin and full of disbelief when he said, "Detective Rein?"

Rein stared back at the man. "Alan? Is that you?"

"You're damn right it is!" Lloyd laughed, throwing his arms wide for a tight embrace. "What are you doing here?"

"I . . . came to see how you were doing," Rein said, stepping back to look him over. "Somebody told me you were a police officer now, and I just had to come see it for myself."

"Coming up on my first year already." He pointed at Carrie and said, "Is he with you? You working again, Detective? Mabel said something about a homicide investigation?"

Rein turned around to look at the clerk sitting behind the window and flashed her a large smile, saying, "Homicide? No, that was just . . . part of the joke. I'm sorry, sweetheart. I just wanted to surprise Alan. Did I scare you?" The old woman laughed nervously and shook her head, holding her hand up to her heart and patting it a few times.

"It worked though, didn't it?" Rein said, pointing at Lloyd. "You came out here ready to raise hell."

"You got me." Lloyd grinned. "Shit. Listen, do you want to come in for a bit? I'm just wrapping things up for my shift, but maybe we could go out, grab a bite to eat?"

"I'd love to, Alan, but unfortunately I have to get going. Here, give me your card and I'll give you a call in a few days. Let's get together."

"That would be fantastic," Lloyd said, pulling his card out of his uniform pocket. He clicked his pen and started writing his cell phone number on the back of it. "I've been doing my own investigations. I'm really getting into it. I'd love to pick your brain about some of the things I'm working on."

"No problem. It would be my pleasure," Rein said, taking the card and handing it to Carrie. "Hey, you still staying with your folks in town here?"

"For now. We don't start making the big bucks until we reach full salary."

"I remember what that was like," Rein said. "How is Mom? Anna, if I recall."

"She's good. Real glad I became a cop and decided to help people."

Rein clapped him on the arm. "It was good seeing you, Alan. I'll be in touch."

Lloyd embraced him again and said, "I'm looking forward to it, Detective."

As they exited the station, Carrie was watching Rein, seeing how his expression hardened the moment he'd turned away from Officer Lloyd. "That was a nice piece of police work, finding out he still lived out here with his parents."

"That was nothing," Rein said. "I can't believe they let that kid have a badge and a gun. What a bunch of assholes."

Carrie clicked on her keys to open the car doors and said, "You think he's our doer?"

"Him?" Rein looked back at the station. "No."

Carrie slid into the driver's seat. "How do you know?"

"The killer knows what he is and what he's done. If it was Alan, he'd view me as an immediate threat, especially if I showed up out of the blue on his home turf. Imagine if someone you'd arrested for a serious crime showed up at your front door one day, asking how you'd been?"

"He seemed genuinely happy to see you," Carrie said, adjusting her mirror before backing out of the spot.

"I wish I could say the same."

"Why?"

"You can't go through what he went through and not suffer severe psychological effects, Carrie. Add all the pressures of the job onto that, the shift work, the trauma we experience, and it's just a matter of time before something goes wrong."

"Maybe he's just on some good meds. Now that I think about it, stunted and underdeveloped is a good way to describe most of the cops I work with."

The front door of the station popped open and Lloyd came out, looking for them. He saw Carrie's car and hurried after it, coming around to Rein's side as he leaned down and caught his breath. "You know, I need to tell you this. It's your fault."

Rein looked up at him. "What is?"

"Me doing this," he said, pointing at his uniform. "Becoming a cop."

"How so?"

"What you said to me in the hospital. Do you remember?"

"Kind of," Rein said. "I think I told you to try your best not to let this ruin your life. Clearly you didn't listen to me when you decided to become a cop."

"No, it was more than that. A lot more than that," Lloyd said. "You told me there were monsters in this world, real monsters, and they bite children. You said that some kids, when they get bitten, they turn into monsters too. You told me you didn't want to see that happen to me. Then you said that sometimes, when a monster bites you, you become immune to it forever after. You told me that it was their job to protect children, because we are the only ones who don't have anything to be afraid of anymore."

Rein stared at the young man but did not speak.

"Anyway," Lloyd said, laughing at himself, "that's why I'm here. I guess you were just trying to cheer me up back then, but I took it serious." He put his hand on Rein's arm and said, "It's good to have you back, sir. We need you."

Carrie waved to Lloyd as he stepped back from the car, keeping her eyes fixed on the road as Rein slumped in his seat, rubbing his temples. "You okay, Grizzly Adams?"

He turned toward her, "Do you even know who Grizzly Adams was?"

"I know he had a big beard."

After a few minutes, Rein said, "You know, that person he's talking about, that's not me. Not anymore."

"Of course it is."

"Not after what I did. When you do something like that, everything else goes away."

"I don't believe that. One mistake doesn't undo all the good you did, Jacob. All those kids you saved. All those parents you got justice for. Look what you're doing now. You're still fighting monsters, and I for one am glad, because we need you on our side, just like Lloyd said."

"Monsters," he whispered. "I killed a child, Carrie. A little girl. At night I lay there thinking about what she'd be doing if she were alive right now. I see other little girls her age and I want to claw my own eyes out. I can't ever forget what I am. I won't let myself *ever* forget what I am. To that little girl and her family, *I* am the monster."

19

The sun hung low over the row homes' rooftops, casting golden light over the trash cans and telephone poles on either side. Carrie turned the wheel toward the curb in front of Rein's house, feeling cool evening air sweep through her car's open windows. They'd been driving all day, and she needed a shower. They both did.

Chicano music blared from boom boxes set up in front yards up and down the street. The air was thick with smoke from grills stacked high with meat. It was Saturday night. The whole block reeked of beer.

"You'll check the driver's license photos on all those names from the library to pick out the white males, right?" Rein asked.

"I'll get started on that tonight."

"Then run criminal histories, previous contacts, and pay extra attention to the ones with mental health issues."

"I will."

"And tomorrow night you're going to the club?"

"That's the plan. You're coming with me, right?"

He paused. "I'm not sure you need my help anymore, Carrie."

"Rein, I know you don't think you should be doing this, but I need you to listen to me right now. You killed a little girl. That's what this is all about. You killed a little girl and nothing can make that right."

Rein's jaw tightened, but he did not speak."That guilt has been eating you away for years. Christ, you even went to prison when you didn't have to. It sucks, and there's nothing that will fix it, and I get it." She turned in her seat toward him. "Right now there is a little girl missing out there, and she's probably in the hands of some maniac. A perfect, precious little girl who deserves to live, Jacob. The same way the little girl you feel so guilty about did. That's what I'm asking you to help me do. You accidentally took one life away. I know you're sorry about it, but it can't be changed. What I'm asking you to do now is help me get one back."

"You know," Rein said, "you can't manipulate me that easily, Carrie. But it was a nice try."

"Oh, come on, Rein. That was perfect."

"It was acceptable. A little heavy-handed."

"Can you just help me?"

A broken-down lawn mower was parked near the sidewalk on one of the front yards. Its engine lay disassembled in the grass. No one had bothered to cover it up. The spark plugs were fouled. The oil inside of it had turned to tar in the summer heat. It would never run again. Whoever had worked on it had even left their tools behind. A few wrenches and pliers. Good tools, once, but long since rusted shut. All of it so useless that no one in the neighborhood had bothered to steal it. "I'll think about it," Rein said. "Go home get some sleep. You look like hell."

She watched him get out of the car and said, "*You* look like hell, except with a beard."

As she pulled away, she glanced at Rein in her rearview mirror and saw him staring down at one of the large piles of trash on the street. He grabbed a dirty duffel bag from the trash and started scooping up books and papers dumped on top of the other refuse. Rein lifted his head toward the house and shouted, "What did you idiots do?"

Four dark-skinned men were sitting in lawn chairs on the grass, drinking beers. One smiled at him and said, "You moving out today, man."

"Like hell," Rein said, stuffing his things inside the bag.

"Bed's already gone."

"How is the bed already gone? I paid for the week."

"Since you like *Inmigración* so much, you go with her, huh?" he said, pointing his beer at Carrie's car. The other cackled with laughter.

"Hey, *ese*," another said, "I give you my bed if you send your bitch up here. Tell her I want to see her pussy."

Rein was up the steps in a flash, going for the nearest man's throat. Tires screeched on the asphalt behind him, and Carrie came leaping up the steps, grabbing the back of his shirt, shouting, "Hey! It's not worth it, Rein! Come on, let's go."

She dragged him down the front steps toward her car and opened the door for him, pushing until he was seated. She could hear the men jeering and cursing at her in Spanish but ignored them, wanting only to get back in her car and get the hell out of there. "Those dirty pieces of shit," she said as she slammed the door shut. "Did you get all your stuff?"

"I didn't have much," he said.

"I'm calling ICE Monday morning. We'll see how much they're laughing when I shut their employer down. You'll see."

"It's not worth it," Rein said. "You were right."

"They can't just do that to you."

He slumped back in his seat and said, "No one would blame them."

An hour later, they pulled into the Hansen Terrace Condominiums lot. The security gate was raised and disabled, its long arms extended high over the guard house on either side. "They told us we'd have twenty-four-hour security when I bought this place," Carrie said, easing her car over the first speed bump. "Then the builder's financing fell through."

Rein looked around the parking lot and the multi-story buildings. There were terraces outside of each window, many of them decorated with lights or garden boxes. He grabbed his bag as she parked the car, then followed her to the lobby door. A sign reading KEYCARDS DO NOT WORK was taped to the glass, and Carrie sifted through her keys in the dim light, trying to find the right one.

They made their way up to the fourth floor, and Carrie paused before opening her door. "It's not much, and I wasn't expecting company, so excuse any mess you see."

He stood in the doorway, watching her fling her purse onto the couch and pick up a coffee mug from the table, a magazine from the floor, and a bra draped over one of the pillows. She balled up the bra in her hands to get it out of sight, then looked up and noticed Rein hadn't moved. "Well? Come on."

"I'm not sure this is a good idea."

"You have any other ideas?"

"I could get a hotel room."

"Can you afford a hotel room?"

"What does one cost around here?"

"About a hundred bucks, plus you need a major credit card."

"Then, no. Probably not."

"Do you even have a phone to call someone?"

"No."

"Then that settles it. You're staying here," she said, moving toward the front door to close it behind him. "Can't have you roaming the streets, now, can I?"

He looked around at her decorations and furniture. There wasn't much, but she'd made the most of what she had. "This is nice," he said.

Carrie felt her stomach grumbling and laid her hand flat against it, saying, "I just realized we haven't eaten all day. Christ, I'm hungry. You must be starving."

Rein set his bag near the front door, hovering around it as if he might make an escape at any moment, nervously running his palm over the coarse hairs covering his chin and cheeks.

"You do eat, don't you?" she called out from the kitchen.

"Sometimes."

"What do you eat?" she said, opening her refrigerator and bending over to look inside.

"Lately, just Mexican food."

"I bet." She laughed. "I have pasta. Or I can make

hamburgers." When he didn't answer she looked up and said, "PB and J? I'll even cut the crusts off if you want." She leaned out of the kitchen, seeing that he still had not come in, and put her hands on her hips. "Listen, Duck Dynasty, you can be weird about this if you want, but tonight you're getting a hot meal, a shower, and a place to sleep. *Comprende?*"

"*Sí, comprendo,*" he grunted. "Feels like home already."

"So what's it gonna be? Do I need to keep looking, or should we just order pizza?"

Rein looked down at his dirty boots and said, "Burgers."

"My favorite!" Carrie said. "Excellent choice." She looked down at his filthy, grass-stained boots and said, "Take those disgusting things off and leave them by the door."

Rein scratched his face again and looked down at the laces. They were shredded at the ends, and one was broken so short he could tie only a single loop. He carefully undid the threads and placed his boots next to his bag by the door, looking down at his exposed toes through the large holes in his socks. He had one other pair in his bag, but they were worse. Of the two, these were the good ones. "You know, if you're having a psychotic episode, we should call someone," he said.

She stood up, staring at him from across the kitchen counter. "What the hell are you talking about?"

"You're obviously in a state of hysteria and denial. Delusional happiness, some would call it."

"I'm not delusional," she said, turning back to the stove. "I had an epiphany at the library today."

"Is that right?"

"It was like this voice spoke to me, telling me to hang in there and have faith," she said over her shoulder. "That everything is going to be all right."

"I see."

"And no matter what, not you or anybody else is going to talk me out of it, okay?"

He wiggled his toes, feeling the soft, plush carpet under his feet and was amazed at how good it felt. He worked in his boots and slept in them too, for fear that someone would steal them.

Carrie glanced back at him, then down at the bag, and said, "I'm guessing you don't have much in the way of comfortable clothes in there, do you?"

"Another set of work clothes and some underwear," he said.

"Stand by," she said, reaching into the freezer and pulling out a box of hamburgers. She dropped four onto the frying pan, and said, "Just stand by."

He watched her disappear into the bedroom and come back out several minutes later with an armful of clothing. "I dated this guy last year, and he left some stuff here. These should fit. I always meant to give it all to my dad, but I keep making excuses not to go over there."

He took the pair of sweatpants, a T-shirt, and thick white socks that felt softer than the blanket he slept under at the row home. "You sure?"

"Sure I'm sure. They're yours. Go get changed in the bathroom and I'll get dinner going."

Rein shuffled toward the bathroom, holding the soft clothing close to his chest. He stopped at the door and looked back at Carrie. The grill was on, and steam was coming up from the burgers. "I have a question."

"Shoot," she said.

"What's a Duck Dynasty?"

Two hours later, the lights were off except for the television. Carrie shut it down, laid the remote on the table, and slid herself off the couch. She picked up their plates and cups and carried them into the kitchen, listening to Rein's rhythmic snores. She gathered up a pillow and blanket from her bedroom closet and carried them out, setting the pillow down. She tapped him lightly on the shoulder and said, "Go ahead and lie down. Get some sleep."

His eyes stayed closed as he moved down toward the pillow and stretched out, groggily thanking her.

"Don't thank me yet," she said. "This couch isn't the most comfortable thing in the world."

"I'm used to sleeping on the floor," he said, then his mouth opened and he was snoring again.

She draped the blanket over him and pulled it up to his shoulders, making sure it covered his feet. A long tangle of hair covered his face, and she paused to look at him, then bent down and swept it behind his ear. He did not stir when she touched him. She felt the warmth of his weathered face on the palm of her hand and the softness of his beard, wondering whether to wake him. What would she do then? It was probably better not to find out.

She stopped in the bathroom, staring at the stack of Rein's folded clothes sitting on the floor while she sat down on the toilet. His pants were clean, despite the deep grass stains and shredded cuffs. His work T-shirt was sun-bleached and ripped on the seams along the underarms. After she flushed, she picked up the clothes to throw them out. He would not need them anymore. As she reached for the door, she felt something heavy deep in his pants pocket, and stepped back, making sure the door was shut and locked. She laid the pants on the counter and reached inside, feeling a long, curved metal handle. She pulled it out, staring at it in wonder. There was a loop at the top of the handle, the size of one finger, as if were to be held upside down, with the curve travelling along the inside of the palm. At the bottom, a blade. Some sort of work tool.

She clicked open the blade, a hooked, talonlike claw that curved to a point so sharp it would easily pierce another human's being's skull. She slid her finger through the ring and gripped the handle, realizing that it was now nearly perfectly concealed. The only thing anyone would see was the ring and a small portion of the blade curving out from the bottom of her hand. Not a work tool, she realized, but an instrument of death.

20

Carrie emerged yawning from her bedroom the next morning. She'd slept well, despite being afraid of the dreams that awaited. Instead, there was nothing. A deep, dark nothingness, until her alarm clock sounded at eight A.M.

She staggered out of her bedroom, scratching her stomach, eager for coffee. As she rubbed her face and plucked small flecks of crust from her eyelashes, she was startled to realize Rein was standing across the room, staring at her.

"Oh," she said. "What time did you get up?"

"I wake up early."

She looked around the living room. "You could have watched TV, or made yourself breakfast or something."

"I didn't want to be rude."

"Well, good thing I didn't sleep in, then. Good morning! Are you hungry?"

"I'd like to take a shower, if that's all right?"

"Sure, of course. Towels are in the lower cabinet."

"Thank you," he said, then moved to pick up his duffel bag and head past her toward the bathroom. As he walked past, Carrie became aware that she wasn't wearing a bra, just a long white T-shirt and boxer shorts. She looked down, realizing that her nipples were erect and visible. Before she could cover herself, Rein had already left the room, his head kept low the entire time, his eyes covered by his long hair.

I could have come out of the room naked and he would not have noticed, she thought, unsure if that made her offended or comfortable. The bathroom door closed, and she hurried toward it, knocking twice.

"I'm going to make food. Do you want eggs?"

"Whatever you have," he said through the door. "As long as you have enough and don't mind."

"I don't mind, dude. I'm trying to feed you, is all. What do you normally eat for breakfast?"

The water came on. "I normally don't."

"Bacon or sausage?"

"Whichever."

"Scrambled eggs or fried?"

"However you like them."

Carrie groaned. "Keep it up and all you'll get is a bowl of Cap'n Crunch!"

The door flew open, startling her. Rein was shirtless, his torso deeply tanned and lined with hard-won muscle. She saw softness around his stomach and sides, but his shoulders and chest were broad, and she caught herself staring. Rein's voice drew her eyes back up to his, saying, "Do you have the kind with the berries?"

"Of course," Carrie said, finding herself amused at the idea of the great Jacob Rein eating a bowl of Crunch Berries. "They're my favorite."

"I used to like those," he said, before closing the door.

"It's going to be a good day, Rein!" Carrie called out as she made her way to the kitchen. "I had a dream last night that Molly won the lottery and left so she could surprise everyone. She came riding up to the police station in a big limousine filled with all these balloons. I'm telling you. Today's the day, so don't take too long."

She listened for his response, hearing nothing but running water.

Fifteen minutes later, the water cut off. Carrie was ready, standing by the door with her arms full. "Rein, don't get dressed yet. I need to give you something first."

There was hesitation in his voice. "What, *exactly*, do you mean?"

"Don't get any big ideas, pal. I just have more clothes for you."

The door opened a crack, and his hand came through to take them. Carrie said, "Not so fast. There's one more thing." She pushed the door open and glanced, making sure he was wearing a towel, then set the stack of clothes on the countertop. She laid a pair of long, thin hair scissors on top of them and raised an eyebrow toward him.

Rein looked at the scissors and said, "No."

"Please," Carrie pleaded. "You look like the Unabomber. If we find Molly and Nubs today, they're going to run away again in fear. Anyway, you can't go to that club looking like this. They'll think you're a bear."

Still wet, his hair came down to his shoulders and his beard draped over his chest. He turned and looked at himself in the mirror and frowned. "I'd ask you if you meant that literally, but I get the feeling there's another meaning to it."

"A bear is a big burly gay guy who's superhairy. They'll be so busy trying to dance with you that you won't be able to ask any questions."

He grabbed his beard with one hand and drew it tight, wringing it out and looking down to see how long it stretched. Up close, she could see long silver streaks hidden within its thick mass, and imagined how distinguished he'd look if he turned completely gray. "I've been cutting my dad's hair for years. I promise, I won't mess it up. At least, you won't look any more messed up than you already do." She smiled, then opened the scissors wide to make her first cut.

Rein's fingers came around her wrist. "The beard has to stay."

"Why?"

"It helps people not recognize me."

He let go of her hand and stood holding his robe, looking down, not resisting. Carrie drew out a finger length of his beard and said, "Then just let me re-shape it a little." Hair fell away from his face as she snipped, soon covering her hands and his chest. "I never had a chance to give someone a duckbill. Always wanted to."

Rein grabbed her hand again. "No. No duckbill."

"Do you even know what one is?"

"I know it sounds stupid."

She snipped away another tuft from his chin. "It's just called that because it's short on the sides and swoops down in the front. If you want, we can call it the *300*."

"The three hundred what?"

"That movie, *300*? About the Greek guys who fought the other guys?"

"You mean the three hundred Spartans at the Battle of Thermopylae?" Rein said.

"Something like that. Did you see the movie?"

"No."

"Of course not," she said, leaning close to keep scissoring. "Why'd I even ask? Anyway, they all had this kind of beard, especially Gerard Butler, and oh my God is he amazing."

"Molon labe," Rein muttered to himself, looking down to watch her work.

Carrie stopped trimming and looked up at him. "What?"

"Molon labe," Rein repeated. "A famous saying from that battle. King Leonidas had assembled his men inside a narrow pass called the Hot Gates, and they held off thousands of Persians. Slaughtering them until their bodies were stacked so high, the other Persians had to climb over them. Xerxes, the Persian leader, could not believe what he was seeing, so the next morning before the fighting began, he went down to the Spartans to negotiate. The Persians never took hostages. They never spared anyone, but Xerxes was so impressed with their courage he made them an incredible offer. Surrender, and Xerxes would let them join his army. He would even make Leonidas a general and give him all of Greece to rule over. There must have been a moment where he thought about it," Rein said.

Carrie turned him away from the mirror, cutting up along the right side of Rein's head and removing huge swaths of hair. She worked quickly, only half-listening, trying to get as much of it cut as she could before he realized what she was doing and objected.

"The Spartans were dead men," Rein continued, lost in the story. "Leonidas knew it. They all knew it. And now the most powerful man in the world was standing in front of him, offering more riches and glory than any other person on the planet, but the price was the betrayal of everything he held dear. 'All you have to do is lay down your weapons,' Xerxes said. And that's when Leonidas replied, '*Molon labe.*'"

"I like how you say that. *Molon labe*," Carrie repeated. "So what does it mean?"

"Come and take them."

"But they all died anyway, right?"

"Right."

"Guess he learned *his* lesson," she said. "He should have taken the deal."

Rein scowled at her. "No, he shouldn't have. His sacrifice inspired the rest of Greece to fight so bravely that they defeated the Persians and sent them back across the sea. It probably preserved democracy for the entire human race so that we have it today."

"Yeah, but he was dead."

"He died a hero. I call that lucky."

"How so?"

"We all live in darkness, Carrie. Everything around us is dying, some of it slowly, some of it quickly, but all of it will eventually succumb to the darkness."

"You're a really depressing person, Rein."

"But sometimes," he continued, "on very rare occasions, a person gets to swim up through that darkness, even if only for just a moment. They get to thrust their face into the light. It's something most of us will never know. It's worth dying for."

She made fast work of the rest of his hair, leaving it jagged and shaggy, until his shoulders and chest were piled with trimmings. She spent the rest of the time on his beard, getting it perfect. When it was finished, she turned him around and admired her work in the mirror. Rein turned his head side to side, unsure of what to make of what she'd done to him.

"One problem," Carrie said.

"Now what?"

"The guys at the club, tonight. When they see this? Look out."

"You made it worse, didn't you."

"Oh yeah, totally."

By eleven A.M., they were sitting inside the Coyote Township police station, surrounded by stacks of paper that had been turned into a bizarre geometric formation to all fit on the round table. Something sticky covered the table, getting on her hands and arms, but she ignored it, not wanting to know what it was.

At the top of every stack was a name and driver's license photo of the men they'd identified at the library. Rein pointed and said, "Each one has a criminal history, state ID photo, and prior police contacts, right?"

"For the most part," Carrie said. "Some of the guys live in Bumblefuck USA with police departments that don't work on weekends. I've left messages, but I will probably have to wait until Monday."

Rein pressed his hands together, rubbing them. "Unfortunately those are the ones we need to look at. Tell me why."

"Well," she said, thinking it over. "I guess he'd want to live in a remote location with limited police coverage. Plus, property is cheap out in the sticks, so if he's on any kind of mental health disability, he won't have to work. That leaves a lot of time to pursue his interests."

"Good," Rein said. "Very good. So of these candidates, who do we like?"

As Carrie shuffled through the stack, she heard someone coming down the hall. No one had been in the station when they'd entered, and the front door had not opened, so that left only one explanation. She kept her head low, without looking, and said, "Hey, Chief."

Waylon stopped at the doorway, looking down at the stacks of papers and then at his old partner. His mustache was wet from the coffee cup in his hand. He wiped his mouth, then wiped his hand on his pants, and said, "What the hell happened to you?"

"Apparently, it's called a duckbill."

He looked at Carrie. "I thought that's what you did with your hair, like a pompadour."

"No, that's a duck's ass," Carrie said.

"Well, why the hell do they call it a duckbill?"

"It's short and swoops down in the front," Carrie said. "See?"

Waylon peered down at Rein's beard and said, "It looks more like a ski slope. Like something you eat is gonna roll out of your mouth and take off flying."

"Anyway," Carrie said, turning back to her papers, "what are you doing here? Did someone call out again?"

"I got a very annoyed phone call from the radio room, young lady. A very annoyed phone call about you. They said you were making the data girl run a whole bunch of driver's licenses and criminal histories on a Sunday morning and interrupting their pinochle game."

"And what did you tell him?"

"What do you think I told him?"

Rein looked up. "Given my past experiences with police administrators, probably that you were sorry for the trouble and would shut the whole thing down immediately."

"I bet you think that's real funny," Waylon said. "So tell me what we got anyway. When I heard you were running all this info, I figured you were onto something. I came by to see if I could help."

"You're in luck, then," Carrie said. "We are just about to crack this case wide open!"

Waylon's eyebrows raised in surprise, and he looked at Rein. "She had an *epiphany*," Rein explained.

"Oh," Waylon said. "I see. One of those."

"Don't you take his side, boss," Carrie said. "He lives in darkness. He told me so himself."

"Listen, kiddo, these things are complicated," Waylon said. "You have to be prepared for a long, grueling investigation, and in most cases, they don't turn out . . . like we hope."

Carrie continued searching. "Well, I guess you are going to be shocked then, because all we need to do is figure out which of these people to talk to and before you know it, we've got Molly and Nubs home safe and sound."

Before Waylon could respond, Rein cleared his throat and pointed at the stacks on the table, saying, "We're still assembling data. Trying to find out which locals best fit our parameters. Once we can narrow them down, we'll start checking to see if they had any police contacts in the areas of the two kidnappings and murder. Maybe someone ran their tag. It's not much, but it's all we have for now."

"It's a lot, Rein," Carrie said. "It's *going* to work."

"So how long before we can get enough to start some interrogations? Jacob here might have been the supersleuth, but I always did enjoy a good interrogation."

"That depends," Rein said.

Waylon's brow furrowed, knowing he was being set up. "On what?"

"On whether it's just her and me doing this or if you can get us some extra men."

Carrie's eyes lit up. "Can you get us the Feds? That's what this case needs. Bloodhounds and helicopters, Bill. Thermal imaging shit. Please, just call them. I don't even care if they take the case from us. They can have it, if it works."

"That is not what those people do, Carrie. They wait until the shooting stops and show up at the press conference. Take the case?" He laughed. "You'd better understand something. No FBI regional supervisor wants to be stuck out here in Podunk, Pennsylvania. They want to be where the action is. Someplace with upward mobility! The only way to get out of here is to demonstrate a stellar track record. Now ask yourself, Who the hell is going to risk stepping into this mess? For what? What do we even really have?"

"Well," Rein said, "we have a missing white female, dark hair, twenty-two years old, who has a history of drug abuse and running away. We have a dead white male, midthirties, found in a van in the parking lot of a nightclub."

"How are either of those connected in any way?" Waylon said. He held up his hand to stop Carrie from speaking, "I'm not talking about what we think, or what we suspect, I'm talking about what we can prove. Go on."

Rein continued, "We also have a missing white female, blond hair, twenty-six years old, and her daughter. The little girl is white, also blond, and six years old."

Waylon let out a long, slow whistle. "Can you see me trying to sell this to the Feds, Jacob? Can you imagine what those yahoos are gonna say to me? And no offense, but what do you think their reaction is gonna be once they realize *you're* the one stirring all this up?"

"Then let *me* talk to them, Bill!" Carrie said. "If I can just explain it, they'll have to understand."

"When we worked Krissing, up to our necks in dead kids, you know what the FBI did for us? They sent us a publicity person to handle the press conferences. Am I lying?"

"No," Rein said. "And to be honest, Carrie, that was way more high profile than this."

"This is complete bullshit!" Carrie snapped. "Even if the same guy didn't do the killing at the nightclub, he might still have grabbed Denise Lawson and then Molly and Nubs. We might have two suspects on the loose!"

"Would you listen to yourself?" Waylon said. "We can't substantiate a single thing you just said, except for the fact that a *man* from a *gay nightclub* club got killed, and they are gonna call that a lover's quarrel as sure as I am standing here. We have zero evidence of any abductions. Zero."

"There is no way in the fucking world Molly would take Nubs and run off without telling me, Bill. No fucking way! So fuck anybody who says different, got it? They were taken. Period!"

"Do you see it, Jacob?" Waylon said, turning toward him. "Put your cards on the table, right here, right now. Do you?"

Rein saw the need in Carrie's eyes. "I don't know," was all he could bring himself to say.

It was like someone unplugged the lights inside of her as cold betrayal spread across her face. "The problem is that most serial offenders tend to stick with their preferred type. If they like little girls, they take little girls. If they like Asian men, they take Asian men. They don't typically wander outside of their comfort zone in terms of hunting grounds, disposal methods, or victim type."

"See?" Waylon said, holding his hands out toward Carrie. He was about to continue when he saw Rein raise his finger.

"Unless . . ." Rein said.

"Unless what?" Carrie said. When he paused, seemingly unsure of himself, she pounded the table with her fist. "Unless what? I want to hear it."

"For years, profilers have had a theory about a different type of offender. A chameleon, with no form. No pattern. No one's ever been able to confirm their existence, because how could you? You'd have such a wide mix of victims from such a large area, all taken or murdered in such various methods, that it would never track. As far as anyone can prove, it's just a theory."

"And this theory of chameleons or whatever," Carrie said. "You think that's what we're dealing with?"

"I only came along this far is to make sure it isn't. No offense, but neither of you would have any idea what you were dealing with. I'm not sure I would. We would be talking about the most dangerous serial murderer in existence."

"Which no one has ever been able to say is anything more than a theory," Waylon interjected.

"There's a very good reason no one's ever proven the existence of an omnikiller."

"Why?" Carrie said.

"Because secretly, we all pray one doesn't exist."

21

Carrie said nothing as they made their way back to the car, or when they sat inside, or when she turned the key and began to drive. "It's only four o'clock," Rein said, looking at the dashboard. "Do you want to go set up on the club early, see if any of the staff rolls in?"

She looked at the road, refusing to acknowledge him. "Fine."

"Okay," he said, tapping his fingers on the door frame. "Hey, do you mind if we stop at the store real quick? I need to get a few things if we're going to be there awhile."

They made a sudden left, wheels peeling out on the asphalt, throwing Rein's body sideways. Carrie corrected the steering wheel as they hopped over a curb into a small parking lot. They came to an abrupt stop in front of the Sunoco. "Fine."

"Do you want anything?" Rein asked.

"I'm fine."

"We're going to be there awhile. Some coffee, maybe?"

"I said I'm fine."

"All right," he said, and got out. He went into the

store and came back with two coffees, a large Gatorade bottle, two waters, and two soft pretzels. She ignored the coffees he placed in the cup holders between them. "I wasn't sure how you took your coffee, so I got one of the flavored ones and put the French Vanilla cream in it. If you don't like it sweet, you can have mine. I drink it black. I thought you liked it sweet, for some reason, so I guessed."

"I told you I didn't want anything."

"True," he said. "But drinking coffee on a surveillance is a time-honored tradition. I might be a lot of things, but a man who breaks tradition is not one of them. Do you like it sweet?"

"It's fine."

"I guess *fine* is our word of the day, then." He picked up his coffee and took a sip, wincing at how hot it was, then took another. "Fine by me, then. I can handle that just fine."

"Great. Coffee, water, and Gatorade," Carrie mumbled to herself as she watched him. "Half an hour into this and your old ass going to be crying for the bathroom."

"That's what the Gatorade's for."

"How is that going to help?"

He rolled down the window and poured the brightly colored Gatorade into the street. "I wouldn't drink this crap if you paid me. I just needed the bottle."

"Gross," Carrie said, laughing despite herself. "I hope you don't think you're whipping out your donger in my car and pissing into that bottle."

"Actually, it would be pretty hard with you here," he said.

"Ex-*cuse* me?"

He looked at her, holding the empty bottle. "What?"

She rolled her eyes. "You're a complete ass, you know that?"

Rein turned away from her and set the empty bottle down on the floor, his ears and face flushing with embarrassment. "I meant because if someone is around, I can't go. Even if someone talks to me through the door, I lock up. Not . . . not whatever it is you're thinking."

"Seriously?"

"Yes," he said. "When I was a kid, we only had one bathroom, and my dad used to come barging in on me all the time. He wasn't the type to knock. Guess that's where it comes from."

"The Great Detective is pee shy?"

"I'm hardly that. Except for the second part. I'm very much that."

"So what good is the bottle if you can't use it in front of me?"

"I don't know." He shrugged. "Maybe you could jump in the back and get down on the floor or something. Try not to breathe too loud."

"Like hell! You aren't pissing in my car, Rein!"

He looked around the front compartment, seeing discarded coffee cups, receipts, and straw wrappers. "Why? You're worried I might mess it up?"

"You can go directly to hell. At least I have a car."

"Very true." He raised his coffee cup in salute. "There are a lot of things I do not have."

"I'm sorry," she said. "I didn't mean to make fun of you."

"No big deal. I figure, a man has to know himself, and I try to know the good and the bad. Doesn't do any good to lie about it. I happen to be a former felon, turned dirt-poor landscaper who does not own a car, and who suffers from extreme shyness about peeing. You want to throw in the parts about being friendless, homeless, an embarrassment to my family, and the fact that the only thing I'm good at is dealing with psychotics and molesters, that's okay too. In fact, it's *fine*."

Carrie picked up the warm cup and held it in her hand, inhaling its scent, trying to let it calm her. She leaned down and took a small sip. "Thank you for the coffee. Yes, you guessed right. I like it sweet."

He waited for her to finish her sip and said, "You know, I'm no expert with women. I got divorced back before I even joined the County. Then, all that other stuff happened, and well, I just wasn't very interested in dragging anyone else into this mess of a life. So I don't have much in the way of what you'd call experience with women. My point is, even an idiot like me can tell you're mad at me. What did I do?"

It had been building the entire time they were at the station, and if she started in all at once, she knew it would get ugly, fast. "Well, for starters," she said, "you were supposed to have my back, back there, with Bill. I figured we were sticking together on this, Rein. Everybody else is trying to play this thing down, but if we aren't on the same page. I thought . . . I thought we were partners."

"Go on," he said.

"That's it," she said. "I just feel like you should have had my back and you didn't."

"I'm listening."

"Bill already thinks I'm in over my head on this! But he trusts you, and as far as I'm concerned you just told him you're tagging along with the silly little girl just to see how it plays out! That was not cool, Rein. If you're not one hundred percent on this investigation, what the hell use is it continuing? I'm so sorry we don't have conclusive proof of your super–serial killer yet, but let me just remind you that proof would mean the dead bodies of my best fucking friend and her daughter."

He waited for her to catch her breath, waiting to make sure she was finished, waiting for the color to come back into her face. When it was calm again, he said, "You're right. I'm sorry. I shouldn't have made you feel like I didn't have your back."

She looked at him sideways. "I feel like there's a *but* in there just waiting to come out."

"A wise man once said, 'Never ruin a good apology with an excuse.'"

"Sounds like good advice."

"That being said," he went on, "I need you to understand something. In this job, the worst thing anyone can do is speculate. Especially when it's something serious. In front of the press, on the stand, or to your boss, never, ever shoot from the hip. You have to remember, our job is just to assemble the facts. We must remain impartial."

"I can't remain impartial, Rein. Molly and Nubs are missing."

"That's why Bill should never let you anywhere near this investigation," he said. "But you're here, and you're doing an okay job, so don't blow it now. Bill needs to know you're keeping a level head. That way, when you tell him we've got a real situation, he's going to believe you. Trust me."

"Just an okay job?" she said,

"Passing. For now. I've been grading you on a curve so far, so don't get a big head," he said.

"I trust you," she said, before she had time to think

about it. Saying it because it was true. She took another sip of coffee and added, "Dumb-ass."

They pulled into Club Transmission's parking lot. Rein told her to find a spot in the back, as far away from the door as possible, to give them a clear view of the entrance and any cars pulling in. He bent down to look on the passenger-side floor, then searched the center console, seeing nothing but sticky coffee residue and loose change glued down inside the rubber cup holders by more sticky coffee residue. He spun around to look behind his seat. "Where's your binoculars?"

"I don't have any," she said. "You never said we needed any."

"It's basic surveillance equipment 101. You can't do this without binoculars."

"Well, I don't have any."

"What the hell is Bill thinking?" Rein said. "First he buys this heap for an undercover car, then he doesn't even put the most basic equipment in it."

"Rein," Carrie said.

"It sticks out like a sore thumb, and it's filthy." He ran his hand along the dashboard through a layer of dust and said, "Does anybody use this heap for actual police work, or do they just use it to store their trash?"

"Rein."

"What?"

"This heap isn't an undercover car. It's my car. My personal one."

He stopped and said, "Oh."

"I didn't have time to clean it. I was a little busy looking for my missing friend. Sorry."

"It's . . . not that bad," Rein offered. "Honest. It's nice and roomy."

"Thanks."

"It's better than what I have."

"You don't have a car."

"I didn't say it was better by much." He turned to look at her. "Carrie?"

"Yes, Rein?"

"Get some binoculars."

Darkness set in, and the cars along the highway were turning on their headlights, flooding the parking lot as they passed. Carrie pulled apart the last gooey chunk of her pretzel and offered some to Rein, who declined, so she popped it in her mouth. "Maybe they're not going to open tonight," she said, still chewing. "Maybe they're too freaked out about the murder."

"It's possible," Rein said.

"What do you want to do?"

"I want to wait."

"I hate waiting," she muttered. "I hate sitting, I hate staring at stupid buildings, I hate doing nothing while they're missing."

"Sometimes I wonder how many hours of my life I've spent staring at buildings. Hundreds, probably. That's what investigations are sometimes, though. A whole lot of waiting and sitting and preparing for something to happen. Then when it does?" Rein snapped his fingers. "It's over, like that. All that work for a few seconds of action."

"Reminds me of my last boyfriend," she said.

"The guy whose clothes I'm wearing?"

"No. That guy wasn't really a boyfriend," she said. "Just a way to pass the time."

"Ah."

She unscrewed the cap and took a sip of water, washing down the salt and the dough between her teeth. She needed to keep her mind occupied with something else besides the fear of what was happening to Nubs. She pictured the little girl screaming for help, over and over, and no one coming to rescue her. "So, let me get this straight," she said, trying to concentrate on Rein. "You got divorced before you came to the County? You must have had your son when you were young."

"The girl I was dating after high school got pregnant, and we thought it was for the best. Tried to make a go of it, but when I got on the job, it caused problems. She couldn't understand the shift work, or what I was dealing with. I couldn't understand . . . anything about her, I guess. The dad part was easy. Me and Jacob Junior had a great time. I took him to museums and nature centers and bookstores and zoos, and we loved it, but his mom was never into any of that. Eventually, she told me she wanted to do something different with her life, and I understood. Anyway, we stayed separated for a while. I let her stay on my benefits a few years, trying to make it easy on her, but then she met someone and wanted to be officially divorced."

"And there's been nobody since?"

"Nope. Not really."

"Weren't there a bunch of little mamacitas running around the place you used to live? Seemed like they partied all the time. I'm sure there were women."

"Sure," he said.

"And you never hooked up with one? What's wrong? You're only into blondes or redheads or something?"

"It's not that. In those places, there's no furniture. No beds. They lay out blankets and towels on the floor, and you sleep wherever you can find a spot. I would always pick the farthest one away from the door, because otherwise you'd get stepped on by everyone trying to make it to the bathroom. And a lot of times, they didn't make it."

"Jesus," Carrie said.

"Sometimes the guys would bring a woman back. They'd all be drunk. She'd be drunk. They'd be passing her around and giving her a couple dollars every time, right? By the end, she'd have two fistfuls of crumpled dollar bills and go staggering out the door, and everyone would go to sleep. You cannot imagine the sounds, and the smell."

"I can't imagine any of it," she said.

"I guess, after a while, that part of me just shut off. I figured I'd never use it again, so I let it just wither away."

She looked at him. "You mean *it* withered away, like, literally?"

"No, not literally."

"You could have brought a smaller bottle to pee in, if that's the case. Maybe one of those tiny airplane liquor bottles and just stuff it down your pants, and no one would know the difference."

Another car passed, lights reflecting off the windshield, revealing the hard gleam of Rein's eyes as he stared at the building. Carrie looked at him until the light passed. "What if you met someone, though?"

"I think they're here," he said.

Her eyebrows raised in surprise. "Seriously? You're bringing this up now? I mean, first off, you're a lot older than me—"

"They're *here*," he said, pointing through the windshield at two cars pulling into the parking lot, driving toward the entrance. "They must be employees. We don't want to scare them, so let them park and we'll head up there once they get the door open."

"All right," she said stiffly, trying to get back into cop mode.

"What were you saying before that?"

"About what?" she said, playing it off.

"Something about me being older."

"I said I was surprised you could see the cars coming in from that far away, old man."

"Well, I wouldn't need to if you'd brought binoculars, now would I?"

She eased the car in. A well-built man got out of the first car and headed for the door, dangling a large ring of keys in his hand. He undid the lock and propped the door open, then returned to his car. Another man got out of the second car, heaving a large wheeled suitcase out of the backseat and setting it upright on the blacktop. He wheeled toward the front door, suitcase handle in one hand and a bright red wig in the other.

He called out in a deep, gravelly voice, "I'm gonna go get set up, Zack."

"Sure thing, Matilda," the muscular man said over his shoulder. He took a crate full of records out of his car and set it on the hood, looking up at the approaching vehicle. Carrie stopped, and she and Rein got out, heading toward him. It was dark in the parking lot, and Zack moved back.

Rein raised his hand in greeting. "Hi, do you work here?"

"Yeah. Who are you?"

"We weren't sure if you guys would be open tonight."

"Because of the murder, you mean?"

"That's what we wanted to talk to you about, if you don't mind."

"Are you cops?"

Carrie flashed him her badge and said, "What's your name?"

"Zack. I'm the bar manager." He reached back into his car and pulled out a second crate of records. "I'm surprised nobody contacted me. What took you so long?"

They watched him turn and head for the front door. Carrie picked up the crate resting on the hood and followed him. "I asked Darren, the owner, for a list of employees, but he couldn't give me anything."

"That makes sense," Zack said as they entered the bar. "We have a lot of turnover. People think it's going to be all glamour and sequins when they come here, but it's actually a lot of hard work."

"I'm sure," Carrie said.

A stage with a stripper pole dominated one end of the room, with large stacks of speakers on either side, used to pump pulsating dance music to the audience floor. Tall, winding staircases on either side of the room led up to the bar area, where people could talk and mingle, away from the crowd. The club was used on different nights for different styles of music and dance, with the occasional musical act performing. Mr. Darren was not particular about who leased his venue or what they used it for, as long as they paid.

Zack's arms and shoulders bulged against his skin-tight T-shirt as he leaned forward and said, "So, what did you want to ask me?"

"Did you know the man who got killed?" Carrie asked.

"No. I don't think anyone did. I saw his picture on

Facebook and we were all asking around, but no one knew who he was. He'd never been here before, that's for certain."

"Would you know that?" Rein asked.

"I've been running this club for three years and grew up in the scene," Zack said. "It's not like we're in the big city out here. It's a small group, and we stick together."

"How about anyone else that night who was new?"

"Our deejay brought a few friends in from New York, but they stayed and partied all night. Ran up a four-hundred-dollar tab and shorted me out of a tip. Can you believe it?"

"How about anyone that wasn't part of a group?"

Zack ran his fingers through his hair and looked up at the ceiling, concentrating. He snapped his fingers. "Yep, there was someone new that night. Real pretty blonde calling herself Dominique."

Rein cocked his head at Carrie, letting her know this part was important. She pulled out her notepad and pen and began writing. "White or black?"

"White. Definitely."

"About how old?"

"It was tough to say with all the makeup and the wig. Maybe in her thirties? Maybe not?"

Rein stopped him. "Listen, I hate to ask, I really do, but it's important. I'm not real clear on the right terminology for this, so forgive me if I sound stupid. When you say her, are you talking about someone born with a vagina or a penis?"

Zack's eyes fixed on Rein in irritation. "You really need to work on your understanding of gender and human sexuality. Especially with a beard like that."

Rein's face fell as he resisted the urge to glare at

Carrie, and said, "Can you help me out here? I need to be clear."

"I'm referring to a biological man, as in, born with a penis and testicles. Is that specific enough for you?"

"Yes, thanks," Rein said. "Can you tell us anything about Dominique?"

"She didn't stay long. Had one drink, then left. Seemed new to the whole thing. Not talkative or enjoying herself at all. I tried chatting her up, but she seemed to want to be left alone."

"Did she say anything? Anything at all?"

"She had an accent, I remember that," Zack said.

"What kind of accent?" Carrie said.

"Southern. Real thick, too. Like the kind that makes someone sound dumb, no matter how smart they are. I asked her where she was from, and she said somewhere in Louisiana."

Carrie looked at Rein. "And she just happens to be all the way up here and pops in at the local nightclub dressed to impress?"

"It's not that odd," Zack said. "We get businessmen in here every once in a while, finally far enough away from their families and friends that they can try a walk on the wild side."

Rein was deep in thought, arms folded and right fist pressed against his mouth. Whatever he was searching for, it wasn't coming.

"Well, anyway, it was real nice talking to you both," Zack said. "I hope you catch the person who did it. Everybody's scared it's homophobic hillbillies. I'll be shocked if anyone even shows up tonight."

As Zack went to leave, Rein said, "Where in Louisiana? Did he say?"

"Hodor," Zack replied. "No wait. That's from that show. Um, Horton, maybe?"

Rein looked stricken. His voice was grave as he said the word, "Houma."

Carrie found him in the parking lot outside, at the edge of the woods staring down at the parking space where they'd found the victim. The club's door shut behind her. She shoved her notepad and pen into her pocket as she jogged toward Rein. She winced at the stink of bleach still heavy in the air. The chemical had seeped into the ground behind the parking lot and cooked onto stones in the lot, trapping the copper stench of blood.

Rein did not move. The wind picked up, blowing gently against his beard and ruffling the short, shaggy locks of his hair. "Ronald Dominique," Rein said, staring into the woods. "From Houma, Louisiana."

"Who the hell is Ronald Dominique from Houma, Louisiana?"

"He killed twenty-three men. Men he met at gay bars, raped, and murdered. Bars just like this."

"Did he chop them into pieces, too?" Carrie asked.

"No. He strangled them," Rein said. "Which means something went very, very wrong that night for our killer to react the way he did. The victim must have forced him out of character."

"What character? What are you talking about?"

"That would explain why he struck so soon after this event," he said. "That was the part I couldn't reconcile. For an intricate planner, it didn't make sense to kill just a few days later."

"Would you stop babbling and tell me what's going on here!"

"You don't understand," he said, looking at her. For the first time, she saw fear creeping in at the edges of his eyes, and it turned her insides to water. "The phone call your first victim's mother got. The lamp, the stew, that's all Ed Gein. This victim, the club, the name, the biographical information he gave the bartender, that's all Ronald Dominique. Your friend, posed like Regina Kay Walters."

"What are you saying?" Carrie lost her footing backing away from Rein, feeling her knees loosen.

"After Robert Rhoades killed Regina, he dumped her body in a barn at an abandoned farm. That picture," he said.

The image of Molly backing away from the camera flashed in her mind, but she shook it off. "She's not dead. Fuck you, Rein! She's not dead."

He stood in the darkness, staring at her. "We need flashlights and a list of every farm that's up for sale within driving distance."

Tears spilled down her face as she spat at him, "She is not buried in some fucking barn!"

"Listen to me, goddamn it!" he shouted, grabbing her by both arms. "This bastard doesn't want to be a serial killer, do you understand? He wants to be *them*. He wants to be *all of them*, Carrie! There is only one monster standing at the top of that mountain, and we both know what his name is."

"Oh my God. He's going to imitate Krissing next."

"I think so," Rein said. "And right now, he has a child."

22

Bill Waylon woke up tired. that was nothing new. no matter what time he went to sleep, it was never enough. The sun was coming strong through the curtains and blinds, and there was movement and muffled conversation throughout the house, so he knew it wasn't one of the times when he'd woken up two hours before his alarm and would be able to go back to sleep. He'd slept as long as he'd meant to, and it still wasn't enough.

He stretched out in bed, groaning, feeling pops along his spine when he twisted his hips side to side. He lay there, cracking his joints, thinking about retirement. It was going to be lovely. First thing he was going to do was get rid of his alarm clock and never let another one into the bedroom, no matter what Jeri said. He'd spent his entire adult life needing to be places he did not necessarily want to be. Shifts that had to start on time, or he'd be disciplined. Court hearings that had to get under way on time, or he'd face contempt charges. Now it was meetings with council people and covering the goddamn school crossings, all of which had to be seen to on time, or else.

But not for long, he thought. When I retire, I'm

going to spend the rest of my life not having to be anywhere, or do anything, unless I absolutely feel like it.

He had the age and the pensions to do it. He'd
worked twelve years as a street cop before getting
bumped up to County Detective. Twelve years vested
him to receive a half pension. He worked another fifteen years at the County, which gave him the other
half. Once he started collecting his pension, he'd make
his whole salary sitting on his butt, doing nothing but
grilling burgers, drinking beers, and fishing.

It wasn't long after Rein went to prison that the
flame went out inside of Waylon. He wanted to retire.
To be done with it all. Hand the whole sloppy shit
sandwich over to the younger generation and let them
try to eat it. He told Jeri he was going to work in the
plumbing supply aisle of Home Depot and tell people
where the bathroom was. He could think of nothing
that would make him happier.

She told him if that's what he needed to do, she'd
stand by him. But then, in her gentle way, she reminded him that the girls needed braces still, and
braces cost a lot of money. So did cars and car insurance. And both of them were going to college, whether
they liked it or not.

That's when the mayor of Coyote Township called
him up, an old man whose voice creaked like a wooden
chest. "I knew your father, Bill. He always did the
right thing for us. I'm looking for a new chief, and I
was hoping you might come do the right thing for us
now."

The old man's political connections, bailing him out
one more time, Waylon figured.

Coyote was a small little town with small little town

problems. The cops there were slow and steady, like tortoises. Well, for the most part, he thought. All except Carrie. That kid was a race car, just dying for the chance to let out the throttle. A small-town PD was going to either sap the soul right out of her or drive her mental. He was glad she was getting the chance to dig into a large investigation. He wanted her to get a taste of the bigger picture, and he hoped the day came when she told him she was leaving for the FBI, or the attorney general's office, or even, god forbid, the County detectives.

Once this case of her missing dingbat best friend was settled, he intended on suggesting that Carrie move on in no uncertain terms.

She'd argue, of course. The girl was loyal to him, and he knew it. They had a kind of father–daughter bond, partly because she was only a few years older than his own daughters and partly because of the drunken sad sack she called Dad. He cared about her enough to force her to leave because it was good for her. Somehow, he'd find a way to make her understand that too.

It wouldn't be easy. As a man living in a house with three grown women, he knew what he was talking about.

Waylon knocked on the master bathroom door before opening it. Jeri was sitting on the toilet, flipping through a magazine.

"Hey," she said without looking up. Her red hair was pulled up in a makeshift bun, and her face was still pink from a vigorous scrubbing. She was about to turn fifty, but her legs were still shapely, despite the faint purple lines running up and down them.

"Good morning," he said, walking over to her.

He bent down to give her a kiss, and she pulled back. "I'm peeing."

"You even pee beautiful." He kissed her and started peeling off his T-shirt and boxer shorts. He turned on the water, reaching to feel if the spray was getting warmer. "You want to get in here with me?"

"I can't. I have to drive Kate to softball practice."

"Abby can't take her?"

"She has orientation. She wants to go drive around the campus to figure out what buildings her classes are in."

"Right," he said. He felt the water again and then slid inside, letting it run over the top of his head. "You sure you can't jump in just for a little bit?"

"Hang on, I need to flush."

He stepped out of the way, pressing his back against the wall as he heard the sound of the toilet flushing. The water splashing his feet turned ice cold for a minute, then warmed up again. The shower curtain parted, and Jeri stuck her face in. "Tell you what. Take us out to dinner tonight to celebrate Kate's big day tomorrow, and me and you can take a nice hot bubble bath together after we get home. How's that sound?"

Waylon reached for the soap. "Sounds like the perfect end to a long, long week."

He shaved in the shower, going up and down his neck and sides of his jaw, lifting up the corners of his dangling mustache. After the shower, he peered close to the mirror, making sure it was undamaged. It was still thick and bristling, even though it had more gray hair than black. He could no longer see his upper lip and was tired of tasting his breakfast all the way up to dinnertime. He took a pair of scissors out of the mirror and began trimming. Drawers were opening and shutting inside the bedroom, with the sound of hangers scraping across the closet's metal bar. "Hey, honey?"

"What?"

"Sam Elliott in *Tombstone* or Sam Elliott in *Mask*?"

"Which one was *Mask*?" Jeri asked.

"The one with Cher and the kid with the messed-up face. Mideighties."

"Which one's more bushy?"

"*Tombstone*, definitely."

"I always did like Cher," she said.

Waylon chuckled and leaned closer, snipping the scissors as he went.

The girls were sitting at the table by the time he went downstairs. Jeri had heard him coming and started pouring already, setting a large, steaming mug at the head of the table, almost white with milk and sugar. Perfect.

He kissed his younger one, Kate, on the top of her head while she munched cereal. "Morning, Dad."

"Hey, babycakes." He crossed toward the older one, holding his arms wide. "There she is. My big girl, all grown up." Abby stood up and hugged him, and he kissed her on top of the head too, smelling how clean and fresh it was. He stepped back and looked at her, knowing it made her embarrassed, but he smiled anyway through his thick mustache. "First day of college tomorrow. I can't believe how beautiful you are."

"Dad," she rolled her eyes.

He bent his head toward her, making her look back at him. "But you know what I always tell you, beauty is only skin deep. It's a lot more important to be smart and brave and good. You're all those things, and I know it. So you go to that school and you get as much out of it as you possibly can. This is the whole foundation for the rest of your life, and I know, I just *know*, you are going to do great things."

"Thanks, Daddy," she said, hugging him again.

He patted her on the back and said, "Most important, if a boy says he wants to show you something in the planetarium after hours, you run like hell."

Jeri laughed from the stove. "Ain't that the truth!" Then she added, "Of course, in our case it was a hay barn, and if it wasn't for that conversation, Abby wouldn't be here right now."

"Ew!" both girls said at once. Waylon laughed, crossing toward Jeri and putting his hands on either side of her waist. He leaned close to her ear. "As I recall, it was your idea to visit the overhead loft at the barn that day." Dozens of pancakes sizzled on the griddle, and she'd stacked bacon and sausage across the entire upper row. It smelled intoxicating. "What happened to you all going vegan?" he asked.

"We didn't go vegan." Jeri laughed. "We went pollotarian."

"What's the difference?"

"We can eat chicken," Kate said.

He pointed at the bacon and sausage. "That doesn't look like chicken."

"Shush, it's a cheat day," Jeri said.

"Pollotarian, huh?" he said, taking his seat at the table. "And here I thought we were Presbyterian."

Abby rolled her eyes. "Do they give you a Dad joke instruction manual when your first child is born, or does it just come natural?"

"It's more like a defense mechanism one develops

when you're outnumbered three to one in your own house." He raised his coffee cup in salute. "If I didn't laugh, I'd cry."

The first chords of Waylon's cellphone's ringtone erupted from the foyer. Waylon slumped forward and groaned. "What the heck now?"

"I don't know, but make it fast. We are eating together as a family after I made all this food," Jeri said, waving her spatula at him.

"All right, all right," he said. "Give me one second."

He entered the foyer as the phone pulsated on the cabinet. He muttered he was coming as he lifted the screen and saw it was Carrie calling.

"Hey, kiddo. You got good news for me?"

Instead he heard Rein's voice saying, "Bill. We found something."

Ten minutes later, Waylon was in the car, the phone docked on his dashboard. "The Baylor Farm, do you remember it?" Rein said.

"I think so," Waylon said, stepping on the gas, grabbing the steering wheel with one hand while holding a half-finished pancake and his phone in the other.

"The kid who shot his grandparents with the twelve-gauge? Eyeball stuck to the curtain?"

"I remember," Waylon said. "Off Route 129?"

"Yes."

He turned sharp at the corner, taking a different street, a faster one that would get him closer to the on-ramp. "What makes you think that's the one?"

"It matches the background in the picture. Farm's up for sale. Abandoned. This is the one," Rein said.

"Did you start looking yet?"

"No. I wanted to wait for you. Bill, you'll need a crime scene unit. Someone good."

"You're sure about this? Absolutely sure we have a body there?"

"I wouldn't let her look, but something is dead here. Lots of crows in the area, and it has the right smell."

"Shit." Waylon sighed. "How's Carrie?"

"Freaking out. We found a crate in the back part of the barn, piled over with rotten hay. A lot of insect activity around whatever's inside there. That's where we need to start. There's death in here, Bill. I knew it the second we walked inside. Pretty sure she knows it too."

"God-fucking-damn it! What about the baby?"

"Not sure. There's always a chance he buried the child with the mother, but I doubt it. He's reenacting famous killers, Bill. Trying on their methodologies to see how they feel before he finds his own. He won't give up that child, not yet."

"Why not?" Waylon asked. But even as did so, the image of a dead child bound in chains flashed before his eyes, a dark basement with bloody pieces of a little girl's dress. The screams he'd been trying to forget for all those years. "Disregard," Waylon said. "I understand."

"Can you get Eddie Schikel up here?"

"I can call him."

"Tell him to hurry."

Waylon could see Carrie's car parked near the barn and the two of them circling around the entrance. Rein barred Carrie's way, looking like the free safety on a football team, moving as Carrie moved, cutting off her plan of attack. Her fists were clenched as she glared at the barn, looking for any excuse to run in there and tear the place to pieces. Rein was talking her down, saying, "If it's true, we will need all the evidence we can find. Use your head, Carrie."

"Fuck you!"

"Look," he said, pointing toward the Waylon's car. "Bill is here."

She looked over her shoulder, eyes red and broken by thick veins. They'd been searching barns all night until they'd found this one. She was fueled by pure rage, huffing like a wild beast, eyes fixed on Waylon but not actually seeing him as he parked the car and got out.

"I don't care!" she shouted. "Get out of my way."

"Hang on," Waylon said. "What's going on here?"

"She's in there, Bill!" Carrie snapped. "She's in that goddamn crate and this motherfucker won't let me see her."

"If she is, you don't want to, kiddo," Waylon said.

"No, Bill. That's my fucking right, you understand?" Her voice broke, cracking high like a piece of dry timber. "It is my *right*."

"You're not going in there," he said.

"Who the fuck are you to say that to me?"

He leapt forward. "Officer Santero! I am the chief of police in this jurisdiction and I'm declaring this a crime scene. You will stand down or you will be removed, am I clear?"

Carrie's jaw quivered. "Sir, yes, sir," she said, jaw clenched.

"Secure the outer perimeter and begin a crime scene log," he said, looking at his watch. "Oh eight fifteen hundred hours, Chief Waylon arrived on scene. No one in or out unless I authorize it, is that clear?"

He waited for her to remove her notepad and begin to write, then headed back to his car, popping the trunk from the key fob in his pocket. He grabbed a camera and a box of gloves, carrying both over to where Rein was standing and dropping them at his feet. "Glove up, and get me pictures of the scene before we go in," he said.

"Sir, yes, sir," Rein repeated as he reached for the gloves.

"Don't give me that look. She needed that."

Rein tugged the gloves over his fingers, glancing back at Carrie, who was now pacing. "Is that what she needed?"

"You ever deal with military people when you were on the street? They'd be ready to fight you over nothing, but the second you bark at them all they see is a drill sergeant. It's a mental realignment."

"She's going through something neither of us ever went through," Rein said as he raised the camera and peered through the eyehole. "You can't realign that."

"Well, I need her to be a cop right now, not a basket case."

Rein snapped off a series of pictures and said, "This must be something only bosses know about, Bill. How to mindfuck your people in ten easy steps."

"You don't talk this way around her, do you? Is that where she picked up all this cussing all of a sudden?"

"You're not her father, Bill. Stop coddling her. It isn't helping."

Waylon checked to make sure Carrie was not standing nearby and leaned close to Rein. "Like you're one to talk. I've watched you mindfuck more people than I can count. If there's a mindfucking hall of fame, you're the all-time champion."

"Only the bad people, Bill." Rein set the camera down and said, "Well, and bosses, too. But I guess that's kind of redundant."

Waylon headed for the barn, then stopped and waved for him to follow. "Well? What are you waiting for?"

"How are you going to justify taking a civilian in there? A convicted felon."

"By not giving a damn what anyone else thinks. You coming or not?"

Light poured through the torn-down slats of the barn, a shambling wreck of rotted wood and loosely assembled beams. The door hung sideways on bent, rusted hinges, and it screeched as Waylon pulled it open. Rein leaned inside the door and snapped several more pictures, all directed toward the crate and the pile of hay in the rear corner.

The barn's floor was nothing more than rows of disjointed beams, and most of the far wall had broken away, leaving a clear view of the green fields beyond. The girl had been standing right there in the picture, Waylon thought. This is the place.

A cloud of flies filled the space between the floor and the exposed beams, the sections of sky covered by black, buzzing insects.

Both men moved toward the crate.

They cleared away the blackened hay straw piled higher than their waists on top of the crate, grabbing it with both hands and tossing it onto the floor. Both of them squirmed and clenched their eyes as they invaded the vortex of flies, waving them out of the way with their hands. In the straw gathered around the crate and going up the sides of the crate, dozens of maggots quivered. Rein pointed down at them and looked at Waylon, both of them knowing what it meant.

The crate had no lid. It was just straw piled on top of straw as they worked to clear it, knocking it away, getting closer and closer to the crate beneath. Waylon's hand brushed against something cold and stiff and he stopped. It was the unmistakable feel of dead flesh.

He looked down between the straw and saw the length of a young woman's leg, her skin blue, dotted with tiny hair follicles. He swept away the straw covering her legs, exposing her high-heeled shoes, and looked up at Rein, making sure he saw.

Rein paused over the head of the crate and brushed aside the remaining wet straw, uncovering the strands of long blond hair and the bloated face of the young woman below. They recognized her from the photograph.

Waylon lowered his head. "God-fucking-damn it."

Molly's eyes were wide and swollen. The deeply imprinted rings around her throat were molded into her skin. Rein bent close to the body, running the tip of his finger along the grooves in the ligature marks, feeling for any signs of the instrument of strangulation.

"Anything?" Waylon asked.

Rein shook his head. The skin was too deteriorated to tell if the killer had used a belt or rope or wire. All that remained were the ringed grooves around her neck. He plied her stiff fingers up to check under her nails, hoping to see dried blood beneath them, that maybe she'd managed to scratch and claw her killer before he took her life. He saw nothing but dirt and tiny maggot eggs there.

Where was the child when her mother was dying,

Rein wondered. Did the killer keep her in his car, telling her they'd be right back? Did he have her tied up in his house? Did he make the little girl stand there and watch her mother die?

Waylon tapped him on the arm and waved him toward the door, telling him to come on. Rein let go of Molly's hands and followed him, waiting until they were clear of the flies. "She's been here at least a few days. The cold weather kept her preserved pretty well, but he killed her right after he took the picture."

"Eddie Schikel should be here any minute. I want him to work the scene as best he can. No need to disturb anything else," Waylon said.

They could see Carrie standing on the opposite side of the barn, staring at them through the broken boards, barely restraining herself from running in after them.

"So much for epiphanies," Rein muttered. "Do you want me to talk to her? You were always terrible at death notifications."

"I'll do it," Waylon said, making his way for the barn door. "About time I stopped coddling her, right?"

Rein unsnapped the gloves from his hands as Waylon pushed the door open, filling the barn with the sound of creaking hinges. He turned around and looked at the open crate, seeing the dead young woman inside, her arms and legs constricted to make her fit inside the box. The killer had not posed her, or mutilated her remains, or taken any sexual indulgences with the body afterward. He'd simply dumped her where no one would see her and covered her with rotting straw.

Waylon had both his hands on Carrie's shoulders then, telling her what they'd found. She collapsed on her knees in the grass, face buried in her hands, and

Waylon moved to drape his arm around her shoulders, staying close. Carrie's face emerged purple with fury as she raised it to the skies and screamed and screamed until there was nothing else but the sound of her screaming.

But the silence of the heavens is infinite and absolute.

III
THE HOT GATES

23

The sky was dark, each cloud swollen and heavy. their ominous shapes hung low on the horizon like an invading armada, big enough to consume the crops and livestock and people. All the people, Rein thought. It was late in the afternoon. He'd wanted to wait until the last faint flickers of orange and red vanished over the tree line before getting out, but the darkness had set in too quickly.

Rein stroked the daisies resting on his lap as he sat in his car, running his thumb through their soft white petals but careful not to break any off. The cemetery had emptied out for fear of rain. Gone now were the joggers and women pushing baby carriages throughout its winding lanes, ignoring the piles of bones rotting nearby under their dull brass markers.

In the rear of the cemetery stood the mausoleums, most of them crumbling, monuments erected long ago to people no one remembered. He strummed the daisies, pondering the hubris of it all. Families wealthy enough to hire expert masons, instructing them to build a tall, solid structure worthy of the dead person's memory. Something that would last. Well, now it was just an old building, he thought. The person inside had long ago turned to dust and their descendants, if they hadn't been wiped out by flood or famine or disease, had gone from this place.

Time moves on, he thought. That's what it does. It's a river, flowing from beginning to end with such force that it will take you under in seconds and pop you back up someplace completely different if you let it. Time the merciless. Time the nonnegotiable.

He bent forward over his steering wheel, searching for signs of movement, seeing none, but deciding to give it a few more minutes. For each of us, he thought, each of them, even all the ones buried under the ground, our brief moment in time is a fixed position. Our entire concept of reality is rooted in petty conflicts and loves and disappointments that matter less than a pile of earthworms when you go into the ground. Emperors, striving to conquer more and more pieces of dirt and stone. Kings, looking to use one tribe of hairless apes to conquer another. Corporate executives wasting their fleeting lives by grabbing as much of the meaningless and futile as they can. All of them destined for the same fate as the poorest degenerate or hopeless drug addict.

The cemetery had been founded in the 1800s, and life was still much the same as it was then. For all our technology, the world is still run by the barbaric and the wealthy, and everyone else gets ground up as food for the machine. It's probably been that way since the first organisms squiggled their way out of earth's muddy puddles. One struggled. One lived in constant fear of being eaten, or murdered, or left behind by the tribe, until one of those things eventually happened. All individual life was fleeting, futile, and then it was over. The only good thing about it, he thought, at least once you were finished with it, you never had to do it again.

All of our good, all of our bad, it all winds up deep in the ground as food for the worms.

He got out of the car, holding the flowers close to his chest as he looked around once more, checking the trails and valleys around him. Nothing but dried leaves scraping against the stones and wind on the grass.

The path toward her grave was well worn. Many feet had scaled the hill from the road leading up to that grave, leaving the grass flat and smooth and bare. Rein looked around again, making sure he was alone as he approached the brass marker. He dropped to one knee and laid the flowers under her nameplate, running his fingers over its letters, and closed his eyes. He had never seen her in life. Not even at the accident scene. He'd been taken away by the police before the rescue team could cut her out of the car.

He'd seen pictures of her, though. Multiple pictures in the newspapers next to his photograph, sometimes from the Krissing hearings, sometimes his arrest mugshot. All of it tied together, as if she was just another victim of just another monster. She was not just another victim, though, and he knew it. She was a living, laughing, bright, and beautiful child who deserved more.

His first thought, long before he was found guilty, was of killing himself. He was going to walk out into the woods and stick the barrel into his mouth and pull the trigger. To trade his life for hers. But he knew that was the coward's way. He knew everyone would say he'd chosen an easy death over going to prison and living with what he'd done. They would have been right.

So, prison then. He pled guilty and refused to even let his defense attorneys enter his police service record into the proceedings.

"I go in tomorrow," he told the grass and the brass placard and to the tiny coffin far below filled with the corpse of a child, none of which could hear him, he knew, but said it aloud anyway. "I just wanted to stop by one last time."

A man's voice shot out from across the hill, so loud and angry it startled him, "Hey! Hey, get the hell away from her!"

Rein looked up at the two figures coming toward him fast. He could see only their outlines in the dark— a man and a woman—but he knew immediately who they were. He stumbled back from the grave.

"You get the hell away from her, you son of a bitch!"

"I wasn't—" Rein tried to say.

The woman shouted at him then, her voice constricted like someone was clenching her throat. "You do not *have the right* to see her. Do you understand me?"

The man's fists were balled as if he meant to fight. Rein backed away even farther, saying, "I didn't mean to cause any problems. I understand."

Spittle flew through her clenched teeth. "You do not *ever come back here.* Ever!"

"All right." Rein swallowed anything else he had to say and turned away from the grave, starting back for his car.

He heard the whisper of flower petals soft against the brass engraving of a little girl's name, and the rustle of wind as the bouquet came hurling after him. "Stop coming here, Rein," the man shouted after him.

"Stop bringing her flowers. You think she needs your flowers now? You think they mean anything?"

Rein scooped up the flowers and kept moving, his gain stiff and awkward. His hands dripped wet from the crushed stems, and the parents were still shouting at him, telling him to get away from there, to never disgrace that sacred place again.

He ran for his car door, desperate to get away. His hands trembled as he fumbled with his keys at the lock, trying to get in. The father was running down the path, chasing after him, his face filled with open rage as Rein struggled to get the key into the lock, but it was closed up tight. The slot was gone, leaving nothing but solid metal. He slammed the key against it again and again, trying to force it into the slot. When he looked up, he saw the father was not alone.

The little girl was coming down the hill now, covered in dirt, spilling worms and bugs as she staggered toward his car. "No," Rein moaned. "Please, no."

He felt the car rock and looked up to see that the dead were surrounding him on all sides. They'd filled in the road on both sides, a horde of dead children and murdered housewives and men he'd accused of crimes who shot themselves before going to jail. He spun around in horror as they came for him, calling his name.

"Rein?"

His head jerked around as he searched for the approaching figures, seeing nothing in the darkness except the dim numbers on the cable box. He let out a deep breath and leaned back against Carrie's couch, feeling the fabric behind him, damp with sweat. He'd slept for four hours after being awake for almost two days straight. He could have worked longer, but Waylon ordered Carrie to leave the crime scene and not return until eight the next morning. She'd told him to go fuck himself.

"You both found the body," Waylon had said. "That's all anyone could have expected from you. Me and Eddie will process the scene."

"Go fuck yourself," she'd said.

"Carrie, do you really want to see her like this?" Rein had said. "If you do this, you're going to regret it. You have memories of her where she is happy and smiling, and those are going to be the things you cling to for a long time to come. She wouldn't want you to remember her like this."

What about Nubs? A thousand questions died in her throat. Things she couldn't bring herself to say. Is Nubs buried in there too? Or somewhere nearby? Why did he take her? What is he doing to her? Why didn't I believe Molly? Why did this happen? Oh my God. How the hell did something like this happen and I didn't even believe her?

"We will turn over every rock in this place for any sign of the little girl," Waylon had said. "Listen to me, kiddo. I need you fresh and I need you rested so you can both get back into this fight as soon as possible. You stay awake too long, you will start hallucinating. You want to find Nubs and get the bastard who did this? Go home, get some rest, and be ready to work tomorrow morning."

"I have to go tell Penny. Someone has to go tell her that her daughter is dead."

"Someone will. But it won't be you, kiddo. Go home."

"Jacob?" Carrie called out from the bedroom, her voice soft in the darkness.

"Coming," he said, struggling to get up from the cushions. He stumbled around the side of the couch in the dark, feeling his way down her hallway toward the bedroom's open door.

"You were talking," she said. "Did Bill call? Did they find something?"

"No, I'm sorry," he said. "I was talking to myself. Go back to sleep."

"It sounded like you were upset. Were you dreaming?"

"No. It was nothing."

"It woke me up."

"I won't do it again."

He could see the lights of her eyes staring at him through the darkness. Her voice was hollowed out, like the dry husk of cicada after it abandons itself. Something inside of her had left, and neither of them were sure it would ever return. "If I asked you to sleep in here, would you do it?"

"No."

"Why not?"

"It wouldn't be right."

"Rein?"

"Yes?"

"I don't want to be by myself right now. Come on."

Her fingers brushed against his hand and wrapped around it, pulling him toward her. He resisted as long as he could, but she would not release him, dragging him toward the bed and then down on top of it. She slid sideways to make room, pulling the covers back. "When's the last time you slept in a real bed?"

"The night before I went to prison."

"How does it feel?"

He stretched out under the covers and maneuvered

the pillow under his head, feeling it curve ever so per-fectly. "You know how a domesticated animal some-times gets loose and goes out into the wild? You have to find it in time or else it can never come back home. Once it's been away from its family and home for too long, it turns. It changes. It doesn't belong around peo-ple anymore."

She turned away from him, pressing her back to him and settling in. She grabbed his hand and pulled it across her chest, then cupped it around her left breast and held it there. Rein tried to pull away when he real-ized what she'd done, but she would not let him. "Keep your hand there. I want to feel it over my heart," she said. "I need to thank you."

"For what?"

"In all this time, you never lied to me. You never said we'd find them. You never said this would all be okay. Even when I was stupidly telling myself it would all be. I get it now. It was all a big lie, and I told it to myself. Molly was dead the whole time, and you knew not to get my hopes up. I guess tomorrow we'll keep looking, and the day after that, and do the best we can. That's all we can do." Rein listened to her breathing slow and settle, her legs twitching gently as she de-scended into sleep.

He'd learned early on that there was no use in faith. If prayers worked, he often thought, no child would ever die of cancer.

There was no such thing as good luck or bad luck. No such thing as destiny, no such thing as karma. There was only chaos. Complete random chance, born of a universe that was devoid of any interest in the tiny, tiny people of a lowly planet inhabiting one of its end-less supply of solar systems. Here we are, stuffed in the back pocket of a meaningless galaxy, surrounded by the endless expanse of infinite, cold space. Humanity is less significant to the cosmos than ants are to us, he thought. Less significant than a single amoeba. The only reliable thing in all of existence is entropy. Everything, no matter how beautiful or unique or well loved, is constantly dying, always decaying, and eventually reduces to dust.

He'd learned it all a long time ago, accepted it as fact, and moved on. That understanding had guided him throughout his entire career. Shielded him from emotional injury. It had also numbed him inside and cut him off from any true feelings. It had cost him his wife and an adult relationship with his son.

Rein looked down at Carrie. She'd found him in the wasteland. He'd been wandering the barren desert of his own life for years until she'd convinced Bill Waylon to come for him. In return, he'd escorted her to the brink of the void, watching as she accepted it and let it crawl within her. Soon, it would begin to dissolve her own light.

Unless you find the child, he thought. Maybe if the little girl could be found, it might yank Carrie back hard enough to free her.

And if the child could be saved, if Nubs could be wrenched from the gnashing teeth of the void before it snuffed out her light, he thought, what then? Was it possible it might lead him away from the nightmares as well? After all this time, was it even possible to be set free?

Memories of the little girl he'd killed washed over him. The way her father screamed flowed through his being like toxic bilge water. He could still smell the scent of her blood in the cool night air. It was mixed with the sweet stench of radiator fluid and stinking burnt rubber. He thought of Emily Cross and knew that the answer was, and always would be, no. Of course not. Redemption is an impossibility, he thought. There is no such thing.

Images from the farm flickered like old film reels across his mind, showing him Molly's body again and again. Where had the little girl been when her mother was killed? The Omnikiller had likely sent her away. He'd told her to go play and Mommy would be fine. Then he'd told Molly to put on the dress and pose for the picture and everything would be fine. Then he'd told her to do all of his filthy little acts and the child would be fine, and if she didn't the child would do them instead.

Rein wondered what the man had told Nubs when she asked where her mother had gone. "She left you with me," he'd probably said. "She didn't want you anymore." Then he'd held out his hand and led her into the void.

He closed his eyes and lowered his head next to Carrie's, breathing her in, feeling her heart beating inside her breast. He fell asleep searching for a place of solace, knowing it could not be found, and went down toward the dead and the dark that awaited.

24

Morning found them entangled. legs wrapped together, bound up in sheets, arms numb from being buried under each other's bodies. Rein's eyes opened at the soft vibration of the phone on the nightstand. "Carrie?"

She pushed him away, rolling into a tight ball, and clenching the blankets up to her face.

"Your phone," he said. He slid his arm out from beneath her and propped himself up, seeing *Chief Waylon* appear on the screen. "It's Bill," he said, prodding her. He reached over her for the phone. "You need to take this. It could be important."

"Hello?" Waylon's voice on the other end said, the phone answering on its own.

Rein looked at the phone in confusion, unsure of what he'd touched to turn it on or how to turn it back off. "Carrie?" Waylon said. "It's the chief. Are you there?"

"It's Bill," Rein whispered urgently. "Take the phone!"

"Who the hell is this?" Waylon said. He inhaled

sharply, and his voice dropped to a menacing grumble. "Son of a bitch. Is that you, Jacob?"

"Uh," Rein said, pressing the phone to his ear. "This isn't what it sounds like, Bill."

"What the hell is wrong with you? I sent you back with her to make sure she got some damn rest."

"That's what I did."

"You listen to me and you listen good, Jacob. I've overlooked a lot of shit over the years with you, and I stayed your friend when a whole lot of other people threw you to the wolves."

"I know you did."

"That girl is like a daughter to me. You got it?"

He looked down and saw her staring up at him, wide-eyed. "I got it," he said. "Nothing happened. I promise."

"It better not have. Put her on the phone."

Carrie took the phone, glaring at Rein, silently mouthing, *Why the hell did you pick up?* "Hi, chief," she said. "Any word on Nubs?"

"No, but I've got good news and bad news. Good news is, once word got out we had a dead body, I was up to my behind in people willing to help. Bad news is what kind of help we found. I need you both at the district attorney's office in one hour."

Carrie's eyes slid sideways toward Rein, to see if he'd overheard. "Are you sure about that, sir?"

"Hell, no, I'm not sure. He's not going to like it one bit, either. But I need you both here so we can explain to these idiots what's going on. One hour," he said, and the line went dead.

She put the phone down and drew up her knees to her chin, resting her face in the thick blanket. "He said—" she began.

Rein cut her off. "I heard."

He pushed up from her bed, groaning as he stood. His body ached from sleeping in such unfamiliar comfort. His joints cracked as he stretched out his arms and twisted his back. "This appointment's been penciled in since the day you found me."

Vieira County Courthouse was the same as he remembered. Ugly brown panels stretching up and down the length of it, an idea someone thought looked current when it was built in the seventies. A long line formed on the right of lawyers and witnesses and jury officials waiting to pass through the metal detector. A large sign hanging on the wall near the entrance read ALL VISITORS SUBJECT TO SEARCH.

Two bored-looking women in cheaply made blazers worked the metal detector, with a court security officer sitting at his desk far behind them, arms folded over his bulging stomach, eyeing the people being allowed through. Rein could not see the front of the man's gun belt beneath his stomach's overhang. People dropped watches and keys and wallets into a plastic bin held by one of the women and were waved through the metal detector by the other.

Carrie left him in that line and went to the other side of the security desk, greeting the fat guard. "Officer Santero," she said. "I'm armed."

"Do you have your ID?" he asked.

She held her wallet open for the guard, who had to bend forward in his seat to see it. "I'll need you to sign in," he said. He opened up one of the lockboxes behind his desk and wrote down the number next to her name.

"I'll need all your weapons. Taser. Knife. Bazooka. Rocket launcher," he said, laughing at his own joke.

Carrie came around the side of the desk, drew her gun from its holster, and slid it inside the lockbox, waiting for the guard to seal it and hand her the key. "Don't lose this now," he said.

"I won't."

Rein's turn came. He drew out the folded metal blade with the curved handle and dropped it into the bin. "What is that thing?" one of the women asked. "Some kind of box cutter?"

"It's for work," Rein said.

"Well, you can't bring that in here."

"I know. That's why I put it in the bin."

"But you can't bring that in here."

"So how about you hold on to it here for me?"

The fat guard was coming forward then, wheezing as his gut swung with each movement. "What's the problem here?" he said.

"No problem," Rein said, holding up his hands. "I just want to know if you can keep this for me."

The guard looked down. "What the hell is that?"

"Some kind of box cutter," the woman said.

The guard picked up the blade and snapped it out, staring at its deadly curve. "Be careful with that," Rein said. "It's extremely sharp."

"He's with me, sir," Carrie called out, coming around the guard's side. "Can you just lock it up with my gun? We have to get to the DA's office."

The guard fumbled with the blade, trying to get it shut. Rein closed his eyes, waiting to hear the man shriek in pain as he severed his finger. Instead he gave up and handed it to Carrie, blade extended, and said, "Get that thing away from me."

"Here, let me close it," Rein said, trying to take it from her, but she worked the lock and snapped it back into place in one easy motion.

He passed through the metal detector silently and headed for the elevator, scowling as he pushed the up button, waiting for her to catch up to him. "What's the matter with you?" Carrie said.

"Since when do they make cops surrender their weapons to come in the courthouse?"

"Since before I started," Carrie said. "It's something the judges decided as part of a new safety program. Courthouse security and sheriffs are the only ones who get to carry guns."

"That's just perfect. So when a maniac comes through here with a machine gun, the real cops will be defenseless, but that's okay because the security guards will handle it," Rein said. "I can't wait to hear how *that* turns out."

The elevator door opened, crowded with people, and they both stepped in. "Fourth floor, please," Carrie said to the man nearest the button.

"This place is a joke. Always has been, always will be," Rein muttered. "A group of clueless pencil-pushers choosing the illusion of safety over cold reality."

"There you go. That's the right attitude to have before our meeting," she said. "Do you mind not dumping your personal issues on me right now? I had kind of a rough day yesterday."

He looked up at the numbers, shifting aside as the doors opened and people maneuvered around him to get on and off. At the fourth floor, the bell rang and the doors began to slide open. "I guess I'm a little uncomfortable being here, is all," he said.

They started for the DA's office and she said, "It's

not like I'm really looking forward to talking about my dead friend."

The office had not changed in the years since he'd been there. Heavy carts stacked high with papers and case folders were parked outside of the small offices housing two assistant district attorneys each. They sat back to back, so cramped that one had to tell the other when they were getting out of their seats to let the other one through. Interns and secretaries hurried through the narrow corridors and in between the rows of cubicle dividers, and unattended phones rang on every desk. Rein did not recognize anyone, and no one looked at him.

"I guess we're in the conference room," Carrie said, looking around.

She turned, and he followed her down the next hallway. They passed no offices until the end, where a single door opened into a large, windowless meeting room. Carrie entered first, seeing Bill Waylon seated at one end of the table and Harv Bender at the other. Waylon had her case file open, with the crime scene photographs and reports assembled in front of him. The first photograph on top was Molly, packaged inside the crate, still dressed in the shoes and dress the killer had forced her into. Waylon immediately tried covering the photograph with his arm, but it was too late. Carrie forced herself to look away and focus instead on the men sitting around the table, seeing who she recognized.

A half-dozen men in shabby-looking suits filled in the seats along the table between them. County detectives and deputy district attorneys, playing with their phones or reading the newspaper. They looked up at her as she entered, and Bender leered at her. "There she is. I'm sorry to hear about your friend, hon. That really sucks." His voice fell away as Rein came in behind her.

Waylon rapped his knuckles against the table and said, "All right, everyone. This is Carrie Santero. She's my lead investigator on the homicides." He looked down at his file, adding, "And I'm sure you all remember Jacob."

A few murmurs came from the others. Rein greeted them silently, trying to remain out of the way, but Bender called out, "The work release program at the prison has sure made progress, hasn't it?" He waved his hand and laughed. "I'm kidding. It's good to see you, Rein."

"Thanks, Harv," Rein said.

"So Bill was just telling us about this new serial killer theory," Bender said, pointing at Waylon. "I guess we're all starting to see where he got that idea."

"I asked Jacob to be here so he could explain it to you all," Waylon said. "I want you to listen to him."

"Sure," Bender said, smiling. "We'd love to hear all about it. Please, tell us how the homosexual victim at the nightclub and the young woman in the barn were both killed by the same person. I'm dying to know." A few stunted laughs and hushed comments came from around the table. Bender said, "I'm serious. Please tell us how this is not just two separate events, with two totally unrelated victim types."

All of the faces were turned toward him. Rein swallowed. "We're dealing with something called an omnikiller." He waited, looking around at them to see if the word meant anything to any of them. It didn't. Carrie stared at him, willing him to go on. "A killer who has no victim type," Rein said. "He's reenacting famous events from the past. Using their methodology, their fetishes. He's probably been doing it for a while, but no one caught on."

"Because the Great Detective wasn't here to show us all the way," Bender said.

"Because the victims are so completely different," Rein replied. "Look, this isn't about me. There is a missing child, and if we don't act fast she's going to suffer in ways none of us can fathom."

"A little girl, you say?" Bender said, eyes digging into Rein.

"Yes."

"Well, I'm sure I speak for everyone when I say that none of us can stand anyone who'd hurt a little girl. In fact, I'm pretty sure I speak for every single person in this office when I say that any piece of shit who kills, or even harms, a defenseless little girl is the worst piece of shit on the planet. Actually, I'd consider it a disgrace if such a piece of shit ever came into this office and tried to pass himself off as something he isn't."

"That's enough," Waylon said.

"Oh, I agree," Bender said. "Now, let me be real, real clear about this so there's no mistake. We will be conducting the follow-ups on both homicides from here on out, given that you've completely lost scope of these investigations and bought into some fairy tale concocted by a megalomaniac who thinks that by getting his name back in the papers, the public might forget what he did. But I've got news for you, Jacob. No one will forget what you did. Now get the fuck out of this building. You're a disgrace to everything it stands for."

Rein stood fixed in place, hands at his sides, eyes locked with Bender. Then his head twitched and he relaxed, keeping his voice low and even as he said, "You're right. Good luck and I hope you get the guy." As he turned to leave, Carrie reached for him, but he kept walking.

He went down the elevator, shutting out the people around him. Lawyers talking to clients about plea agreements they should make. Fathers telling their sons to tuck in their pants before they went in to see the judge. Behind him, two uniformed police officers talking about how much overtime they were making to stand around at court that day. He shut each of them out, one by one, closing the doors on their conversations and closing the doors within himself to the places that cared.

He walked through the courthouse lobby, steering clear of the security guards and the lockboxes. He'd leave it for Carrie. It did not matter. He told himself he would close all of the doors.

All of the darkest ones he'd unlocked, journeying down into the depths of his psyche with the child rapists and teenaged killers. All of the ones that helped him connect with the haunted spirits of the people he needed to make confess. He would close all of those doors first, sealing them off, and then he would close the rest.

The ones that let him feel anything at all.

Cars passed by him on the street, filled with people focused on getting to work, waiting to see if their checks cleared, wondering who their husbands were screwing, worried about medical test results, none of them concerned about killers or the killers' victims. Bodies could be decomposing in the windows of every building they drove past and none of those people would have noticed. He craved that oblivion. He'd sought it all that time he was pushing lawn mowers and cutting up logs, but something had always dragged him back toward the past. Something inside of him would not surrender, no matter how much he begged.

No longer, he thought, walking down the street, watching the cars, deciding he would be like these people from now on. He'd learned his lesson. There is no redemption. There is no going back. Once you have left the garden, there is only the wasteland, and it is a place without allegiance to anything you've left behind.

He has taken a child. Her name is Natalie. They call her Nubs.

(I don't care.)

Another sweet, beautiful child who deserves to live.

(It's someone else's job now.)

You're already responsible for the death of one little girl. Wasn't that enough?

He pictured Carrie's face when Waylon told her about Molly. Watched her fall to her knees screaming, the lines of spittle connecting her teeth, the inhuman howls of anguish. He'd heard them before from too many parents, too many husbands, too many children who would never see their mothers again. The screaming would not stop. Ever. The killings would not stop, ever.

"It's finished," he said aloud. "I'm finished."

What about the girl? You've given her enough that she could begin tracking down the suspects. She might find him.

(Bill will watch over her. He won't let her go alone.)

She won't wait for Bill. You know she won't. She'll rush in at the first hint of finding the little girl, and the killer will take her, too. But he'll do it slow. So slow. His fury at the nightclub will pale in comparison to what he does when she invades his den. He'll make her watch as he kills Nubs. He'll make her watch, and participate, and eat the child's cooked organs. Anything to make the horror stop. Anything to get him to turn off the blowtorch and pull out the nails and let go of the pliers ripping off chunks of her flesh. He will make her—

Rein gasped, unable to breathe. He clenched his eyes shut and bent forward, gulping at the air that would not go into his lungs. Images flashed that he could not escape, crimson-soaked bodies and wide-eyed children staring lifelessly at the ceiling, but this time he was speeding down the highway at eleven o'clock at night. This time he was feeling the warmth of alcohol coursing through his system. This time he was desperate to get home and turn on all the lights in his apartment to shut out the darkness, to spend the rest of the night sitting in his living room, clutching the sides of his chair, terrified of falling asleep.

He clenched his eyes shut, trying to shut out the images, gritting his teeth and whipping his head side to side trying to shake them loose. He never saw the car coming toward him at the intersection. Nothing before the screech of tire rubber against the road, and a sudden, deafening impact.

Metal crumpled under metal, whipping him face-first into the steering wheel, cracking him across the forehead so hard there was an explosion of bright white light. He was knocked backward, thrown into a vortex as the car spun. Both of the cars, spinning and spinning, turning from the point in space where they were joined together in a tangle of metal and smoke.

The spinning finally stopped and he opened his eyes, sitting up, peering through the clouds of dark vapor, eyes watering from the impact, still dazed, and he saw what he'd hit. Long lengths of fine blond hair stuck up through the shattered glass of the other car's rear window, smeared dark with blood. Just behind the door, the top part of a child's safety seat.

Rein grabbed his door handle, trying to force it open, but the frame was bent, and it snapped free in his hand. He dropped onto the seat and kicked the window wildly, screaming and screaming and screaming for help.

Rein stumbled over to the nearest lamppost, pressing himself against it, clutching it like a man at sea would pieces of wreckage. In the shimmering haze, he saw the front door of the courthouse burst open and Carrie come running through it, searching for him.

He wiped sweat from his eyes and face, huffing and panting, seeing Carrie's head turn side to side, looking up and down the street. Looking for him.

You fool.

She saw him bent over at the end of the block and came running.

I am the door that cannot be closed.

25

The windows were down, bathing his face in cool air. cool air against his damp hair and beard. Cool air rippling through his shirt, helping it to dry. Carrie turned around to look at him. "You should have seen it. I thought Bill was going to toss a chair across the room at Bender."

Waylon grunted as he drove, trying not to smile. "Come on, now. I only gave him a little bitty piece of my mind." He looked in the rearview mirror. "You all right back there? Don't puke in my car."

Rein closed his eyes, listening to the wind. "I'm fine."

"Can you believe those assholes tried to hassle me about giving me back my gun?" she said. "I was trying to get out of there to go find you, and they'd switched guards at the front. The idiot couldn't find the sign-out sheet for me to leave the damn building." She snapped her fingers and said, "That reminds me."

Waylon watched her stick her hand into her front pocket and saw her take Rein's knife out. He looked in the rearview mirror. "Jesus H. Christ, you took that in there?"

Carrie went to hand it to him, but Rein had not moved.

Waylon scowled in disbelief. "Are you crazy? Do you have any idea what would happen if they ever matched that weapon to the injuries?"

Carrie looked down at the folded metal claw. "What injuries? What is this thing, anyway?"

"It's called a karambit," Waylon said. "Put it away and don't let anyone else see that. Especially those idiots from the County."

"All right, all right," she said, sticking it back in her pocket.

"I can't believe you were dumb enough to keep that thing," Waylon muttered, eyeing Rein. "Son of a bitch, Jacob. That was stupid." He looked at Carrie. "As soon as we get back to the station, that thing is getting destroyed. I don't want to see it ever again."

"What are you mad about? I thought it was something from his work," Carrie said.

"It was for work, all right," Waylon said. "Just not the landscaping kind. You tell her what you did with that?"

Rein's eyes were still closed.

"I don't know why I'm complaining. At least if she has it, I know you won't cut anyone's nuts off with it this time," Waylon said.

"You were the one that shot him," Rein said.

"I shot him because that's what normal people do. Normal people holding guns shoot bad guys doing bad things. We do it all the time. Normal people do not reach inside the open wound and start cutting another man's privates out."

"Normal is limited, Bill. Your problem is that you are normal. You think rationally and you are confused and afraid of a world that isn't," Rein said. "That's why you've always needed me."

As they spoke, Carrie laid her hand on the outside of her pocket, feeling the karambit's outline against her palm. Now that she knew its pedigree, it felt like a talisman and she would not let go of it. She touched it, thinking of how Walter Krissing must have screamed when it entered him. She touched it and wondered how Rein's face looked when he performed the first cut. She touched it, feeling the curved spine and hinge where the curved talon's peak of blade folded into the handle and tried to imagine why Rein had brought it with him now.

Waylon's voice brought her out of her thoughts, saying, "Grab the case file." When she'd reached into the leather bag near her feet and drew it out, he said, "Give me the rundown on the suspects you developed."

"These on the top all have mental health records, rap sheets, and a history of interest in serial killers. They live in remote locations where they'd draw less suspicion."

"How many are there?"

"Ten or so."

"That's no good," Waylon said. "The County isn't going to help us on these follow-ups. They're stuck on the separate incidents theory. Bender assigned half his men to round up every person going in and out of that bar and see if they can't beat a confession out of them."

"Asshole," Carrie muttered.

Waylon looked in the rearview mirror at Rein. "So what's the play? Which one do you want to talk to first?"

"None of them," Rein said.

Carrie looked back, "What?"

"We don't have time to talk to all of them. Not while he still has that little girl. Every second we waste, he's getting closer to his next identity."

"Krissing," Waylon said, spitting the name out.

"Walter always liked to groom his victims. To form a relationship with them and make them care for him. What condition we find the little girl in depends on fast we act."

"Why did Krissing try to bond with them if he was just going to torture them and kill them?" Carrie asked.

"It made their suffering sweeter to him if it contained the element of betrayal."

Carrie gritted her teeth at the idea of Nubs being groomed by her mother's killer. "I'm going to kill this bastard when we find him. I swear to God, even if he didn't touch a hair on Nubs's head, I'm going to kill him."

"Let's just find her first," Waylon said. "So if we aren't going to start interviewing these suspects, what are we doing, Jacob?"

"Sociopaths come in contact most with mental health agencies when they are children," Rein said. "Parents, neighbors, teachers at school, the parents of other kids, Children and Youth agencies—they all form a sort of protective shield around juveniles. Society works very hard to keep children safe. It's the one thing we do right. Once they turn eighteen, we cast them out into the world."

"That all sounds great, but are you going to tell me what we're doing or not?" Waylon said. "I'm just driving, so at least tell me if I'm going the right way."

"You're going the right way. We need to speak to the doctors at the Vieira Juvenile Center. They will tell us who our most likely candidates are."

Waylon weighed the idea, pursing his lips together until his mustache hung down to his chin. Eventually, he said, "Not bad. I had the same idea. Just wanted to make sure you were on the same page."

"Bullshit," Carrie said.

"That hurts my feelings, young lady," Waylon said.

"Your heart will just have to go on."

Vieira Juvenile Center was another boxy, gray government building built by the same contractor who built all the other boxy, gray buildings in the region. The genius of closed-contract projects where high-level elected officials were allowed to decide which of their cousins or nephews would be awarded those contracts. Half the money allocated for the building actually made it there, with the other half being doled out behind closed doors.

In Coyote Township, the head of the Board of Supervisors had been loyal to the Republican party for long enough that he'd been awarded a position at the County, overseeing roads and highway maintenance. In return, he hired all the sons-in-law and cousins of other Republicans in the county who had not been smart enough or had a clean-enough record to become deputy sheriffs or courthouse security guards.

County jobs came with pensions and benefits, paid well, and were hard to lose. In the nearby cities, the scams and leeching were the exact same, but instead they called themselves Democrats. The party did not matter. It was just a façade that the people in charge used to disguise themselves. Corruption runs deep in any government; it is just more apparent in the smaller ones.

Rein followed Carrie and Waylon up the winding concrete steps, past the barren hill where grass did not grow. The windows were blacked over, revealing only the outlines of figures standing behind them like apparitions. Rein could see someone's hands pressed flat against the window and heard a loud thump that shook the glass, and then a second thump that made Carrie and Waylon both turn their heads. They heard a muffled scream. The hands withdrew from the window, and it was empty once more.

"I hate this place," Carrie said as they neared the top.

"Believe it or not, they do good work here," Waylon told her. "At least, they do the best with what they have."

An abandoned basketball court sat to the side of the entrance, a rim with no net drooping from its bolts on a ruined backboard. The pole was eaten through with rust, and grass grew up through the court's cracked asphalt. Unused picnic tables sat on one side of the court, outside of the windows, within full view of the locked rooms inside. Rein remembered the County's proud announcement that they were installing an outdoor recreation facility at the Juvenile Center for the low cost of $2 million, including a garden and patio and tennis court and picnic area for families to spend time together, to foster bonds that would carry them into the future once they were reunited.

The public had fought the project, claiming the little burglars and sexual deviants did not deserve such coddling, and the County seemed to cave, scaling back the original design to something much less costly. They let enough time pass for the public to move on to other pressing matters before construction began. Somehow they'd still run over the original $2 million budget building just the half-court and picnic area.

Waylon held the door open. "After you."

The lobby was a wide, open room with secondhand couches and garish orange paint with diagonal lines of green and tan striped from one wall to the other. Framed cartoon drawings showed small children holding hands beneath a smiling sun. The secretary at the counter sat behind thick glass that she did not slide open as they approached. Rein waited as she turned the pages of a slick entertainment magazine, then said, "Hello," waiting for her to look up.

At last she did, saying, "Can I help you?"

"Yes, we'd like to speak to the doctor in charge of sexual offenders."

"And you are?"

She eyed Rein, trying to decide where she knew him from, her head tilting clockwise as if the weight of her brain was making her head lopsided. Waylon nudged him aside, slapping his large, gold chief shield against the window and said, "Chief William Waylon, Coyote Township. We're investigating two homicides. Call the doctor, please."

"A chief, huh?" she said, looking at the badge as she picked up her phone. "I didn't know chiefs investigated crimes."

"In all fairness, he's not really doing much of the investigating," Rein said.

Waylon turned his head between the two of them and said, "All these years, and you're still not funny."

"Oh, I'm funny," Rein said.

"You are the least funny person I know."

"Then you must know some really funny people."

"You're not funny."

"Ask her," Rein said.

Waylon looked at Carrie. "Is he funny?"

"Kind of," she said, casting an eye on Rein. "I guess so?"

"She's just being polite," Waylon said.

"Well, is Bill funny?" Rein said. "I mean, aside from that mustache?"

Carrie laughed, then covered her mouth. "Sorry, Chief."

"See?" Rein said. "Funny."

The door opened next to the reception glass, and a dark-skinned woman with short hair looked out at them. She addressed Waylon first. "I'm Dr. Shelly, can I help you?" Her voice slowed to a trickle as she looked past him and saw Rein. "Jacob?"

"Hello, Linda."

Her large eyes turned toward him. "What are you doing here?"

"The usual," he said.

She inspected Waylon and Carrie, assessing them both and determining they were police, her face bearing the natural distrust all social worker and mental health professionals have for them, then back at Rein. "Is that the right thing for you to be doing?"

"This time, yes."

She opened the door, allowing them to enter. "What can I do for you?" she said over her shoulder, leading them down the pale yellow corridor papered with motivational posters. Someone moaned from behind one of the doors and slammed against it, twisting the knob, but the door did not open. Each of the doorknobs was bolted from the outside.

"Keep your head down and don't look in any of the windows," Shelly said, looking back at Carrie. "Just ignore anything you hear."

"I need you to look at a list of names for us, see if you can give us some direction," Rein said.

"Direction toward?"

"A highly adaptive personality. Very traumatic past. Too many disorders to name, but mainly the really bad kinds."

"You're describing half the kids in my unit, Jacob."

"Not this one. This one was special."

Fists banged against the doors as they passed, followed by voices shrieking to the point of breaking and low, disjointed snarls. Shelly pulled a set of keys from her pocket and said, "This whole section's been on lockdown since this morning. One of the children bit a nurse through her cheek. Her teeth were showing. She's going to need a skin graft." As she inserted her key into her office door, the screams and banging sounds grew frantic and louder. "The others are unhappy at being confined."

She shut the door behind them, drowning the noise from the hallway to a low roar and said, "How many has he killed?"

Carrie raised an eyebrow in surprise, but Rein seemed unfazed. "Two that we know of. Possibly more. He has a little girl now." He looked at Carrie, watching her for signs of emotion as he said, "The daughter of his last victim."

"Methodology?" Shelly said.

"He's adopting the techniques and preferences of

other killers. Probably their personalities as well. My guess is that he started this as a child, probably in a place like this. Pretending to be other people as a coping mechanism. Maybe characters from a movie, comic books, anything to forget who he really is."

"You said you have a list of names?"

Carrie removed the packet of information from her case file and handed it across the desk.

"Where did you get them?"

"We started at the library," Carrie said. "Then whittled them down by previous offenses, location, and recent activity."

"You gave it one of your sludge tests?" the doctor said, smiling at Rein, who half smiled back.

Carrie looked between the two of them. "I don't understand. What's a sludge test?"

"Jacob always told me that criminal investigations were like sludge tests. Remember when you were in middle school and the science teacher gave you a test tube of goo and said, 'Figure out what's inside it'? You had to see what reacted to certain chemicals, see what evaporated when you heated it. By the end, you were able to identify all the pieces. Right?" Shelly said, looking at Jacob.

"That's right," he said.

Carrie's mouth tightened in annoyance. "I guess you must have left that part out when you explained it to me."

Shelly took the papers and laid them out on her desk, sifting through them one by one. As she peered down at the names on the pages she said, "You realize what you're asking me to do is a serious violation of federal law."

"I do," Rein said.

"It's a breach of County protocols and would result in my being fired."

The pages were spread out from left to right, and she selected one, put it on top of the one next to it, took it away, and put another one on top instead. "Which is why I expect you to tell us no," Rein said.

"In fact, I will be making a note of this interaction, and if the need arises file a report with the appropriate body," she said, now stacking the packets into two halves. She turned the half on the right facedown and stacked the other one on top of it.

"Perfectly understandable," Rein said.

Shelly folded her hands across the stacks of paper, dark eyes centered on him. "I tried to reach you, but the number was disconnected."

"I wrote you," Rein said. "I still have the letter. I meant to send it, but . . . you know."

Shelly's face fell. "I thought something happened to you."

"What else could possibly happen to me, Linda?" he said.

She stared down at the papers on her desk, needing to look away from him. "Well, it's good to know you're still alive." She lifted the stack and passed it across the table toward him. "I'm sorry, but I cannot assist you in this."

"In that case, we'll be going." He got up from his chair and stepped aside as the doctor went to her door to let them out.

"Wait," Carrie said, but Waylon grabbed her arm and squeezed it tight enough to stop her from speaking further.

"Follow that hall straight back to where you came and knock three times. Someone will let you out," Shelly said.

Rein looked back at her, holding the stack of papers under his arm. "Thank you for your time, Dr. Shelly."

"Good luck," she whispered, reaching to touch his hand, then she shut the door.

Carrie's jaw flexed as they drove, her teeth clenched as she stared forward. She had not spoken since they left the juvenile facility, and Waylon knew better than to try. He looked in the rearview mirror. "So, you want to fill me in on what just happened in there? I'm not sure if the doctor helped us or not."

"She put them in order," Rein said, looking down at the first name. "The ones on the bottom are the names she didn't recognize. The ones on the top of the stack are the ones she did."

"And you caught all that?"

"It wasn't that hard, Bill," Rein said. "If you were paying attention."

"Or maybe they just had a special connection," Carrie muttered. "You certainly seemed well acquainted."

"We used to work together," Rein said.

"Oh, I'll bet," she replied.

Waylon watched Carrie from the corner of his eye, seeing the barely contained anger waiting there, ready to strike at anyone or anything. "What job did we have with her?" Waylon said, trying to change the subject. "Was it one of the Krissing kids?"

"I met her in prison. She chaired the volunteer program I was part of. We spoke quite often."

Carrie's eyes were fixed on the road ahead, her right hand gripping the armrest handle next to her. "Well,"

Waylon said loudly, trying to change the subject. "So we got us some names, then. You all ready to talk to some lunatics?"

Rein flipped through the first few pages and said, "First up is Barclay Folds. Lives out by the old coal mines." As he scanned through the pamphlet he said, "Arrested for stalking, attempted rape, and another rape that was withdrawn when the victim went missing. Did time at the state penitentiary for burglary. Six foot two."

"Jesus," Waylon said. "That our boy, you think?"

Rein tapped the page and said, "He's certainly a good candidate."

Carrie's jaw came unlocked just enough to say, "If Barclay Folds did all this, I'm going to make what you two did to Old Man Krissing look like an act of kindness."

26

The small house sat alone in a barren wasteland of dirt and rock, with a bent stovepipe sticking up through the roof. The shingles had been patched, re-patched, and finally given up on. Now they were just covered over in places by pieces of tacked-down tarp. The car parked next to the house was covered by the rest of the tarp. Someone had removed the wheels and replaced them with cinder blocks so long ago, there was rust spilling down their sides.

Rein went around the side and checked the back-yard, looking for piles of fresh dirt or power tools or bags of lime or sand. Anything a man would need to dispose of a full-grown human body composed of flesh, bone, muscle, organ, and blood. No fire pits or burn barrels either, he thought. Nothing but unplowed dirt. There's always basements, he told himself. Or off-site locations. He pressed his ear to the wall beneath the side window, listening, hoping to hear a little girl's voice. There was nothing.

Carrie knocked on the door, did not get a response, then knocked again.

"This is how you teach them, Bill?" Rein asked.

"Excuse me, young lady," Waylon said, hooking his belt with the undersides of his fingers and hoisting it up over his belly. "There's the visiting knock and the felony knock," he said. "Your knock said, *Hey, we're just visiting*. This is the felony knock." He grabbed the door handle with both hands and kicked the bottom as hard as he could with the toe of his boot, sending loud booms rattling through the front of the house. "It says we ain't going away."

They could hear someone shuffling toward the door, and all three of them stepped back, getting clear. Waylon's hand went to the gun on his side. When the door cracked open, he bladed away from the entrance, keeping most of himself behind the wall. A man's face appeared in the narrow opening and said, "Who're you?"

"Chief Waylon with the police department. Are you Barclay Folds?"

"Yeah."

"I'd like to speak to you a minute."

Folds was still hidden behind the door, not opening it, not wanting them to see something. "What about?"

Rein slid his foot in the space of the doorjamb, keeping it from closing. "About an investigation. Is anyone else in the house besides you?"

"No."

"Open it," Rein said.

"What's this about?"

"Open the goddamn door!" Carrie shouted. She smacked it hard with the flat of her hand and pushed. "We're not asking again!"

Folds limped aside as they shoved through the door. His left arm was clutched tightly to his chest, the fingers crooked and stiff, his thumb bent at the wrong angle. His whole body was tilted and withered, like someone had let the air out of his left side. His left leg was bent inward and his foot dragged on the dirty carpet as he slid out of Carrie's way, watching in confusion as she burst into the living room. "Nubs! Nubs! Can you hear me?"

"Wha—who's Nubs?" Fold stammered.

"Where the hell is she, you sick motherfucker?" Carrie shouted.

"I don't know w-w-what you're talking about."

"Bullshit!" She grabbed him by the collar, pulling him so close her spittle flew in his face. He shrunk away from her, too busy shivering to wipe it off. "You a rapist, Barclay? You like to hurt women? Where is the little girl? I'm going to ask you one time, and then I'm going to start hurting you real, real bad."

"Carrie," Waylon said, coming up behind her. He laid his hand on her shoulder and eased her back, saying, "Houses like this make a lot of noise, and I swear I heard something from one of the back rooms. I'm sure Mr. Folds here don't mind if you do a safety sweep real quick to make sure everything's all right. We'll deal with him."

She let go of Folds's shirt and raced toward the back of the house, checking every closet and opening all the cabinets in the kitchen.

"What do you people want?" Folds whimpered. "I didn't do nothing."

Waylon and Rein closed in around him, looking down at his disfigurements. The man grimaced as he pulled his bad hand in close, the muscles in his ruined arm tight and corded. "What happened to you?" Rein said.

"I had a stroke when I was at Graterford," Fold said.

"State didn't want to pay for any more operations, so they paroled me early and sent me home."

"Is that right?" Rein said.

"What's this all about, anyway?"

"A few dead women. A little girl missing. Just your type of thing, Barclay," Waylon said, peering down at the man.

"No way," Fold said. "No way, no how. I changed in prison, sir. This stroke here was a blessing in disguise. I couldn't hurt nobody if I wanted to."

"When did you have the stroke?" Rein said.

"Two years ago. No, wait, three."

"Who was your doctor in the hospital?"

"I don't know."

"How long were you in the hospital?"

"A few . . . a few weeks."

"How many?" Rein said.

"What was the hospital's name?" Waylon snapped.

"I don't recall, officers!"

Rein and Waylon pressed against him, moving in unison, cutting off any lines of escape. Waylon snarled, "You're a lying rapist, Folds. You think we're buying this cripple routine? You're faking it."

"I swear to God! No!"

Waylon looked at Rein, breaking character for the briefest of seconds, silently asking him if the stroke was an act. Rein's hands shot forward into the center of Folds's chest, knocking him backward on his bad leg. Both men watched the crippled man topple and slam his bad knee into the nearest side table. Folds flailed out, his good arm waving in the air as he tried to stop himself from falling, but it was too late. His ruined arm stayed tight to his chest as the back of his head cracked the floor and his eyes fluttered, dazed. Folds moaned, his good leg extending and withdrawing against the carpet like that of a crushed insect, his bad leg still bent, bad foot turned inward. He convulsed violently as the left side suddenly constricted. "Please, I need my medicine!" he cried out through clenched teeth. "Help me. I didn't do nothing. Please help me!"

"Carrie," Waylon called out.

The sound of crashing drawers and fluttering papers from the rear bedroom stopped. "What?" she shouted.

"Time to go."

"But I'm not done looking." She came out from the bedroom, confused by the sound of whimpering, and looked at Folds writhing on the floor. Waylon and Rein leaned down and scooped him up, dropping him into the nearest seat.

Folds tried to catch his breath as he grabbed his medicine from the couch and unscrewed the cap. "Where are you all from, anyway? I want to see your IDs," he said, but they had already gone.

Waylon took the main road back to the courthouse, not bothering to throw on his lights as he flew through each stop sign. "What's the next name on the list?"

Rein flipped through the pages. "Travis Berry. Twenty-five years old. Multiple arrests as a juvenile for prowling and loitering. Probably Peeping Tom activity. One for animal abuse. That's interesting."

"Like, beating his dog?" Carrie said.

"A lot of these guys mutilate animals," Waylon said.

"Or have sex with them," Rein added. "Or both."

"Jesus." Carrie grimaced.

"Kind of ruins the whole Jack the Ripper romantic killer thing, don't it?" Waylon grunted.

"Just tell us where he is, Rein," Carrie said.

Rein raised the pages to read them in the fading light. The sun was balancing over the horizon like a large orange circus performer doing a final high-wire act. He studied Travis's mouth and eyes, asking himself if this was the face of a man capable of becoming something he'd feared his entire professional life. He decided he was not sure. "Last known address is on Bores Road, out in West Croatan."

"Do you know where that is?" Waylon asked Carrie.

"I think so. My uncle had a cabin out that way when I was a kid."

"Good," Waylon said as he pulled up beside her car in the parking lot. "Take your car. We'll see you there."

She looked at him, confused. "We're not all going together?"

"I want you to have your own car in case we find the girl. Me and Rein will have to stay at the house with the suspect, and you'll want to go with Nubs, right?"

"You're right," Carrie said. "Thanks for thinking ahead like that, boss."

"That's why I get paid the big bucks, kiddo."

Carrie jumped down from the seat, saying, "Just make sure you keep up, old-timer. I won't wait for you when I get there."

"You most certainly will," he called out. "I will be right behind you the whole time."

They watched her get into her car and turn on the headlights. Rein got into the front passenger seat, holding the stack of papers in his lap. He looked at Waylon, seeing the man's expression harden once Carrie was out of sight. Rein grunted and shook his head. "I wish you'd been that good at playing people when we worked together, Bill. I wouldn't have had to do all those interviews by myself."

Waylon's eyes were fixed on him, hard points of light. "You better not be doing what I think you're doing."

"What do you think I'm doing?" Rein asked.

"You know exactly what I think you're doing." Carrie's car headed out of the parking lot, and Waylon watched it leave without moving. "Listen, we both know I was no angel back in the day. I did a lot of stuff I regret. And you never judged me or turned me away when I showed up with a bag and slept on your couch. I am acknowledging that right here, before God. But Jacob, that girl is like a daughter to me. She's young. She's vulnerable. She's fucked up over her friend. She's got a piece-of-shit father who left her with some kind of, I dunno, issues toward older men."

"Listen to yourself. Around her it's all *golly heck* and *Is that why she's cussin' so much*, but the second she leaves, you become a different person. I've got news for you, Bill. You're not her father. You're not her savior. You're her chief, and she sees right through your little act. You should have never, ever let her anywhere near this investigation, and we both know it."

"She will make a good cop."

"Not with the level of training she's gotten so far."

"Man, fuck you. You don't get to come back in and act like some moral authority over me."

"I'm not a moral authority over anyone," Rein said. "I know exactly who and what I am. You should try doing the same. If Carrie is fucked up, it's because you let her on this case. But instead of worrying about that, you're worried that I'm playing along just so I can sleep with her."

Waylon grimaced at the notion. "Jesus, Jacob. Did you?"

"No. And fuck you right back for asking me that."

"Listen, goddamn it. I know you been through a lot. A pretty young girl like that showing some attention would drive anyone crazy. I'm just saying. She's not in her right frame of mind to be making good decisions, so I'm asking you, as a friend, to leave her be. She doesn't need someone like you making it worse."

"Oh, don't worry, Bill," Rein said. "The second we find the little girl, I'm gone. You can all go back to your perfect lives and never have to worry about me again. Bender was right, okay? You want to hear me say it? I'm a disgrace to the job and everything it stands for. I get it. I make myself sick just being here. There? You happy?"

"That isn't what I meant."

"I know exactly what you meant." Rein pointed at Carrie's vanishing lights down the dark street. "Are we going to let her go interview Travis Berry by herself, or are you waiting for me to get out?"

Waylon shifted the car into drive and stepped on the gas. "You know all that shit is not what I meant. You're twisting it all up! For Christ's sake, man, I'm grateful you came back. You hear me? It was never the same once you were gone."

Rein watched the road ahead of them for signs of Carrie's car, letting things cool back down. "So," he said, "you went and saw Jacob Junior?"

"I did. He looks real good. Doing a hell of a job with the DA's office."

"I try to keep up as best I can. It's hard without a computer or phone, though. The papers out my way didn't cover much about Harrisburg crime."

"Plus, all the newspapers where you were living were in Spanish, I bet," Waylon said. He laughed at the notion, not meaning to but unable to help himself.

"Yeah, pretty much. Hey, just so I'm clear," he said, sounding more serious. "Carrie's like a daughter to you?"

"That's right."

"Good to know," Rein said. "Because, you know, if this all ends, and she and I become a thing, I intend on calling you Dad."

"You even think about it and I will kick your ass so hard your grandmama will fall down."

"Don't be like that. It's wrong for future family to fight."

"That part I said about being glad you're back?" Waylon said. "I didn't mean it."

"I'm just glad we can have these kinds of conversations. It's hard for a girl's father to talk to his son-in-law sometimes."

Waylon glanced at him. "I don't know what I'm worried about anyway. Nobody who has a beard like that can possibly be interested in women. Real men have mustaches. Everybody knows that."

"Are you mocking my duckbill?"

"Yes, I do believe I am."

Rein scratched his chin, feeling the length of his beard. "Well, the ladies love it. One in particular. I think you might know her."

"Shut your ass," Waylon said as he accelerated, trying to catch up to the car that had already faded into the distance. "Duckbill. What kind of a stupid name is that for a beard, anyway?"

The road signs were obscured by tall corn, or they'd been knocked down and never replaced. The people in West Croatan did not seem to care. The only people who visited the area were people with a need to be there, who already knew their way around—others should not have come. The houses were unnumbered. There were no mailboxes. Carrie saw newspapers and mailing circulars piled around people's front porches, most of the publications old and yellowing, surrounded by large coffee cans filled with cigarette butts. West Croatan was one of the unincorporated parts of the county, covered by state troopers who did not patrol and, when they were called, might not be able to respond for hours.

Carrie's cell phone had stopped receiving or sending messages forty minutes before she turned down the long dirt stretch that was Bores Road. Road was a generous term for the unpaven, leftover horse trails that wound in around the cornfields of West Croatan.

She rolled down her window and smelled death. Her headlights picked up the carcass of a fawn splayed out in the middle of the road, its white ribs sticking up through its open chest. Birds and bugs had been feasting there, stretching long lengths of intestines from the crumpled body in every direction. Carrie's lights shined on the white spots on its fur as she drove past, maneuvering her car around it.

The crickets were symphonic, loud and surrounding her on all sides. Her car emerged from the fields, its headlights spread wide across sudden, flat darkness, showing her several feet of the road ahead and a sky without stars.

She saw the house at the end of the road and stopped.

She cut off her headlights and watched, listening, waiting. The living-room lights were on but the blinds were drawn tight. The house had two stories, with windows along the second floor, also covered in blinds, also drawn tight. The yard was vast beyond the house, but the fences had long since fallen away, so where its property line started and other unused farm lands began she could not tell. She saw trees and scattered scrub growth in places but nothing planned or tended to. In the driveway sat a white work van.

She looked at the van, feeling something stir deep within but not trusting it. She put the car in park and shut it off, stuffing the keys down inside her pocket, where they would not jingle. The road was dark behind her. She pulled out her phone, saw no signal, but texted Waylon anyway. *Where are you guys? I'm at the house.*

The message indicator swirled uselessly. She put the phone in her pocket, slid out of the car, and eased the door shut behind her. A shadow moved behind one of the first-story windows, a blotch of darkness that sent Carrie flat to the ground, chest deep in dirt. There was no cover in the open field. Nothing to hide behind. She watched the shadow move away from the window and stayed low, creeping across the field as quickly as she could.

She went wide around the front of the house, checking the side and as much of the rear as she could see from that angle. The air was heavy with moisture. Rain was coming. The fields stunk of leaking septic tanks and squished beneath her boots. She looked over the rotting woodshed and garage set behind the house. Both were overgrown with brown vines that crept in and around the dozens of scattered tools leaning up against their walls.

She crept farther onto the property, close enough to see the house's crumbling stucco façade and the ugly yellow sealant bubbling up beneath it. She slid her feet as she walked, using old tricks from when she and Molly used to hide from the cops in the woods, finding branches that would crack with the tip of her boot and stepping over them, finding clumps of rock and dirt that would crumble and toeing them out of her way. As she came to the back of the house she saw something parked beside the garage: a newer model red tractor. Carrie looked around the landscape surrounding the house. Nothing looked plowed or turned. Nothing even looked mowed.

The window nearest her darkened, and she looked up to see a large shadow standing behind the blinds, big enough to fill the entire frame. She froze in place, the tendons in her legs tightening like steel cords rooting her in place. The shadow stopped, then moved away, and the light filling the window went out.

One by one, the lights in the downstairs turned off, removing all ambient light from the yard. Carrie backed away, moving toward the edge of the road, away from the house. She squatted in a large dirt rut, wanting nothing more than to hear Waylon's car coming up the road.

It didn't come. There was nothing but her and the sound of crickets.

She cursed and slapped the side of her neck, plucking a beetle from her skin and tossing it to the ground. Damn bugs, she thought. They probably don't get many humans to feed on out here. Me sitting in this field is like ringing the dinner bell to them.

She watched the house for signs of movement, thinking maybe they've just gone to bed. Not unusual for a working man. Depending on his trade, he probably had to be up before dawn to get to the job site. She looked back at the van and frowned, wondering what kind of work it was used for. It could be for anything, from carpet cleaning to painting to plumbing. It had no logos, nothing but plain white panel along the sides. Then again, almost every police dispatch reporting an attempted child luring involved a suspect driving a white van. So, there was that.

Carrie turned and looked down the road, searching for signs of Waylon's car. She slid her phone out of her pocket and checked for new messages. Signal lost.

"I'm going to wait," she said aloud. "They'll be here soon. Bill said to wait. So I'm going to wait."

She moved in a crouch, circling around the front of the property back toward the van, wanting to get a better look at it. She went to the driver's side and peered in. The front compartment was empty and completely clean. There was a heavy black curtain behind the front seats, blocking anyone's view of the back. She tried the door handle, but the locks were down on both doors. She looked again. Even the cup holders were empty. For a working man's van, this was unusual, she knew. Working men spent a lot of time in their cars. They ate fast food going from one job to another. They scribbled addresses on little bits of paper that they discarded when they didn't need them anymore. They collected receipts. This van was empty.

Carrie went around the back of the van and tried the

rear door, already knowing it would be locked. The windows were blacked out.

Not unusual, she told herself. A working man would want to keep his tools and equipment out of view.

She tried the rear door again, jiggling the handle, but it was locked tight. She stepped back, staring at the house, trying to make up her mind what to do next, when she felt another bite on the side of her neck. She smacked the bug away and felt a bump forming on her skin, starting to swell where she'd been bitten. She looked at her fingers, seeing drops of blood and scowled, but then stopped. Something was wrong.

Carrie lowered her head and smelled her fingers, unsure at first. She went back to the van and grabbed the handle with her other hand, wrapping her fingers around its length, then took her hand away and pressed it against her nose, inhaling deeply, and was certain. On the handle was the unmistakable smell of bleach.

A soft, audible click sounded from the house, and she looked up to see the metal doorknob turning ever so slightly. The front door opened an inch, revealing nothing but pitch black inside the home, and stopped. Carrie's heart pounded hard in her chest as she drew her weapon, aiming it at the dark space behind the door.

She took a deep breath and said, "Aunt Carrie is coming, baby."

She started forward, taking short, sharp breaths. The abyss beyond the door was inviting her in.

She squeezed the gun's handle as she nudged the door the rest of the way open, jerking back out of the way as she turned side to side, checking for signs of movement. Nothing. She switched the gun to her left hand and searched the wall with her right, finding a light switch and flicking it up and down several times, but no lights came on. She inched forward, as quietly as she could, not to avoid being heard but to hear anyone approaching her.

You always hear people say it is so dark I can't see my hands in front of my face, she thought. This is the first time I've ever seen it in real life.

She could see only three bright dots forming a triangle at the top of her weapon. Two years prior, Bill Waylon had blown half his equipment budget on installing tritium sights on every gun in his department, and now it was the only visible thing. She continued deeper into the house, scanning, scanning, moving around the entryway with her gun, searching for anyone inside. She told herself the wind had blown the door open. The owner was already in bed.

I smelled bleach, she told herself.

He uses it to clean his equipment. You've broken into someone's house without a warrant and now you're about to shoot the first thing you see. You're a scared little girl. Put your gun away, back out of the house before it's too late, and wait for your chief.

There is bleach on that van. Strong. That's no coincidence. There are no such things as coincidences.

She heard a creak above her head and looked up. Something had moved across the floorboards above, a distant, muffled sound, but she'd heard it. Then she heard it again. She crept across the room, keeping her free hand extended to search for the staircase, and found a warm wooden length of handrail just as her foot bumped against the kickboard of the lowest stair. She looked up, seeing a faint, flickering green light at the top of the steps. She stared at the light, trying to understand what it could be, and the metal pad affixed to the light began to clarify beneath it. A metal pad with a series of numbered keys beneath it. An electronic lock, she realized with a start. "Nubs?" she called out. "Are you up there?"

Another thump on the floor, louder this time. Carrie started up the stairs, keeping her gun centered on the door, ready for it to open. One step, then another, moving upward toward the blinking green light. She hurried as she drew closer, eager to be through the door, to confront whatever waited there. The door appeared to be nothing more than a plain white hardware store model, hollow and flimsy, but when she touched it, it felt cool. Reinforced metal.

She wrapped her hand around the doorknob and turned, keeping her gun trained in front of her, ready to fire. It opened. A door that locks in whoever is inside the room, she thought. She pushed forward, into the impenetrable darkness, too dark for her to see who or what was inside of it. She grimaced and clenched her fists, tired of being cautious. She shouldered the door open the rest of the way and barged forward, twisting and turning in every direction with her weapon, until a tiny voice, spoken through cracked lips, managed to utter words that struck her like bright streaks of lightning.

"Aunt Carrie? Is that you?"

27

A hundred kisses and frantic embracing as she ran her hands up and down the little girl's body, checking every inch of her, making sure that she was all in one piece. Words tumbled out of her mouth as she kissed Nubs on the forehead and face, wet tears on her lips, not knowing who they belonged to. Promises spilled out of her, swearing they were getting out of there, everything was going to be all right.

"My mommy," Nubs whispered, clutching Carrie.

Clenching her eyes shut. Her teeth grinding together in outrage. "I know, baby, I know. No one is going to hurt you again."

"Mommy told me to be brave."

"You are so, so brave, baby."

"Where is she?"

"Just hang on a little bit longer. Just a few more minutes, and everything will be okay."

A sound behind the door turned both of their heads, something creaking on the stairs, and Nubs cried out, "He's coming! No! Tell him to leave us alone!"

Carrie pushed the little girl behind her and raised her weapon, listening, trying to hear over Nubs's whimpering and the rush of blood pulsating in her own ears. She'd never heard her own heart beating before. Now it was a pounding drum.

Another creak on the stairs, closer this time, and Carrie fired. Two bullets, center mass on the door, flame spouting from the gun's barrel that lit the entire room for one instant. Nubs covered her ears and screamed, her cries muffled by the painful ringing in Carrie's ears from the gunshots. She waited, holding the pistol steady, ready to fire again. If the bullets had hit the target, a body would be falling backward down the steps. There would be a giant crash, then hopefully the sweet sounds of a murderous freak sobbing at the bottom, crying that his femur was sticking out through his flesh or his neck was broken but he was still alive. Instead, there was nothing but the ringing. Carrie waited, holding her position.

"Sweetheart?" Carrie said.

Nubs only whimpered in reply.

"You have to stay here for a second."

"No!" Nubs cried. "Don't leave me!"

Carrie felt her tiny arms clench around her leg, but she did not move, did not lower her pistol.

"I need to make sure the bad man is gone, okay? I will not leave this room without you. I promise."

The hold on her leg only got tighter. The little girl was crying so hard that Carrie could feel tears soaking through her pants leg. She tried to talk, found her voice locked inside her throat, and the door grew blurry from the thick tears forming in her eyes.

Carrie.

The awkward teenager rolling her eyes at everything their math teacher said, making her laugh uncontrollably.

Carrie.

The two of them shaving the sides of their heads in Penny's bathroom. Stealing from the used CD store. Working odd jobs together. Making out with their boyfriends in the same car.

Molly, the one person she'd always had in a life filled with shitty people you could not rely on.

You take good care of that little girl, Carrie. That's my sweet little angel, and you protect her, goddamn it. I'm watching you, bitch.

"Baby?" Carrie said, forcing herself to breathe. "Mommy said to be strong, right? That's what she said. Well, this is what she meant. I need you to let go of my leg, because I have to open the door. After that, we are leaving this place forever. Can you do that, baby? Just be strong, one more time, for Mommy, okay? One more time for me."

She felt Nubs's arms release from her, enough for her to move her leg, and she inched forward. Her arms ached from holding the gun up for so long; they were starting to shake. She gripped the handle with one hand and reached for the doorknob with the other, twisting it slowly, slowly, until it popped open and she pulled it inward.

She kept the gun in front, moving it as she moved, looking with it as she looked. As she came around the corner of the door, holding it outright, something grabbed her wrist. Carrie twisted and squeezed the trigger again, the gun's deafening bark echoing in the stairwell, but the man's grip was like iron. He wrenched her forward, slamming her arm against the door's steel frame so hard that she felt her fingers loosen around the handle. She struck out with her knee and stomped with her foot, driving the heel of her boot into his shin, his ankle, any part of him she could find, whatever it took to keep the gun in her hands.

She cried out as his elbow slammed down on her wrist, driving down on her again and again until she felt something snap inside her hand. She watched in mute horror as the gun tumbled out of her fingers over the side of the staircase. She lost sight of it as the bright, glowing dots disappearing into the darkness.

The man pulled at her, trying to drag her out of the doorway, using his awful strength to pull her aside to get to Nubs. "Aunt Carrie!" Nubs screamed, her words ringing throughout the darkness, filling Carrie with renewed strength. She battled the man, beating him with her fists and claws, and in the frenzy she felt the thick metal object in her pocket swinging against her leg.

She fumbled to get her fingers down inside the pocket and pulled, hearing the metallic click of the karambit's blade locking into place. She swung and the man howled in pain, giving Carrie the leverage she needed to break free.

She dove back inside the room and slammed the door shut, panting with the knife trembling in her hand. The sound of soft electronic beeping on the other side of the door was quiet. Carrie stepped backward, trying to catch her breath as the door's loud magnetic lock activated.

The little girl flung her arms around her, pressing her face against Carrie's leg, crying into it.

"You should not have come here," a man's voice said through the door.

The knife danced in Carrie's jittering hands, no matter how hard she gripped it. She clenched her teeth and forced herself to think past the child's weeping, the dark room, and the man on the other side of the door. This was his lair, and she'd invaded it. The more time he had to plan, or to equip himself, the worse it would be.

"Well, I did," she said. Her voice was shaking, and she knew it, hated it, but continued on. "You don't like it when someone interferes with your plans, do you? It makes you crazy, right? That man at the nightclub. You had a plan with him, and something went wrong. What did he do to make you so mad?"

"Shut up about things you know nothing about!"

It was working, Carrie thought. "Well, now it's happening again. You had a plan for this girl, didn't you? You were going to be her friend, right? Get her to trust you and believe you wouldn't hurt her, just like Old Man Krissing, right? Because you're a phony, aren't you. A faker! A nothing! Well, I'm here now, and I'm not leaving." Her fingers tightened around the knife. "Open the door, unless you're afraid."

She watched the door, waiting for the first sign of movement, ready to slash and cut anything that tried to come through it. "Come on, pretender! Open the door!"

The door did not move. "I can see you, you know."

Carrie turned to look around the room, searching for cameras. Of course he had cameras. He wanted to record what he did and save it for later. He wanted to watch his victims suffer as they waited for him to return. "Good," she said, raising her middle finger in the air. "Why don't you open the door and see me up close."

"You have a knife," he said. His voice flat and hollow. "Do you think that will protect you or the child? You're a fool. Now you will both pay dearly for your interference."

She could hear him going down the steps, leaving them trapped in the dark room. She bent down to Nubs and wrapped her arm around her again, kissing her on the head and holding her tightly. The room had no windows, and she realized she could not hear anything outside of the house. No wind. No crickets. Even the sound of the man walking downstairs had vanished.

It's soundproofed, she thought. It has to be. He wouldn't want the mailman hearing someone scream for help.

There was nothing left to do but wait for him to open the door, and then, she thought, she would fight until she was dead. But even if it was with her last breath, she would claw out his eyes or cut through his throat just enough for Nubs to get away. Just enough for that, even if it was not enough for anything else.

28

Rein pointed at the car parked in the middle of the road ahead of them. "There she is."

Waylon leaned forward, squinting. "Why the hell did she park there?"

"She must have wanted to walk up to the house on foot."

"Goddamn it," Waylon said. "I told her to sit tight and wait for us."

"Well, maybe she got tired of waiting."

"It's not my fault the cell phone lost its signal."

"Yet *she* still managed to find the place," Rein said.

Waylon stopped the car and cut it off, hurrying out of the driver's seat and running up to Carrie's car. He ducked down to see if she was inside it, saw that she wasn't, and smacked his thigh. "Son of a bitch. I told her to wait."

Rein eyed the front of the house. "Door's open."

Both of them stared at the darkened windows. "You think she's dumb enough to have gone in there alone?" Waylon said.

"Is there any doubt in your mind?"

"Not one." Waylon drew his pistol. "Let's go get our girl, then."

They moved toward the house, and Rein crouched beside him, empty-handed. "I wish I had something for you," Waylon said.

"You were always the better shot."

The two of them flanked the door on opposite sides, Rein hanging back as Waylon inched forward with his gun, cutting the angles through the door's small opening. "I can't see shit," Waylon hissed in frustration.

"Wait," Rein insisted, pulling Waylon back onto the porch as he leaned forward and pushed it open the rest of the way. He stood facing the dark living room and closed his eyes, slowly inhaling, holding his breath as he tilted his head forward, listening. The crickets in the fields all around them. Waylon's labored breathing. The buzzing of a fluorescent light beneath them, and then the sound of a metal-edged tool or weapon being picked up and laid back down on a wooden workbench. "The basement," Rein said. "Someone is down there."

"How the hell do you know that?"

"Sleeping in a jail cell surrounded by people who want to kill you," Rein said. "You learn how to listen."

Waylon raised his gun and entered the house first, both of them crouched low as they advanced across the floor. Rein tapped Waylon on the shoulder, pointing him in the direction of the basement door.

They could barely make out the door's white frame. Someone had left the door wide open, but the lights were off below. Both of them stood, staring down the flight of narrow steps that descended into nothingness. Rein reached above the door frame and the walls around it, feeling for a light switch, then shook his head. They could hear one another breathing heavily, panting as they began down the stairs, both of their chests skipping and jumping, but still they moved forward, traveling down one step at a time. Waylon scanned the room with his weapon blindly, the bright glowing dots of his gunsights glaring in the darkness.

Rein grabbed Waylon firmly by the shoulder, stopping him.

They were perched on the steps, suspended over the concrete floor, and Waylon looked back at him in confusion. Before Rein could answer, something rolled toward them, a round metal cylinder that rattled and clanked, stamped *Flashbang – 1.5 Second Delay.* Rein only had enough time to cover his face before he realized what it was. The sudden explosion of light and sound knocked both of them sideways. Rein's hands grasped frantically at the nothingness, but all he found was Waylon, and even as he tried grabbing on to him, both of them were already falling.

Waylon landed flat on his chest, the air knocked out of him. He gasped like a dying mule, straining to get air back into his lungs. Rein struck the floor with his jaw so hard he felt his teeth loosen. He lifted his head, staring in shock at the bright light. He saw the empty flashbang canister on the basement floor near the steps and wiped his nose. Blood was leaking out of it like a faucet. Someone was coming toward them.

Rein groaned as he tried to get up, barely able to make out the man standing over him. Instead, he saw a bright white butcher's apron and the cruel, comical frown of the Greek face of tragedy. Underneath the mask Rein could make out the same shape of the mouth and eyes he'd seen in the photograph of Travis Berry.

Travis bent down and grabbed a handful of Rein's hair, gripping it tight and pulling back as he slammed his fist into Rein's face, once, twice, the impact crushing his nose and splaying his lips. Rein's head slumped down. He was barely conscious as he was dragged across the floor, feeling its cool concrete against his skin. He heard, rather than felt, the metal shackle snap tight around his left wrist, and it stirred him, but it was too late. When he pulled his arm forward to grab for the apron, he realized he was bound to the wall by a thick metal chain.

Waylon's choked breathing filled the room as Travis picked up Waylon's gun, turned it around in his hands to inspect it, then tucked it down inside his apron pocket. He walked past Waylon toward a workbench filled with ugly-looking tools and devices. Long metal needles and iron pokers, thick shears and jagged handsaws. He selected a long machete and flicked his thumb against the blade's edge, testing its sharpness. He looked back at Rein, his tragedy mask tilted sideways as he stared at Rein's face.

Rein steeled himself as the man came toward him, machete in hand, and then bent down, looking at Rein from behind the large cutouts in his mask. "I know you," he said.

"I know you too, Travis," Rein shot back. "Let me go and we'll get to know each other a lot better."

"I thought I would have to come visit you, but instead you've come to me. You see, I've been studying you for a long time, Jacob Rein."

Rein lunged forward against the chain but fell short

and backed up to the basement wall, saving his strength, knowing he would need it. The masked man turned and looked at Waylon, still lying facedown on the floor. "Leave him alone," Rein shouted, rattling his chain as loud as he could. "Bill! Bill! Get up!"

"The little girl has beautiful eyes. I will bring them to you as a present first. And then I will bring her something of yours." He looked down at Waylon. "I don't think we need to worry about him any longer."

"Bill!" Rein screamed, watching in horror as Travis bent down and grabbed a handful of Waylon's hair, raising his bloody face off the basement floor. Travis placed the machete's blade beneath Waylon's jaw. Rein's voice died in his throat as the long knife's edge slit Waylon across the neck. Waylon's feet kicked and he pounded his fists on the floor until the blade reached the underside of his other ear and he collapsed facedown, not moving.

"I will be back for you," Travis said, pointing at him with the dripping machete. He stepped over Waylon and started up the basement stairs.

Rein could not look away from his friend's motionless body, unable to control the burst of grief welling inside of him. He lowered his head and sobbed, letting it out, letting it consume him. As he wept, he heard something stir in the basement and opened his eyes, seeing Bill Waylon's right hand extending out.

Waylon gurgled and sputtered blood as he raised his head. The open wound under his neck pulsated rivers of crimson, but he extended his left hand. His legs moved, and he was crawling across the floor.

"Bill?" Rein whispered.

Waylon's words were a clotted tangle of grunts as he forced himself forward, large bubbles of blood popping from his severed throat, but still he crawled. He flailed with his hands, grabbing for the workbench until finding a narrow bracket between its legs.

Rein watched in amazement as Waylon lifted himself upward, gurgling as he reached for the bench's ledge with both hands, rocking it back and forth until it began to sway. Rein stretched toward him as far as he could, pulling on the chain with all of his might, calling out, "Come on, come on!"

The workbench tilted like a large oak tree being hacked by an ax. He rocked it, trying to tip it. Dozens of metal objects fell from the bench, clanging on the cement floor, until the entire structure came loose and crashed down on top of Waylon.

In the dust and darkness, Rein could not see his friend anymore, or hear him, but the effort had been enough. Thick metal spikes and knives lay scattered on the floor all around Rein. He sorted through them, tossing aside what he didn't need, until there, shining in the shadows, was the large rectangular blade of a meat cleaver. He was ready for when the bastard came back.

As Rein reached for it, he stopped, hearing creaking stairs above him. The man's heavy footsteps as he went to find Carrie and Nubs. The horrors they would have to endure while Rein stayed trapped in the basement, clutching his weapon uselessly. There would be no great battle. When the man realized Rein was armed, he'd simply shut the door and wait. It would only take a few days of dehydration to make Rein too weak to defend himself. He would force Rein to listen to what he was doing to the girls. Rein knew that. He would send pieces of them down into the basement like scraps in a processing plant.

The footsteps were getting more faint then. Travis

was going upward, farther away. That's where they must be, Rein realized, forming a map of the house's interior in his mind. Find the room on the second floor.

He gripped the meat cleaver's handle and looked at his left arm, seeing where the shackle was bolted to him. He squeezed his hand into a fist and pressed his arm flat against the basement wall, trying to get his hand high up from the cuff.

Emily Cross, he thought. The little girl whose life he'd taken and could never give back.

Natalie Michaels. Nubs. The little girl he'd been tasked to find, and come so far, only to have her torn from him at the very last.

He shifted his hand upward from the shackle as far as it would go, giving himself half an inch of wrist before the bottom of his palm. He lined up the cleaver's blade against his skin and took a deep breath, telling himself the fight was not finished yet. A roar erupted deep from within his chest as he raised the cleaver high in the air and swung.

The steps creaked outside of the upstairs room. Nubs clenched Carrie ever tighter, her entire being wracked with tremors. "You stay behind me, baby," Carrie said. Rein's knife was sticky in her hands, tacked to her skin with dried blood.

That won't be the last of you on this blade, you son of a bitch, she thought. I will put it inside of you and let it drink.

The keys on the electronic pad outside of the door beeped one at a time until the locks holding it shut disengaged with a click. As the doorknob turned, Carrie reached down and touched the top of Nubs's head, caressing her. "I need you to be brave one last time, baby. Can you do that for Aunt Carrie?"

The child's arms were clamped around her, refusing to let go. The door was opening. Carrie could hear her own voice trembling and forced herself to say, "When I say, you have to run down the stairs and get out. You keep running, no matter what."

"I can't!"

"You have to, baby."

"He's going to hurt you!"

Yes, he will. But he won't get you, Carrie thought.

The door opened fully. The man standing there was outlined by the dim light of the house beneath him. Carrie's eyes had adjusted to the darkness, and she could see his butcher's apron, slick with fresh blood, and his grotesque mask, the eyes and mouth darkened by shadow.

"Remember what I said, baby," Carrie told her.

Travis raised his machete and leveled it at Carrie. Its size dwarfed the small blade in her hands. "Rein should not have brought you to this place. He has led you to your destruction."

Carrie clutched Nubs to the side of her leg, keeping her hand pressed down over the girl's ear, hoping she couldn't hear the man speak.

"Give her to me. I will show you mercy."

The knife was shaking in Carrie's hand.

"If you do not, I will skin her alive as you watch." The machete turned sideways, aimed between her eyes. "Give me the child."

Carrie stroked Nubs's hair one final time as she raised her own knife. "You come and take her," she roared. "*Molon labe*, motherfucker!"

He leaped forward with the machete raised, his long

apron sweeping against his legs as he moved. Carrie crouched low, ready to spring forward with the knife, to strike as hard and fast as she could, as many times as she could, to scream while she was able for Nubs to run, and run, and keep running, when she saw something metal flash through the air behind the man. It circled wide over his shoulder and landed with a deep thump inside the right side of his mask, the sound of an ax sinking deep into the stump of a tree.

His legs wobbled beneath his apron at the impact, the length of the meat cleaver's blade stuck out far enough in front of his face for him to see it. He reached up, feeling the cleaver's spine and handle, feeling where it had severed his ear in half, feeling where it had bitten into his right eye.

Carrie stared in amazement as Travis took two steps forward and collapsed, his body flopping like he was being jolted with electricity, slapping the floor with his feet, hands, and head. A half-naked, bloodied figure stood in the doorway, clutching the severed stump of his left wrist. Jacob Rein looked first at Carrie and then at the little girl hiding behind her. "Is that her?" he asked.

Carrie reached down for Nubs, peeling the tiny arms from around her leg and saying, "It's all right. The bad man is gone. He can't hurt anyone now."

The child looked at Rein in confusion, horrified by his severed hand and all the blood, but all he saw was her long blond hair and soft angelic features. How, even in her horror, she was very much alive. Very, very much alive.

He stayed in the shadow of the door, not wanting to frighten her. "I guess you must be Nubs."

He heard her reply as he closed his eyes. It was a soft, angelic voice. His legs gave out beneath him.

Rein fell backward through the door, tumbling down over the top stair and rolling. Descending through the darkness. The void opened its maw wide, waiting to swallow him. Its long, slimy tentacles slithered toward him, cinching around his ankles and wrist and neck, and he surrendered to it. It was time, he thought. He was too tired to fight it any longer.

Far off in the distance, something crackled across the horizon and streaked toward him. It peeled through the darkness as it came, splitting it open and casting it aside, and warmth radiated throughout his entire being, holding him, lowering him gently down into an infinite light.

29

Carrie scooped Nubs into her arms and leaped over Travis Berry, landing just inches from his thrashing legs. He was clutching the cleaver's handle, trying to wrench it from his head. Every pull brought a high-pitched shriek from him, inhuman sounds as he worked the blade back and forth, sawing through his own skull and the flesh to get it free.

Carrie slammed the door shut behind her, burying Nubs's head against her chest to muffle the sounds, hurrying down the staircase to where Rein lay sprawled. She stared in mute horror at his bleeding stump and bare, blood-soaked torso. Nubs was clenched around her neck with both arms, and Carrie had to force herself free, pushing the child away, pulling her back to kiss her on top of the head, telling her it would all be over soon.

She unbuckled her leather belt and ripped it from her waist, working it around Rein's forearm in a tight loop, twisting until it would not twist anymore. The blood leaking out of his raw stump slowed to a trickle, and she propped his forearm across his chest to keep it elevated. "Stay there," she ordered Nubs as she walked

around the living room, searching for the three glowing dots of her pistol. She snatched the gun from the
floor and raced back up the stairs, two at a time.

Carrie grabbed the doorknob and twisted, trying to
force it, but the door would not budge. The light over
the electronic keypad had gone steady red. Carrie
pressed her ear to the door and listened, trying to hear
if the man was still moving inside. The screams had
stopped. Nothing was bashing against the floor any
longer.

"Still alive in there, Travis?" she called out.

No response came. She closed her eyes, drinking
the sweat from her lips as she pressed them together,
forcing herself to try to breathe quieter. She pressed
the barrel of her gun against the door, feeling the trigger's smooth curve with the tip of her finger, ready to
fire through it at the first rattle of the handle. The first
footstep. Come on, motherfucker, she thought.

"Does it hurt, Travis? I hope it does," she said, the
gun shaking in her hand. She heard a low, gurgling,
moan come from within, and smiled. She pressed her
lips against the wooden door, projecting her voice into
the room beyond. "That a boy, Travis! Stay with me
just a little longer. This is how you die, you son of a
bitch. Not a famous serial killer. Not a monster. Just
another pathetic asshole wearing a cheap mask, filling
up his pants with his own shit, screaming like the terrified pussy you really are! They're going to try to find
you in time to save you, Travis. But I'm not going to
tell them. No. Not for a long time. I'm going to wait."

She pressed her ear against the door again, listening,
and this time there was something. No more moaning,
not sawing. The sound of struggle. The sound of wet
slithering across the room's wooden floor. The desper-

ate grunting of a wounded animal trying to claw toward freedom.

Carrie leaned back and kicked the door handle, trying to smash the lock, but the sturdy metal held, cracking the thick rubber sole of her shoe. She could hear
sputtering pleas from within the room, Travis Berry
begging something to open. To not let this be the end.
Carrie pressed the barrel of her gun against the door's
lock, clenched her eyes shut, and fired.

Sparks showered her arm from the bullet striking
the lock's metal. Jagged splinters exploded from the
door and frame, spearing her in the arms and neck. She
fired again, her ears ringing now, deafened from the gunshots, but the door's handle collapsed, hanging from
its housing by deformed screws. The area she'd shot
smoked and flickered with red-hot embers, and Carrie
stuck her fingers inside the lock's guts, digging around
its sharp edges until the blood from where it had sliced
her open hissed on its hot metal. She kept digging, finally finding the length of the steel bolt and pulling it
free.

She rushed into the room, past the door, and was en-
veloped in its total darkness. She turned in each direction, the gun moving with her, searching for Berry,
seeing nothing. Hearing nothing except high-pitched
ringing.

She turned the gun to the wall across from her and
fired twice. Two brightly lit .45-caliber-sized holes appeared in the wall. Moonlight streamed through them,
cutting the darkness.

"Where are you?" she shouted. She fired four more
rounds as fast as she could pull the trigger, punching
light through the wall and searching. The intrusive
moonlight revealed a trail of wet, shining blood smeared

across the floor. Carrie followed its trail, heading toward the far wall, and stopped, realizing what she was looking at. A dark mouth, formed by an opening in the wall. A hidden panel that had been pulled aside, with bloody handprints spattered across its surface.

At the hole's entrance, a pair of pale ankles were kicking. Travis Berry, wriggling to get the rest of himself inside the wall. Carrie fired through the wall, not knowing where she'd hit, but his yelp of pain was loud enough for her to hear it.

She latched on to his ankle with her free hand and pulled, screaming at him to come out. He kicked as she pulled, smashing her fingers with his heavy boots, but she wouldn't let go, twisting the bottom of his pants leg in her grip, using it to drag him forth.

Travis Berry emerged from the darkness, screaming and thrashing. He grabbed the edges of the panel with one hand, the other swinging the meat cleaver, slashing the air and spraying the walls with his own blood.

He kicked Carrie in the knee, hitting her right on the knob of bone, and she felt his ankle slip from her grasp. Her leg gave out beneath her, sitting her down on the wet floor, staring at the sole of Travis's boot as he reared his foot back, about to smash it into her face.

Carrie thrust her gun forward into the closest part of his body she could reach, jamming the barrel into the soft, squishy center of Travis's genitals. He paused, his bent leg hovering in the air, frozen in place, his one good eye open wide. Carrie pulled the trigger.

She rolled out of the way as Travis screeched, clutching himself between the legs. A spurting font of blood erupted between his fingers, a hot geyser that had been struck true.

Carrie leaned against the wall, catching her breath.

She was sickened by what she saw, amazed by such raw, open agony, but she forced herself to watch. Travis's face contorted, his mouth staying wide open in a soundless scream. His lips were strung with lengths of spittle and his tongue bulged forward, flopping around his mouth, out of his control.

She waited. Watching until the blood spitting out of him slowed to a trickle and his contortions came to rest. She inched closer to him, staring down at his face, his once boyishly handsome features now ruined. He stared back at her with his remaining eye, words bubbling up from his mouth in pink, foaming bubbles. He let out his last—a long, rattling gasp—and went still. Carrie stood bent over him, watching everything, listening, trying to hear as much of it as she could. She wanted to remember every detail of his death for the rest of her life.

30

Sitting in the driveway on the ambulance bumper, Carrie watched the flurry of activity at the house's front door in silence. Nubs was in her arms, her tiny face pressed against her chest, snoring lightly. There were not enough EMS units there yet to worry about taking Nubs to get checked out at the hospital. That would come. She stroked Nubs's hair and kissed her again.

Dozens of police cars from local jurisdictions, state police, and county detectives were scattered across the lawn, along with ambulances and first responder SUVs. Two fire trucks were parked in the front yard, using their powerful search-and-rescue equipment to flood the house with light.

Two metal gurneys parked next to the front entrance, empty. Carrie had seen the EMS teams hurrying into the house carrying bags of gear, and now they were emerging. The first team came running out, carrying Jacob Rein on an orange Reeves stretcher, running lines of fluid into his arms, the monitors hooked to his chest beeping as they laid him on the gurney and buckled him down. As they rolled Rein across the lawn toward the nearest ambulance, she saw another EMT come running through the doorway carrying a small cooler.

She watched them load Rein into the ambulance, along with the cooler, and slam the doors shut. The interior lights in the back of the ambulance stayed on as they continued to work on him, even as the siren erupted and the driver sped away.

A second team emerged carrying a second Reeves stretcher. Carrie sat up, trying to get a better view. Nubs stirred at being moved, and Carrie stroked her hair, telling her it was all right as she sat back down. She could make out Waylon's body being set down on the gurney. They'd hooked IVs to him, and that was a good sign. She could see Rein's blood-soaked shirt sticking out from beneath the neck brace they'd wrapped around Waylon's throat. Rein had packed his shirt into the injury and tied it tight before coming upstairs to rescue them, she realized. It had not been much, but it had been all he'd had, and he'd done it one-handed.

Carrie could not unsee the spray of blood across the basement wall, or the severed hand lying on the floor. She could not fathom the act Rein had committed to save them. It was nothing she could put into words. She watched Harv Bender come through the door, following the gurney as the EMTs continued to work on Waylon. At least they hadn't given up yet, she thought. Hadn't draped a blanket over him and zippered him up inside a black bag, either. It was something, she thought. Not much, but something, and she decided she would take it.

The EMTs rolled Waylon toward the next ambulance and loaded him in, the gurney's metal legs clanging as they shuttered upward to roll him into the rear. Bender stood by, waiting for them to close the ambulance doors before making his way over to her.

He reached out, running the tips of his fingers through the little girl's hair. "How is she?"

"This is probably the first sleep she's had in days," Carrie said.

"Listen," he said. "I know what I said before."

"It's all right. It's over."

"No, it's not all right. I was wrong," he said. "What you all did here, it was a miracle. An absolute miracle. And Rein? I mean, goddamn. That was just a hell of a thing."

"Will Bill make it?" Carrie said. The words sounded empty to her, devoid of any emotion. She'd been wrung out like a wet sock, left hollow.

"I have to believe he will," Bender said. "He's too damn strong to let some son of a bitch kill him like that."

"Did you send someone to tell Jeri and the girls?"

"Dave Kenderdine's on his way over there. He's going to drive them to the hospital. How about her? Will you reach out to her grandmother?" he said, nodding to Nubs.

"In a few minutes. I just needed to collect my thoughts."

Bender patted Carrie on the arm and said, "That's a good phone call you get to make. Enjoy it. We don't get to do that too often."

She watched him walk back into the house, shouting, "Is that son a bitch in a body bag yet? I want to take a picture holding his head up like a trophy." She reached into her pocket for her phone, holding it up to see if there was any signal. One bar. She kissed Nubs again and pressed Penny's name on the screen, holding it against her ear, waiting for it to ring.

The old woman answered, her voice a mixture of surprise and dread. "Carrie? Oh my God, what is it. Did you find something?"

Carrie closed her eyes and took a deep breath, steadying herself. "I—" she started to say, the words catching in her throat. She wiped her face and forced herself to swallow, holding Nubs so tightly the little girl began to stir, and said, "Penny, I've got her."

ACKNOWLEDGMENTS

Brandon and Julia, Mom and Dad, my sisters, all friends, all family. The readers who have stayed with me since the earliest independent days. My partners in CID, the members of the Warrington Township Police Department, all surrounding agencies, prosecutors, child services, and the criminal investigators I have worked with, learned from, and been inspired by for the past twenty years. Tony Healey, my constant companion on this journey, and so many others. Dystel, Goderich & Bourret LLC. Literary Management. Kensington Publishing and its staff, for giving this book a place it can be proud to call home. This book would not exist were it not for these next three people. I could not have done it without Sharon Pelletier, Steve Zacharias, and Michaela Hamilton. Their support, hard work, and trust make me want to be a better author.

Don't miss the next superb thriller in the
SANTERO AND REIN series
by Bernard Schaffer

AN UNSETTLED GRAVE

Coming soon from Kensington Publishing Corp.

Keep reading to enjoy an excerpt . . .

*O*ut in the long stretches of road beyond the lights of the supermarkets and shopping centers, she drove. True darkness waits in the places with no streetlights. Her high beams dissolved into the fog. Monica Gere wiped the inside of her windshield with her palm, doing nothing but smearing wetness across the glass, and turned up her defroster. It was fall. The days were still warm but the nights turned cold. Sweat cooled on her bare arms and legs and left her shivering. She turned up the heat on the defroster, hoping it would help her see better. It didn't.

Monica went slow. Her headlights connected with eyes along the side of the road. Deer turned their heads, staring as if they might leap in front of her car at the last second to make a run for it. She had a fear of hitting a deer at high speed. A friend of hers hit one and it came barreling through the windshield. The damn thing kicked and thrashed, all antlers and hooves, destroying the car and slicing her friend into a bloody mess. Deer were stronger than they looked. They were large, powerful animals. She passed two others and slowed down even more.

She crossed over the double-yellow lines into the oncoming lane, giving the animals a wide berth. It was ten o'clock at night and she hadn't passed another car since she left the gym. Out here in the woods, cruising under a canopy of thick nighttime cloud and fog, she thought she could have driven in the left lane the entire way.

Unknown to her, the vehicle behind her moved as she moved, changing from lane to lane and closing in. Its engine whined as it raced to catch up to her, never turning on its headlights as it cut through the fog. Monica squinted into the rearview mirror, trying to see what was making the noise. As she looked, brilliant white light blossomed inside the glass and blinded her.

The car behind her activated its high beams, and a light bar mounted across its roof spun to life with dizzying red and blue LEDs. The driver aimed a spotlight at her side mirror, and its glare reflected straight into her face. Monica raised a hand to shield her eyes and skidded to a stop on the gravel road.

She put her car in park and heard someone coming up behind her. She could not see him. Only a shadow, the shape of a man, blocking out the light between his car and hers. In his silhouette, she saw the bright crimson flare of a cigarette. The man flicked it away, sending it into the grass beyond Monica's car.

She rolled down her driver's side window. A flashlight activated inches from her face, the LED burst of a thousand lumens blinding her. Even when she flinched and clenched her eyes shut, all she could see was its white halo.

"Please," she said, but he spoke over her, commanding her to hand over her license and registration.

Monica reached across to undo her glove compartment and fumbled for the paperwork. "I've only had this car a few months," she said. "I'm not sure where anything is."

She could see the flashlight waving around the interior of her car, checking, no doubt, for drugs. It lingered over her chest and stomach, shining against the droplets of sweat above her sports bra. Looking to see if I have my seatbelt on, she thought. Good thing I do. The hand holding the flashlight came in through the open window and aimed downward, straight down at her lap, so bright it revealed the fibers of her yoga pants. The stitching of the seam that ran up her crotch. She closed her legs together, telling herself he was checking to see if she'd tried hiding any weapons.

Cops, she knew, had every reason to be cautious. Night after night, in some part of the country, a police officer was murdered, just because he was doing his job.

Monica handed over her license and the pink registration paperwork marked *temporary*. She smiled politely and said, "I've never owned a new car before. Is this because I went into the other lane? I was trying to go around the deer. They're everywhere."

The officer stepped out of view, his flashlight still aimed at her face while he read her information. "Have you been drinking tonight?"

"No, I'm coming home from the gym," she said.

He went behind her car, standing off to the side of the road, out of view. She heard him say, "Can you check that again for me? Make sure you have the spelling right. Monica Gere, with a *G*."

She couldn't hear anyone respond, but then he came

back to her window, his flashlight back to her face. "Ma'am, are you aware there's a warrant for your arrest?"

"What? That's impossible."

"It may be just some procedural error," he said. "Sometimes the computer gets mixed up." He read her info back to her, making sure he had the right name and date of birth and address.

"Yes, that's all correct."

"Well, apparently, there's a drug warrant out for you. Did you get any paperwork in the mail?"

"What kind of paperwork?" Monica asked. Had there been? She normally threw out anything that looked like junk mail. Would she have even recognized an envelope from some kind of court appearance? "No," she said. "I don't think I did. Listen, this is crazy. I've never done drugs in my entire life. There has to be a mistake."

He reached for her door handle and opened it. "Ma'am, step out of the car."

"No, wait a second," Monica said. "I run marathons and work out five nights a week. Do I look like I do drugs?"

"Ma'am, don't make this any harder than it has to be."

He reached for her arm and she yanked away, saying, "Listen to me, sir. Just listen for a second. I respect the police, and I know you have a job to do, but this doesn't make sense. I do not have any warrant."

"Get out of the car now!" he shouted.

It was the tone of absolute authority. An angry school principal. An irate father. A boss with his employee's financial security in the palm of his hand. She got out of the car.

He spun her around and pressed her, face first, against the door. "Spread your legs," he said, pulling her hands behind her back. "Do not move. Understand?"

"Yes, I understand," she said, trembling. "I didn't do anything wrong."

He grabbed her by the back of the hair, making her gasp. "Say that again. Say that one more time, and see what happens."

She felt the handcuffs cinch down, crushing her wrists until she cried out, begging him to let her go.

He kicked her feet apart wider with his boot. His hands went to her hips, fumbling with her waistband, coming up along the sides of her ribs, rubbing across her chest. He yanked her sports bra up, exposing her breasts to the cold air, and squeezed them. "What are you doing? You can't do that!" she shouted.

He smacked her across the back of the head, cracking her so hard she felt dizzy. He shoved her toward the back of the car. She stumbled, trying to get away. He threw her down on the road, holding her handcuffed wrists and twisting. The metal cuffs ground against her bones.

He grabbed the back of her yoga pants at the waistband and yanked them down from her backside, revealing her, and spread her open. She screamed, her voice echoing through the woods, but the road was empty and the fog was thick. He raped her while pressing her facedown into the dirt, telling her he was the cop and he had the power and it was what she deserved.

* * *

She lay in the darkness, unable to move, not remembering when the man had left. The night air was cool against her bare, exposed flesh. She heard a car coming and couldn't lift her head. The car stopped. Doors opened. People came running toward her, their voices panicked.

What happened to her?

My God, I think she's been raped.

Someone dropped a sweatshirt on top of her half-naked body, and someone else said, Call the police.

"No," Monica moaned, forcing the sound from her throat. She could hear the police dispatcher on the other end of the phone asking, what's your emergency?

"No!" she screamed, trying to roll over and get away, but they held her down and told her it was going to be okay, the police were already on their way.